ISLA'S OATH

BOOK TWO

Also by Cassandra Page

Lucid Dreaming

The Isla's Inheritance trilogy
Isla's Inheritance
Isla's Oath
Melpomene's Daughter

ISLA'S OATH

BOOK TWO

CASSANDRA PAGE

www.cassandrapage.com

To my mother and father, Lorraine and Fred.
For everything.

CHAPTER ONE

"**R**eady?" Jack asked, standing beside me. He was wearing board shorts and a tank top, his feet bare on the sandy path. Blond hair stirred in the evening breeze, brushing his shoulders. He looked like any Australian male on holiday at the beach.

Except your average male didn't have long ears protruding from sun-bleached hair, each easily four inches long from scalp to tip.

"I guess." I took a deep breath, savouring the briny smell that evoked memories of summer vacations with my father. I picked my way down the path to the beach, thongs clicking against my heels as I stepped between the weathered log retainers. Jack followed. The plastic bag he was holding rustled faintly.

When we reached the beach I shook off my shoes and picked them up, hooking them over one finger. The sand was cool under my feet; the radiant heat of the hot summer day had almost faded. "Where to?"

Jack pointed towards the worn, even stones scattered at the feet of the towering headland. The water pounded, working patiently to undermine the rocky bluff and send it crashing into the sea. A deep rock pool shimmered in the moonlight, connected to the ocean by a winding channel that surged and retracted with the tide.

We picked our way across the stones to the empty pool. I glanced at Jack. "This is the place," he assured me.

I nodded, trying not to feel nervous. Jack seemed calm—his aura was a uniform light blue, like a winter sky—and I resolved to try and emulate him.

I could have taken a sample of that light blue calm to help me relax, but I didn't know how to do it without damaging him. That was why I was lurking on a south coast beach in the middle of the night in the first place.

One of the shadowy rocks in the pool moved, floating towards us. I jumped, staring. The shape drifted from the shadows into the moonlight, revealing that it wasn't a rock but a head, hairless and with tiny, round ears. Two solid black eyes opened wide, examining us for a long moment before their owner stood.

Water streamed off its—his?—naked body, splashing into the pool. His skin gleamed silvery blue and his chest was broad and flat, tapering to a narrow waist. He didn't have a bellybutton. Mercifully, the water was opaque and reached the middle of his taut belly, so I didn't have to avert my gaze from an ironclad confirmation of his sex.

"So this is your half-breed master?" The creature spoke to Jack with a watery hiss, slow and deliberate.

Jack bristled. I stepped forward. "I'm Isla."

"The half-breed *aosidhe*," the creature insisted, narrowing his eyes.

ISLA'S OATH

I shrugged. His tone was insulting but the words were true. My mother was an *aosidhe*, a noble faerie, and my father was a human. "If you say so."

"I do." He smiled, showing two rows of serrated white teeth, like a shark's jaw they'd shown us in science last year. What would it be like to be torn at by such a set of teeth? The worrying thought was more insistent now than it was in school, because the jaw was still attached to its owner.

The creature chortled, enjoying my reaction to his appearance. Irritation surged, making me scowl. "And you are?"

"I am Mako. A full-breed siren."

I ignored the jab. "Jack says you've agreed to teach me how to manipulate emotions."

"I agreed to talk to you," Mako corrected, waggling a fine-boned finger at me. "I need a couple of things from you before I agree to be your teacher."

"We have the meat." Jack reached into the plastic bag and pulled out a tray of pork chops. He held it up so Mako could inspect the contents.

The siren ran a blue-grey tongue over his teeth. "Oh yes. It's been a long time since I've had land-meat. Very good."

"Here." I pierced the transparent wrap with my finger and pulled a chop out, tossing it to the creature in the pool. He caught it dextrously, tearing a piece of raw flesh free and chewing it with disturbing enthusiasm. I was glad the poor light bleached the colours from the world, so I wouldn't have to see the red-brown of the blood that trickled down his chin.

"Another?" Mako asked when he finished the first chop. There were two more in the packet.

"You can have one more halfway through the lesson, and the last at the end," I said, handing the tray to Jack. I rinsed my fingers, which were faintly sticky from handling the raw meat, in a rivulet of seawater that ran past my feet.

Mako stared at me. Worry knotted in my stomach—would he refuse? But after several heartbeats he smiled that toothy smile. "Very well, half-breed. I will be your teacher. But you must swear me an oath first. That you will not harm me."

"Will you swear the same oath to me?" I asked, mindful of the speed with which he'd devoured the raw pork chop.

The siren stiffened, glaring at me with outrage. "Do you mock?"

I glanced at Jack, who shook his head. "The sirens swore an oath generations ago not to harm any living thing not born in the sea," he murmured. "He cannot harm you, even if he wishes to."

"I'm sorry," I said to Mako. "I didn't know."

This mollified him. He gazed at the tray of meat, and I felt sorry for him … until he spoke. "We used to be able to hunt our own land-meat, but now we only get to eat it if it falls into the water, already dead."

I knew what he meant. Drowning victims. Dumped animal carcasses. I shuddered before biting my lip, steeling myself. This was the only teacher Jack had been able to find me. I had to be polite.

I recited the words Jack and I had agreed on beforehand. "I, Isla Blackman, swear not to harm you, Mako, in exchange for you teaching me how to control my ability to see and manipulate emotions."

Mako nodded, considering, his thin lips pursed. "Agreed,"

he said finally.

I felt the oath settle over the two of us, shivering against my skin as it bound me to uphold my word.

And so my lessons began.

More than five hours later, Mako declared we were done for the evening. I stood, groaning, my backside numb from sitting on the edge of the pool for hours and my feet icy from the long submersion in the salty water. Jack steadied me with a warm hand as I stretched out the kinks before tossing the last piece of pork to the waiting siren.

"Same time tomorrow," Mako mumbled around a mouthful of food. He vanished beneath the water between one breath and the next. An incoming swell broke up the ripples from his departure.

I trudged beside Jack across the beach, head hanging low. The sand was warmer than the water, but not warm enough to dispel the chill in my feet. I wriggled my toes gratefully when we reached the dunes and I could slip my shoes on.

Jack glanced at me. "What is wrong?"

I sighed, stuffing my hands in my pockets. "That didn't go as well as I'd hoped." Mako and I had spent most of the evening coming to grips with the different ways our abilities worked. I saw emotions as colours in people's auras and manipulated them by touching the person and willing the colours to change. Mako smelled them as scents on the air and through the water and manipulated them by singing, even at great distances. The siren insisted the differences were cosmetic, simply the way our minds processed something beyond the five senses. We'd only just started figuring out the common ground when he'd halted the training.

"It should be smoother tomorrow night." Jack sounded upbeat even though his shoulders drooped. He'd been the guinea pig for our experimentation and, although it wasn't physically taxing, it was emotionally draining. Literally.

"I hope so. We've only got four more nights."

"It will be fine." His tone was reassuring. I kept my gaze on the path so I wouldn't have to see whether he believed his words. I wanted to think he did.

Jack stayed by my side until we reached the caravan park, stopping at the end of the row of dark cabins. "See you tomorrow night," he whispered.

He kept a cautious eye on me until I unlocked the cabin door and crept inside. Ever vigilant, just as he'd been since we first talked on Mount Ainslie several months before. When I glanced back from the stoop, he waved and disappeared into the shadows. I brushed the sand off my feet, wishing I dared to have a shower to bake the chill from my bones. But I didn't want to wake everyone.

The cabin we—me, my boyfriend and my cousins— were renting had a small kitchen on one side of the open lounge, as well as a combined bathroom and toilet, and only two bedrooms. Dominic and Ryan shared a room lined with bunk beds, while Sarah and I had the master bedroom, the two of us bunking down in the queen-sized bed. Would she steal the sheets the way she had when we were twelve?

ISLA'S OATH

I crept into the bedroom. Sarah curled on her side, red hair fanned across her pillow. She snored gently.

Snoring seemed like an excellent idea, so I quickly changed into a clean T-shirt and boxer shorts and crawled into bed. I was asleep as soon as my head hit the pillow.

CHAPTER TWO

The sound of banging cupboards dragged me from my sleep. The bed was empty. Sarah's and Ryan's voices were audible from the kitchen, their words muffled by the hiss of the shower from across the hall.

I rolled over to look at the clock. Nine o'clock. I'd had just over four hours sleep.

Craptastic. I closed my eyes and groaned.

The door to our room opened and closed again. "Good morning, sunshine!" Sarah trilled. The smell of cooking bacon followed her in, making my stomach rumble.

I ignored it and her, pulling my pillow over my head. She snatched it away, holding it out of reach of my flailing hand.

"How'd it go?" she said. I scrunched my eyes closed more tightly. "Talk to me, Isla."

"You aren't going to go away, are you?"

"Nope."

I sighed and gave up, rubbing my eyes. "Okay, I guess. Slow."

ISLA'S OATH

"So you have to go out again tonight?"

"Probably every night we're here." I sat up with a groan, smoothing the rumpled sheet over my knees. "I really could use some more sleep."

Sarah shook her head. "How would you explain that to Dominic? As far as he knows, you had an early night last night."

"I'm eighteen. Do I need an excuse to sleep?"

The corner of her mouth twitched and her aura flickered with amusement. But instead of the laugh I'd been angling for, I received a frown. "He'll smell a rat. He's a bright boy."

I grimaced. Sarah was right. If I wanted to stop my boyfriend from figuring out something was going on during our holiday, I needed to behave normally.

"You could just tell him, you know," she said, putting the pillow at the foot of the bed and sitting on it so I couldn't reclaim it. She meant everything—that I was half-*aosidhe*, why we were here, Jack's true nature. We'd had this argument before. Sarah and Ryan knew Jack had come down to the coast to meet me, and why. Dominic didn't. "Then you wouldn't have to sneak around, or worry about him being jealous of Jack if he catches you together."

"He's not jealous of Jack," I said.

"You know that's not true, aura girl."

"Well, he shouldn't be."

"Tell *him* that." Her aura flared with the same irritation that glittered in her eyes.

I bit my lip. Sarah had only just accepted my apology for not confiding in her sooner about how my heritage had affected Ryan. Our argument about whether to tell Dominic anything had reopened the wound.

9

I had a few reasons for not wanting to tell him yet. The biggest was the *duinesidhe*—the term used to describe the fae races more broadly—preferred to keep their existence a secret. I'd known and trusted my cousins all my life, whereas I'd only been dating Dominic for three months. That level of deep trust wasn't there yet.

Besides, what if he decided I was a freak and dumped me? My stomach roiled at the thought.

"There's real coffee," Sarah said, relenting. "We found a percolator under the sink." I blinked, realising I was staring at her, lost in my thoughts and a haze of fatigue.

"You're the best." I smiled.

"Don't you forget it." She gave me a fleeting grin and left the room so I could dress.

The shower stopped running and footsteps padded up the corridor, signalling that Dominic had returned to his room. Sighing again, I clambered out of bed and grabbed an armful of clean clothes, ducking across to the bathroom to have a quick shower and brush my teeth. I wiped the steam from the mirror with my forearm and stared at my tired reflection.

Maybe if I brushed my teeth hard enough the weariness would wash away.

"Time to harden up, Isla," I told myself sternly after I'd rinsed. I'd made the decisions that led me here: to keep a secret from my boyfriend, and to invite him to the coast with us in the first place. I was just going to have to deal.

I squared my shoulders and plastered a bright smile onto my face as I walked out into the lounge. "Good morning!"

Ryan waggled his fingers, curiosity swirling around

him so vividly it amazed me that the others couldn't see the mix of colours. But he didn't ask how my midnight excursion went. Sarah handed me a cup of coffee before returning to the frypan and its sizzling bacon and eggs. I inhaled deeply.

"Morning." Dominic kissed the top of my head as I sipped my coffee. He was a good eight inches taller than my measly five foot four. I'd read somewhere that I was only a little below average height for a female. I wasn't sure I believed it. Taller women surrounded me. Even Sarah was only a couple of inches shorter than Dominic.

I liked the fact he was so much taller. His hugs made me feel safe. However, I drew the line at him resting objects on the top of my head … as he was doing now.

"Hey!" I swatted him away, ducking out from under the glass of orange juice so it didn't spill.

"What?" His grin was cheeky and his brown eyes gleamed. I laughed.

Keeping secrets from him would be easier if he wasn't such a good guy. Of course, then we wouldn't be dating in the first place, I supposed. I sighed.

"What's the plan for today?" Sarah asked as we sat down to breakfast, all wedged in around the small table.

"I was thinking of taking my sketchbook down to the beach," Ryan said around a mouthful of toast. He was a painter when he wasn't working at the supermarket. He hadn't made any money from his art yet, unless selling sketches and occasional tattoo designs to his friends for a few dollars counted. "Might see if I can get some, um, inspiration from the locals."

"Take a photo. It's quicker," Sarah said with a raised eyebrow. Now Ryan had clipped his hair short to remove the black-dyed ends, the two of them were peas in a pod. Their red hair and blue-green eyes matched, as did their pale skin and smattering of freckles.

"Drawing someone with a pencil ... well, you get to know them better. It's more intimate." Ryan waggled his eyebrows.

"Perv." She threw a teaspoon at him.

"The beach sounds like a good idea," I said before they started to bicker in earnest. "We should go soon, before it gets too hot."

"What's the forecast?"

I grinned. "Hot." I'd checked my smart phone the night before, while I was waiting for the others to go to bed.

"Could be worse," Dominic said, eyes twinkling. "It could be scorching."

"That's easy for you to say." I poked him in the ribs and he squirmed. "You're not going to burn to a crisp in five minutes like we are." My pale skin was the only thing I had in common with my cousins. I didn't even have the freckles.

"It's true." Ryan nodded with a hangdog expression.

Dominic and I washed the dishes while Ryan took a quick shower. Sarah put her swimsuit on under her clothes and curled up on the couch to study a map she'd found tucked under the phone, memorising the local facilities and how to get to the beach. With my boyfriend beside me, I couldn't really point out I'd already walked down there once.

Washing finished, I left Dominic to dry up and hurried back to our room to change. Given this was my first beach holiday with my boyfriend—any boyfriend—I'd bought a new swimsuit before we left Canberra. I was uncomfortable in a bikini but felt frumpy in a one-piece, so I'd settled for a tankini. The one I'd chosen was a deep wine red the salesgirl swore suited me—especially given the other colour in that style was white, which made me look like I'd seen a ghost. Or like I was one. Neither seemed like girlfriend-to-a-hot-guy material.

After I slipped the tankini on, I checked myself in the mirror, making sure everything was sitting right, before putting the same T-shirt and shorts on over the top. A pair of thongs and sunglasses, a towel over my shoulder, and I was ready to go.

The others were waiting out the front of the cabin when I emerged. Dominic leaned against the balcony railing, smiling when he saw me. Sarah had a canvas bag embroidered with a giant pink flower slung over her shoulder. Ryan held a new sketchbook and a small pencil case as though they were precious. Although he also carried a towel, he hadn't put his swimming trunks on. I guess he wasn't planning on getting wet.

The five-minute walk between the cabin and the beach seemed shorter in the light of day with my chattering companions than it had the night before. I made sure to follow Sarah's directions, giving no clue that I already knew the way. Holding hands with Dominic as we strolled along the side of the road, I studied the houses lining the streets. Most of them were newer, two-storey build-ings that would have cost their owners a small fortune. A few older, weatherboard houses resisted the trend towards modernisation, but even the weatherboard houses were well loved, neatly painted and with green gardens even in the middle of summer. Many of the houses, new and old, had quirky signs: *Bad Manors* and

Love Shack made us groan out loud.

Finally, we passed between the last rows of fences and crossed a small road. We stopped at the top of the dunes and looked down. The cove was small and didn't have a lifesaver station. However, a breakwater just off the coast softened the waves to a gentle roll—at least according to the information I'd read on the internet when choosing a caravan park convenient to Mako.

The beach wasn't crowded. Several families explored the sand; young children constructed castles and dug for seashells, crabs or buried treasure. A woman with sun-bleached hair jogged along the wet sand at the water's edge, a Border Collie trotting behind her with its head high and tail wagging. Occasionally it snapped enthusiastically at an incoming wave, but it didn't stop moving. The woman was either ignoring or hadn't seen the No Dogs signs at the top of the dune.

I could see the emotional auras of the people on the beach, but the dog was a mystery to me—although it was clearly happy enough. Why was that? The power extended across some species; I could use it on the *duinesidhe*, and my mother was able to use it on humans.

She used it on my father, at least, I thought sourly.

Maybe it was because of the closer relationship between *duinesidhe* and humans. It made sense; after all, my mother and a human male had been able to make a mixed-breed baby.

The others were halfway to the sand. I followed them down the dunes, trying not to look too hard at the rock pool, suspended high above the waterline due to the retreating tide. Empty. At least Mako wasn't lurking in there, watching. My gaze drifted out to the vivid blue ocean. Was that a shape, out beyond the waves? A watching face? It vanished with the next swell, and I chided myself for paranoia. But I wasn't sure—despite Jack's reassuring words about the sirens' oath—that I wanted to go into the water. Visions of sentient sharks flashed behind my eyes.

Ryan spread his towel high up the beach, placing his sketchbook carefully in the centre. He started a fresh one every year. The pages on this one still sat flat and didn't have little smudges of lead on their edges from twelve months of handling.

Gazing at the rolling waves as though mesmerised, Sarah shed her tank top, shorts and shoes, placing them in a messy pile. Her emerald swimsuit stood out like a jewel in the bright sun, bringing out the flecks of green in her eyes. I hesitated, my ears burning with embarrassment, before doing the same.

Dominic stared at me, eyes wide and mouth agape. I hid a smile behind my hand, pleased he didn't give my taller cousin more than a passing glance. Scarlet flashed in his aura. Did it represent what I thought it did? I turned my face away to hide the blush that warmed my cheeks.

Sarah squirted a generous amount of sunscreen into her palm before offering the bottle to the rest of us. With painful experience to urge us on, Ryan and I took similar portions and made sure we didn't miss an inch of exposed skin—although Ryan made sure not to get too much on his fingers so he didn't smear his sketchbook.

That was going to make for an uncomfortable sunburn if he wasn't careful.

Dominic hesitated when I offered him the bottle. He'd

removed his T-shirt and thrown it down on the pile with the rest of our clothes. "I want to work on my tan a little." His skin already gleamed golden brown.

"Don't be an idiot," Sarah said, one hand on her hip. "We're not going to baby you if you get burned."

"I won't!" he protested, offended.

I squeezed some more sunscreen into my palm and, before Dominic guessed what I was about to do, splatted it onto his bare chest. He squeaked and drew a breath to object. When I started to rub the white lotion across his chest, though, he smiled and held his arms out. His skin was warm and smooth under my fingers. I glanced up; he was gazing down at me, eyes hot.

My stomach fluttered.

"Lucky bastard," Ryan muttered.

"I know, right?" Dominic grinned back at him.

Sarah rolled her eyes and walked down the beach to the surf.

"Don't they say you're not meant to swim within an hour of eating?" I asked Dominic as we followed Sarah down to the water. Had it been an hour since breakfast?

"You can," he said, weaving his fingers through mine and kissing the back of my hand. He used to swim competitively for our school. "You just want to avoid heavy exercise, like doing heaps of laps, or you could get sick."

"No heavy exercise. Check."

When we got to the water's edge, I stopped with my toes in the water.

"Coming?" Dominic said, brown eyes crinkling with amusement at the corners.

"I like to get in slowly. You go ahead."

I shaded my eyes against the sun and watched as he

strode into the waves, heading out to where the water was waist-deep. When the next wave rolled in, he dove under it. Sarah was already further out, beyond where the waves started to break. Her red hair swirled around her as she floated on her back over each swell of surf.

Right on the shoreline the water was warm, but as I edged in it grew cooler. Wriggling my toes in the swirling sand, I waited until I'd adjusted to the temperature before taking another step. After a couple of minutes of watching my inching progress, Dominic waded back to where I was standing, only knee-deep.

"Hug?" He held his arms wide, dripping.

"Oh no." I backpedalled. He chased me through the water, parallel to the shoreline, both of us laughing. The water sprayed up around me as I ran, droplets glittering in the sun.

The race was short—I was tired, and Dominic's legs were much longer than mine. He scooped me up and carried me deeper into the water. I struggled half-heartedly. His arms were cold and wet behind my back and under my knees, but it was the touch of his sun-warmed chest against my bare arms that made me shiver.

I didn't get to enjoy the sensation for long before he tossed me into the waves. I came up spluttering and laughing. Then I cupped my hands and tossed a scoop of water at his face.

The water fight was inevitable after that.

Our splashing attracted the attention of a pair of children, a boy and girl about ten years old. They gazed on with wide brown eyes. Would their parents—who watched from the shoreline—be annoyed if we splashed their kids?

"Bluebottle!" a man's voice yelled.

Forgetting the fight, I whirled. The man was in his sixties, and stood a good twenty metres to our left.

He was pointing towards us.

Dominic and I looked around wildly, scanning the frothy surface of the water for the telltale blue of the Portuguese man o' war, or bluebottle jellyfish.

The jellyfish's bobbing bladder was a couple of metres away from us, drifting closer with each swelling wave. Tentacles trailed behind it, deceptively benign.

"Time to go," Dominic said grimly, wading for the shoreline.

"Uh huh." A bluebottle sting wasn't fatal, but it hurt like fire. I'd stepped on one when I was fourteen. The welt had been visible on my heel for days.

The brown-eyed girl backed away, eyes so wide I could see the whites all around. She tugged at her brother's arm. He stood still, stiff with fright. Freckles stood out like dark spots on his suddenly pale skin.

If they didn't move, the bluebottle was going to reach them in seconds.

"Toby! Molly!" Their parents ran into the water.

I waded over to the boy. Behind me, I heard Dominic splash back towards us, calling my name.

"Time to go, Toby," I said, taking the boy's arm.

Heightened by our physical contact, his emotions flooded into me.

I'd seen fear before, sickly yellow and pulsating. This boy's fright was beyond that, a blazing orange that hit me like a punch to the gut, knocking the wind from my lungs. Bile and the ghost of agony rose in my throat. A bluebottle had stung Toby before, and badly. The memory quivered through him. I couldn't see it, but I felt the emotional resonance, a frantic shadow that paralysed him.

"Toby!" the girl sobbed, yanking on his hand. The bluebottle was right in front of us, tentacles inches from the boy's bare stomach.

Before I had the time to second-guess myself, I *pulled* the terror out of his aura and into myself. The dread shot through my hand and up my arm. My heart thundered in my chest and a metallic taste flooded my mouth.

His feet freed at last, Toby splashed for the shore, his sister keeping pace with him. Wobbling on my feet, I followed, staying between them and the slowly bobbing jellyfish. Dominic reached me, taking my arm as a wave rolled by.

He looked startled when his fingers touched my skin.

We splashed out of the surf seconds later. The children's parents hugged them fiercely. Molly shook with fright. Toby, however, looked at me with calm eyes. "Thanks, lady," he said.

"Yes, thank you," his mother echoed. Tears glittered in her eyes; her aura shone with relief and a fading terror the same colour as the emotion I'd just absorbed from her son. "He's allergic."

"No problem," I said, leaning against Dominic. He wrapped his arm around me. Would the woman be so grateful if she knew I'd taken a big helping of her son's feelings, as though I were a psychic vampire from a story? I shivered.

"Are you okay?" Sarah asked, jogging along the shoreline towards us.

"I'm fine," I said.

"You're shaking," Dominic corrected me.

"It's just adrenalin." My teeth chattered.

"Come sit down for a bit." He led me up the beach towards our towels, Sarah on our heels.

Ryan was sitting upright, peering down the beach. "What was it?"

"Bluebottle." Dominic grimaced. "No one was stung. Isla saved a kid who freaked out."

Ryan's gaze, when it met mine, was full of questions. But all he said was, "Good. Bloody things."

"He wasn't just freaking out," I murmured, feeling like I needed to defend Toby. "His mum said he's got an allergy."

"You'd think they'd take their kids swimming at a pool instead," Sarah said with a shrug, shaking my towel free of sand. She wrapped it around me. The sun-baked warmth of the fabric seeped into my limbs as I sat, and slowly my shivering subsided.

"Do you want anything?" Dominic sat beside me. "There's water in the bag."

I opened my mouth to reply. Sarah spoke first. "I think she needs an ice cream. Don't you, Isla?"

"Uh. Sure," I said. She glared at me. "I mean, yes. That would be lovely."

"There's a little store just up the road." Sarah smiled sweetly at Dominic. "We passed it on the way here, remember?"

He raised an eyebrow, amused. "I guess you want one too then?"

Sarah batted her eyelashes. "How sweet of you to ask! Why yes, I would!"

"You'll be okay?" Dominic asked me.

I nodded. "No more playing with bluebottles. I promise."

"Good. Come for a walk?" he asked Ryan.

Ryan hesitated. I knew as clearly as if I'd read his mind—although my powers didn't extend that far—that he wanted to talk to me while Dominic wasn't around, to find out what had happened the night before. At first, Ryan had been bemused by the notion I was part-fae, but he had since developed a fascination with the supernatural. I wouldn't have guessed that about him before the past couple of months.

Although, when I thought about it, Ryan's curiosity made sense. The revelations of my heritage had changed him more than anyone else ... except me.

He wrinkled his nose and stood. "Sure, why not? Girls, can you guard my stuff?" He patted the sketchbook.

We nodded. My gaze followed Dominic as the pair walked up the beach. He had forgotten to put his shirt back on, and the muscles moved in his shoulders as his arms swung at his sides. Beside him, poor Ryan looked pasty.

"What happened?" Sarah murmured as soon as they were out of hearing distance.

"I thought you saw?"

"I saw enough to suspect you—" she lowered her voice to a whisper "—did something to that kid."

I stared. "How can you tell?"

"You get this distant look in your eyes, like you're looking at someone but also right through them. If that makes any sense. And you touched his arm. So I'm right? You did something?"

I gazed down at my hands, where they curled around the edges of the towel. "Yeah," I admitted. "I couldn't get him to move and he was terrified. Paralysed with fear.

I've never seen anything like it."

"You probably could've picked him up."

"I don't think so," I disagreed, glancing over at the boy. He was sitting with his sister under a beach umbrella, drinking a juice popper and trying to ignore his mother's fussing. "I reckon he's at least thirty kilos."

"He would've been lighter in the water," my cousin pointed out, her lips a thin line.

"Oh." She was right. "I didn't think of that."

"No."

The word was so loaded that I glared at her. "What are you suggesting? That I took his emotion for *fun*?" I said through gritted teeth.

Her green-eyed gaze was steady. "Not for fun. I just think you need to make sure manipulating people's feelings doesn't become your default response now. Especially since you're getting trained in how to use it properly."

"You used to think my power was cool."

"Yeah, well, I've had time to think about it. You're messing with people's free will."

"Don't you think I know that?" I clutched the edges of the towel closer, wrapping them around myself. "The whole thing feels immoral. Wrong. I need to learn how to use it properly so that I don't ... do stuff to people by accident. Every day of the last three months I've been worried I might hurt someone." Shame burned in my chest as memories resurfaced of the day I'd knocked our nana, Dad's mother, off her feet with an emotional attack. I hadn't touched her; I hadn't needed to. Although I had fixed the situation and she wasn't permanently hurt, the memory still gave me nightmares.

Sarah regarded me with narrowed eyes for a few

moments and then nodded. I saw her emotions shift as she relented. "Good. I'm sorry. I just wanted to make sure you were being careful."

"I'm trying."

She poked her tongue out at me. "I know. Very trying."

I laughed, accepting the joke as the peace offering it was. We sat in silence, watching the other beachgoers. Those still in the water were giving where we'd been a wide berth.

As I warmed up, I noticed something curious—although, remembering what Jack had told me in the past, I should have expected it. My sleep-deprived exhaustion was gone as if it had never been. I wasn't just ignoring it because of the adrenalin rush or the coffee, food and exercise.

My body had internalised the boy's emotions ... and turned them into energy.

I didn't tell Sarah.

CHAPTER THREE

When we got back to the cabin, I had a missed call from Dad. After a quick lunch—ham and mustard sandwiches—I put on more sunscreen and a hat, and set off alone for a walk around the caravan park, phone in hand.

"Hey, pumpkin," Dad answered with a smile in his voice. "How's the weather?"

"Nice. Well, hot." Despite the shady trees lining the road, the air hung heavy with the sun's heat. The gravel underfoot warmed through the soles of my shoes, while the occasional puff of breeze stirred my hair on the nape of my neck, doing little to cool me down.

"And the beach?"

"Good. We saw a bluebottle today, though." I set off towards the part of the park where the permanent residents lived, my shoes crunching.

"Everyone okay?"

"Yeah." I decided not to tell Dad about my encounter

with Toby. I didn't want to worry him. I also wasn't sure whether he'd be proud of me for helping the boy or if he'd disapprove. If it were going to be the latter, I'd rather not know. My disappointment at Sarah's reaction still tasted bitter on my tongue.

Or maybe that was the mustard.

"Well, try not to step on any this time," he teased when my silence stretched on for too long.

I didn't bite. "I won't. Did you get my text?" He'd made me promise to send him a message when we'd arrived the afternoon before.

"Yup. How are your cousins?"

"They're fine." The way Dad was circling around what he really wanted to ask made me grin and add, "Dominic's fine too."

"I hope he's behaving himself." Dad's tone was gruff. He wasn't wild about the idea of my boyfriend coming on the trip when there weren't any adults with us—ignoring the fact Sarah and I were eighteen and Ryan was in his early twenties.

"He's been the perfect gentleman," I reassured my father. "He's sharing a room with Ryan." I lowered my voice, even though the nearest people, an elderly couple dressed in clashing floral prints, were a couple of vans away. "Honestly, Dad, it's not like he could try anything if I didn't want him to."

"I know that, Isla. That's part of what I'm worried about!"

"Dad!" The blush burned my cheeks.

The elderly couple looked up. A trembling white furball of a dog poked its head out from under their caravan and barked, a high-pitched yap. The man patted the dog, glowering at me. His glare spoke volumes—they lived on site and didn't approve of all these tourists coming down every summer and cluttering up their home. With their kids. And their music.

On the other end of the phone, Dad was chuckling.

"You're not suggesting I'd ... take advantage of him?" I muttered into the receiver, hurrying around the nearest corner so that I was out of sight of the floral prints and their nervous pet. "Seriously?"

I hadn't told Dad my belief that my mother had used her *aosidhe* magic to make him fall in love with her when they'd first met. I didn't know if he suspected it, wondering why he still loved her, even though almost two decades had passed since he'd last seen her. Was it possible to love someone that desperately and simultaneously suspect your feelings weren't real?

No, *real* wasn't the right word. Foreign or unnatural would be a better description. Once they were inside you, those artificial feelings were real in every way.

Dad's laughter died when he heard the hurt in my voice. "Of course not, sweetie. Honestly, you wouldn't have to. You're an attractive girl, and he's not blind. I know you wouldn't do that."

"No, I wouldn't." Thinking about the boy at the beach today, I added, "Not out of selfishness."

After an awkward pause, Dad decided to change the subject. "And did Jack make it down?"

"Yes, we went to see my, uh, teacher last night."

"The siren." Wherever Dad was, he didn't have to worry about people overhearing. He knew the reason we'd come to the coast was so I could get training—he'd even paid for the cabin and the petrol, ostensibly as a graduation gift to Sarah and me. Aunt Elizabeth, Sarah and Ryan's mother, had pitched in for food.

"Yes."

"What's it … he? … like?" Dad's involvement in the *duinesidhe* world had been limited, as far as I could tell, to his relationship with my mother.

"He. Ever seen a blue pointer?"

"The shark?"

"Uh huh," I said.

"I've seen pictures."

"Imagine that, only humanoid."

"Oh." He thought about that for a moment. "Jack's looking after you, right?" His voice was anxious.

"Yes, Dad." My path took me to the edge of the park. Scrubby bushland clumped between well-worn paths; cicadas clicked loudly. I added, "He's as bad as you are."

"Good!" He sounded relieved.

"That wasn't meant to be a compliment."

"Well, it was."

When I got back to the cabin after my call, Ryan showed me some tourist brochures he'd picked up from the park's main office. He'd put one about art galleries along the coast to one side for further consideration. Sarah was more interested in visiting the zoo down at Mogo, which was only a twenty-minute drive from where we were staying. Dominic was happy to defer to me, which left me feeling both flattered and awkward, like I was under pressure to come up with something to keep us entertained.

Our cabin wasn't air conditioned or even insulated. The old ceiling fan ran full bore, creaking alarmingly and buffeting us with hot air. We were all perspiring; it wasn't ladylike but at least I was in good company.

"Let's go somewhere with air conditioning," Sarah said finally with an exasperated look at the fan. That, at least, got unanimous agreement, and let us rule out the zoo that afternoon.

Once we'd settled on a plan, we headed out, driving south to the Bega Valley so Ryan could go to the regional art gallery, stopping at several smaller showrooms and tourist traps along the way. We were in my car, which was the newest and actually had functional air conditioning. I didn't have a CD player, so I plugged my MP3 player into the portable speakers Sarah had given me for Christmas. Ryan and Sarah squabbled about the choice of music until I declared the "driver's choice" rule of music selection. Then I put the MP3 player on random.

The galleries were interesting—and air conditioned— although I didn't have enough money to buy anything bigger than a postcard print. We did buy a stick of fresh honeycomb from the heritage centre in Bega, though. By then it was Dominic's turn to drive, so Sarah and I picked at the honeycomb, making happy noises and licking our fingers to make sure they were clean. I didn't want the sticky mess on the car's faded upholstery.

"The last place I wanted to stop is just ahead," Ryan said when we were only twenty minutes from the caravan park. He directed Dominic to turn in at yet another roadside village. Although by then it was midafternoon, the temperature hadn't dropped; the sun glared down from a brilliant blue sky, casting stark shadows onto the hot tarmac under our shoes.

When we reached the little art shop, we scurried inside as quickly as we could, hoping for a breath of cool air.

ISLA'S OATH

We met with partial success. The shop was small and crowded with objects, if not with people. The walls, where we could see them through the clutter, were beige-painted concrete, cutting the temperature by a few degrees. The high, rattan-covered windows provided some shelter, and a half-dozen ceiling fans whirled overhead. Near the counter, an old evaporative cooler trying to chill the air added to the coastal humidity.

An eclectic mix of sculptures, paintings and photography filled the shop. Near the door, a stand of tourist items towered, overstuffed with plush koalas, kangaroos and kookaburras dressed in Australian flags or green and gold. The koalas wore bush hats that dangled tiny corks in their startled marsupial faces, and the kangaroos wielded boxing gloves and glass-eyed scowls.

Ryan wove his way through the stands to the back wall. He skipped over the photographs, stopping when he reached the paintings. Nose inches from the canvas, he examined the images like a scientist studying a rare artefact. Scratching my own nose, I hoped he didn't sneeze. The shop reeked of sandalwood incense, and my stomach roiled uneasily. Had I eaten too much honey?

Sarah found a poorly lit cabinet of cheap jewellery; glancing over her shoulder, I saw hearts, crosses, angels and a single, out-of-place pentagram that reminded me with a chill of my one and only séance experience. Dominic wandered over to examine the sculptures.

"Can I help you all?" A large woman came out from behind the counter, her sudden appearance making me jump. I hadn't seen her until she moved. Her red and gold gypsy-style shirt camouflaged perfectly with the rug hanging on the wall behind her.

"Just browsing, thanks." I smiled at her. She didn't smile back.

"Your friend there like art?" The woman indicated Ryan with a jut of her chin.

"He's a painter."

She brightened—I noticed a few old spots of paint on her jeans—and lumbered over to Ryan. However, she kept a gimlet eye on the rest of us, presumably to make sure we didn't steal anything. Very welcoming.

Bored, Sarah and I waited by the jewellery stand. "I'm dreading getting back to the cabin," my cousin admitted, brushing sweat-damped tendrils back from her face. "It's going to be an oven."

"Why don't we use the barbeques to cook dinner?" I suggested, wiping my palms on my denim shorts. My nausea was growing. I wasn't sure I'd be able to eat dinner. Stupid honeycomb. "At least that won't heat up the cabin any further."

"Good idea." Her eyes lit up. "Then we can go down to the beach for a swim afterwards. To cool off."

"Hey, Isla," Dominic said, walking towards us. He was holding something black in one hand. "I was thinking about getting this as a present for your dad, to thank him for paying for the trip." He held the object out to show me, a lump vaguely shaped like a curvy woman with her arms together above her head.

I squeaked and leaped back, my shoulder thumping into a hanging wind chime. Wooden tubes clanked furiously. The shop's owner shouted something, but I didn't hear it.

The sculpture was iron. And I'd nearly taken it from him. Dominic stared at me with wide eyes, the sculpture still outstretched. The storeowner barrelled over and snatched it off him as though he was brandishing it.

Swallowing hard, I fled.

My mother's race was violently allergic to iron—to the point where the touch of the metal caused their flesh to char and melt away. I'd seen an iron pellet sizzle through a hob's skull last spring, a memory I'd sooner forget. Jack had assured me the *aosidhe* reacted just as violently to the metal. They couldn't even tolerate contact with steel, whereas, because I was half-human, steel didn't bother me and iron didn't have the same dramatic effect. But it still burned.

And its presence made me sick.

Leaning my forehead against a wooden power pole by the car, I closed my eyes and took several gasping breaths. I felt like an idiot. I should have realised that was what had been causing the nausea when I entered the shop. If it were the honeycomb, Sarah would be feeling sick too.

She and Dominic came out a moment later, looking relieved when they saw me huddled by the car. She talked quickly, her tone reassuring. "It was a really thoughtful idea." I hung my head shamefully. Of course it was. Dad was an ironworker himself—although his reasons for choosing that medium were defensive rather than artistic. He would've loved the gift. "Isla was just telling me she was starting to feel a little sick. From the incense." My cousin's blue-green eyes met mine.

"Are you okay?" my boyfriend asked, hurrying over. I took a deep breath of pine-scented air. Now I was further away from the iron, my nausea eased. "Do you want some water?"

"Please."

Dominic fished a half-empty bottle from the back seat and handed it to me. The water was lukewarm but helped settle my stomach. As I screwed the lid back on, I leaned forward to kiss his cheek. "I'm sorry, Dominic. Sarah is right. It was really sweet of you to think of getting something for my dad."

"Did you want me to go back in and get it?"

"No, no," I said hastily, grabbing his hand before he could turn away. "Why don't we buy him a case of a local beer or something? He has an awful lot of iron sculptures already."

"Lord knows that's true," Sarah muttered. Dad occasionally sold his art, but he made far more items than he sold. The rest cluttered up his farmhouse and yard, taking up space ... and deterring *duinesidhe* trespassers. He'd talked about getting rid of it all after my half-breed heritage had manifested itself. I wouldn't let him. Knowing there was somewhere my family could go that was safe from hostile *duinesidhe* reassured me when I lay awake at night.

"Yeah, sure, I guess so." Dominic's shoulders slumped. My chest felt heavy with guilt, and I wrapped my arms around him.

"Maybe we should just head back to the caravan park?" Sarah suggested, coming to my rescue.

We waited for Ryan, who soothed the shop owner's ruffled feathers by buying a couple of paintbrushes and a decorative fan. "For Mum," he said, gesturing with the latter. A rose pattern adorned the black-and-red fabric.

Once we were away from the iron, I felt better—although the shock left me a little shaky. I passed my keys to Ryan and slid into the back seat with Dominic, holding his hand

and staring out the window at the dense forest of eucalypts that closed in around us as we drove down the single-lane highway. Guilt and self-pity warred behind my ribs, making me feel awful.

It could be worse. You could have Jack's condition, I reminded myself. He was a hob, a member of one of the *duinesidhe* races used as servants by the *aosidhe*, and he was as allergic to iron as my mother's people. He went through the world feeling as jumpy about steel as I was about iron. And there was a lot more steel around—although he'd assured me that with the increasing use of alloys and hard plastics in modern construction, pure iron and even steel were becoming less common.

Sarah glanced over her shoulder at me. "Are you feeling better?"

"A bit."

"Good." She turned back to look out the windshield, adding pointedly, "Maybe you were allergic to something in the shop." Beside her, Ryan stiffened but said nothing.

I didn't have to read minds to know what Sarah was thinking. If I'd told Dominic about my heritage, he wouldn't have offered me the sculpture. He wouldn't be sitting beside me, worried he'd done something wrong.

Dammit.

My "illness" at the art shop did have one upside, albeit one that didn't do anything to lessen my guilt: Dominic was understanding when I said I wanted an early night, going to bed after our post-dinner swim at the—now bluebottle-free—beach. The others stayed up reading and watching quiet TV in the lounge.

I set my phone's alarm for eleven that night, put it under my pillow, and lay down on top of the covers. They clung to me, still hot, but my exhaustion soon dragged me under.

Sarah was getting changed for bed when the muffled beeping woke me up. "Good nap?" she said.

"Yeah." I rubbed my eyes. "I figure I won't get much sleep tonight. Might as well catch up while I can." I wasn't planning on topping up on people's emotions every day after getting no sleep the night before. "Are the others still up?"

"Ryan is. Dominic fell asleep on the couch a half hour ago, so we chased him off to bed for you."

"Thanks."

"You're welcome." Her tone was cool.

I sighed and got up, running a brush through my hair and grabbing my thongs. "Good night," I murmured as I left the room.

Ryan sat sideways on the cheap sofa. He had one long leg stretched along the couch, the other bent so he could use his knee to steady his sketchbook. I peeked over his shoulder. He was shading in a drawing he'd started that morning at the beach, a sketch of one of the children excavating the sand for treasure. Ryan's pencil worked to capture the look of furious concentration on the little boy's face as the sand flew.

I sat at the dining table, slipping on my shoes. My cousin raised an eyebrow at me, taking in my slumped shoulders. "What's up?" he asked in a quiet voice.

"Sarah's pissed at me," I murmured.

"Why?"

"This." I nodded towards Dominic's closed bedroom door. "Being sneaky about it."

He shrugged, looking back at his sketchpad. The

pencil made a faint scraping sound as he resumed drawing. "She'll get over it."

"You don't agree with her?"

"Nope. You'll tell him when the time's right."

"How do I know when that is?" I stood.

"You'll know."

I wished I shared his confidence.

The rest of our holiday proceeded more or less as it had started. We went to the beach every day, even on the one day it rained. We visited the zoo, and went bushwalking, and Dominic and I ventured out as a couple a few times, for ice creams or to sit on the pier in the nearby town, Batemans Bay, and watch the fishing boats come and go. My favourite date was our walk on the beach early on the third morning, the sand empty of visitors except for us, the breaking day still peaceful and cool. I did, however, find it hard to shake the feeling we were being watched from beyond the breaking surf. Was Mako out there somewhere, studying us with black eyes?

The siren's lessons occurred every night, starting between eleven and midnight, depending when I was able to get away from the cabin. Each night I was back in the cabin by four at the latest. Despite Mako's often sharp criticisms, the lessons progressed well. Once I was able to identify different emotions, Mako taught me the basics of manipulating emotions with precision—my approach to date had all the subtlety of a paint gun on a small square of canvas. Dubious about the ethics of changing others' feelings, I was reluctant to do this part of the training. The siren insisted. "If you don't master all aspects of this ability, it will master you."

I thought about Nana, unconscious on the hospital floor, and agreed.

Most precious to me, on the final night of our holiday Mako taught me how to block my ability to see people's feelings altogether. I had to concentrate to maintain it, but he assured me it would get easier with time. "It's like a muscle," he'd hissed between mouthfuls of a large piece of raw sirloin. We saved the nicest cuts of meat for the end of each lesson. "The more you practice, the easier it gets. And the stronger you get, the more you can achieve."

"But I can't just leave the ability off all the time?" My heart sunk and I stared down at my bare feet in the water.

He looked at me sideways. "No. Why would you want to?"

I shrugged, unwilling to explain the attraction of being a regular human to this strange creature. At best, he wouldn't understand; at worst, he would decide I was weak. And that could be a very bad thing. "Thank you for your time, Mako," I said instead.

He paused in the act of licking his fingers and blinked. "The oath is complete. Agreed?"

"Agreed." I felt the binding drift from my shoulders, like steam evaporating from a simmering pot.

"Goodbye, Isla Half-Breed."

His head vanished beneath the waves before I could reply.

As Jack and I walked back to the caravan park for the last time, I stretched until I felt my spine crack. "I'm glad that's over."

He gave me a long look. I only caught glimpses of his eyes' sapphire gleam in the poor light. "You are tired."

ISLA'S OATH

I nodded, hiding a yawn behind my hand. I'd clung stubbornly to my decision not to refuel myself on others' emotions, even though Jack had offered after I told him about the incident at the beach. His part in my lessons with Mako already exhausted him, and it seemed unfair to further abuse his accommodating nature. "When we get home I'm going to sleep for a week. It will be so nice to be in my own bed. With my own pillow. Alone."

"Does your cousin keep you awake?"

"Not exactly. She scowls at me." Jack tipped his head to the side, and I grimaced. "She's mad that I won't tell Dominic who we are and what we're doing. Because she and I are sharing a room, the fact I'm sneaking out is sort of in her face. Sometimes I feel like telling him just to make her happy." Sarah had refrained from saying anything else to me after the incident at the art shop, but her pointed looks and icy tone spoke volumes.

I wasn't used to having real arguments with her—while we bickered from time to time, this issue hadn't blown over the way they usually did. I hoped things would return to normal once we got home. I missed her light-hearted friendship.

Jack's eyes were distant with thought. Finally he said, "What is your relationship with Dominic?"

"What do you mean? He's my boyfriend."

"I mean physically. You kiss and hold hands." His lips pressed together for a moment before he added, "Have you had sex with him?"

Shocked, I halted on the grass at the edge of the road.

Jack took a few extra steps before realising I wasn't beside him anymore. "Have I offended you?"

"Uh." My ears burned. I was glad that the only light

was from the silver moon overhead, so he couldn't see how much he'd shaken me up. "Not exactly. But ... well, no. We haven't had sex."

"And why is that?" His large eyes were luminous.

"Because we're not ready. I'm not ready." This was the strangest conversation. I hadn't even had a talk like this with Sarah. Of course, she and I weren't really confiding in one another right now.

"There you are then," he said. I must have looked as confused as I felt, because he took my hand. His fingers were warm—he always felt hot to the touch, as though he'd just stepped out of a scalding shower and his skin was radiating heat. "If you are not ready to give yourself to this boy physically, why would you be ready to share your family secrets with him? Both require trust. You will know when it is time."

I remembered Ryan's comment. Was this what he meant when he said I'd know? If so, I was glad he hadn't been clearer. It was bad enough having this conversation with Jack.

We started walking again. After a few seconds, Jack dropped my hand, adjusting the bandana covering his ears with the ease of practice.

I decided to change the subject. "Why was Mako so surprised when I said thanks? Did he think we had more lessons to do?"

"No. He was surprised because *aosidhe* do not express gratitude."

"Not ever?"

"I have never heard one do so."

"Wow." My mother's people sounded awful. I hoped I never had to deal with them.

CHAPTER FOUR

A few days after we got back from the coast, Sarah and I sat up to watch a chick flick—although neither of us were focusing on it. My cousin had her bare foot on the coffee table and was painting her toenails a dark red. The strong aroma of nail polish filled the lounge room, itching my nose.

The silence between us felt awkward. I could have looked at Sarah's aura to figure out whether she felt the same way, but I was practicing not seeing her emotions, flexing the muscle Mako had taught me to use. I was timing myself to see how long I could do it before I had to relax and let the unwanted information flood back in again. A glance at my watch told me I was up to an hour. I was starting to feel drained and shaky—like I'd been holding my arms out from my sides for too long ... only the sensation was all over my body. I gritted my teeth and kept going.

If Sarah was still angry with me, I didn't want to know. If you'd asked me six months ago whether I'd like to be able to see others' emotions, I would have said yes. Now I knew better. Knowing with certainty that someone was upset or angry when they are working hard to conceal that fact felt like cheating.

Although not as big a cheat as actually changing their emotions would be.

You could make her forgive you. Just a little nudge, a traitorous voice whispered in my head. If the devil was real, that was what his voice would sound like. My eyes widened in horror at how tempted I was to change things back to the way they'd been. *Given what Mako taught me, it would be easy.*

It would also be a terrible breach of Sarah's trust and a violation of our friendship.

I chewed my lip, staring at the television without seeing the action on the screen. I'd changed others' feelings on a few occasions before the incident down the coast. When Dad was attacked by a fierce, blood-soaked *powrie*—a *duinesidhe* ogre of sorts—I forced it to flee, caught in the grip of artificial terror. It had been self-defence, and I didn't feel guilty about it any more than I had about helping Toby in the surf.

However, I was more ambivalent about the incident with my grandmother. Provoked by her deliberate cruelty, I'd struck her with my newly blooming, out-of-control gift. It hadn't been intentional—but, in the course of setting it right, I'd deliberately enhanced her motherly love for my father, like I was blowing on a smouldering coal to encourage it to flame. Dad had been surprised and grateful at the unexpected healing of the rift in their relationship. Nana had since returned to England, but they now exchanged regular phone calls, something they'd rarely done beforehand.

I'd never admitted my part in reuniting them to anyone except Jack and Sarah. If Dad or Nana suspected my involvement, they'd never said anything to me. I tried to assuage my guilt by thinking of the good I'd done, but still wondered if I'd crossed a line.

When Ryan's key rattled in the front door I breathed a silent sigh of relief. Hamish, Sarah's black terrier, jumped off the couch and bounced over to greet Ryan as he walked in.

"Hey," Ryan grunted, throwing his jacket over the unoccupied chair. His supermarket uniform was rumpled.

"Hi." I smiled briefly. Sarah nodded, keeping her gaze on her task. Ryan glanced from her to me and rolled his eyes. I grimaced back at him.

"So, you know Debbie at work?"

"The pregnant one?"

"Yeah, her. She's leaving in a week and they're going to have a checkout job open if either of you are keen," Ryan said. "The boss said to ask." Since graduating, Sarah and I were both searching for work. Aunt Elizabeth insisted we contribute to household expenses—I could've moved back in with Dad at the farm and not had to worry about it, but finding a job would be a lot harder from there.

Also, the farm was riddled with iron.

Sarah looked up, paintbrush wavering over her little toe. A drop of ruby nail polish dangled, growing thicker as it threatened to drip onto her foot. "Full time?"

"Casual. But decent hours, so the pay will be good."

She gazed at me. What was she was thinking? After a brief hesitation, I looked at her aura. Yellow flickered uncertainly. Because she didn't know if I wanted the job, or because she didn't know if she did?

The job was tempting. On the other hand, Sarah had to put up with a lot more nagging than I did. At least Dad was still paying my board while I hunted for work … and continued to educate myself in my *aosidhe* heritage. After Dad came clean with me about my mother, he'd insisted I needed to learn everything I could in order to protect myself. He didn't say what I was protecting myself *from*, but sometimes a *powrie* pursued me through my dreams, turning them to blood-soaked nightmares, its uneven teeth bared in a snarl and its breath stinking like a sewer. I didn't need Dad to elaborate.

Sarah was still looking at me.

It wasn't worth jeopardising my fragile relationship with my cousin to take the job.

"It's yours if you want it," I said with a smile.

"You mean it?"

"Of course I do."

Her grin was as bright as the dawning sun, melting away the frost that lay between us. She put the brush back in the pot and gave me an awkward hug, careful not to move her feet. "Thanks, Isla."

"You can thank me too, you know," Ryan remarked, grabbing the unguarded remote control and flicking channels. His aura was deep pink, glad Sarah and I were getting along again.

A soft tap at the window made us all jump. Hamish yapped. Ryan, still standing, went to the door and peered out. After a moment, he held the screen door open, looking at me over his shoulder. "It's for you."

Jack stepped past Ryan and into the lounge room. He wore denim shorts and a plain blue T-shirt that made his sapphire eyes sparkle. A bandana covered his ears, for which I was grateful. Aunt Elizabeth—who was reading a book in her bedroom—didn't know what he was, and that was a conversation I really didn't want to have.

Jack looked out of place standing in our lounge room, like a fish in a bathtub; he seemed happy enough, but the sight made me stare. I'd never seen Jack inside a house before. I'd seen him in cars and at the hospital when he'd helped me revive Dad from his coma, but never in our home or any other. My relationship with him tended towards secret meetings in outdoor places, usually at night.

Suddenly that fact seemed unbearably rude. I gestured towards the spare seat. "Can I get you anything? A soft drink or some juice?"

"No, thank you." He perched on the edge of the heavy couch, sparing a glance for my cousins. Sarah blew her toes dry, sneaking peeks at Jack out of the corner of her eye. Ryan closed the lounge room door so my aunt wouldn't overhear the conversation. He leaned against the inside of the door, eyes gleaming with curiosity.

I struggled to think of a polite way to ask Jack what he wanted. Ryan found it for me. "To what do we owe the pleasure?" he asked in a perfect imitation of his mother. I flashed him a grateful smile.

Jack looked from Ryan to me, raising a questioning eyebrow. I nodded; he could talk in front of my cousins. "Remember how you asked me last year whether there was anything I could do to identify who had mailed the elf shot to your father?"

"Yes." Dad had been a coma for a week—the memory of it still made my eyes burn with remembered grief. We'd felt so helpless. The doctors weren't able to explain the cause, but Jack did: my father had been wounded by a magical *aosidhe* weapon that causes paralysis in its target. The elf shot was only able to propel itself over short distances, so it had been brought close to Dad via a package he'd received through regular old Australia Post.

"Didn't it come from Scotland?" Ryan asked with a faint frown.

I nodded. "From Edinburgh." I still had the shredded packaging in my room. Sometimes I pulled the brown paper out and stared at it, wondering who Dad's enemy was.

"Are you sure she didn't send it? Uncle David met her there, didn't he?" He meant my mother.

"I thought so at first," I admitted. "She certainly has reasons to hate him. But the hob who was with the *powrie* when it attacked us said he was working for someone else."

"He didn't say who?"

I shook my head ruefully. The hob, Moray, hadn't survived long enough to answer questions, thanks to Nana's amazing aim with an iron pellet. "Have you had any luck, Jack?"

The hob leaned forward, meeting my gaze. "Yes and no. It has been difficult to find someone with the right skills who was willing to assist. But there is a *puca* who would be able to investigate the packaging for you." The *puca* were a race of faerie shape changers.

I frowned. "Can we trust him?" As well as Moray, the *powrie* that night had worked with a *puca* in the shape of a large black dog. The pair had fled the farm when Moray died, and we hadn't seen them since.

"We could bind him with an oath to ensure his trustworthiness," Jack suggested.

ISLA'S OATH

I should have thought of that. "How do we know that he wasn't the same *puca* that attacked you at the farm? We only saw him as a dog."

"It is not the same *puca*," he said with certainty. "They look different, even in their shape-changed forms."

"Yeah, Isla, you racist," Sarah teased, nudging me with her elbow.

I poked my tongue at her. "How would I know? I've only ever met one, and he was busy trying to bite Jack's face off at the time."

"Not all *puca* are violent," Jack said. "We know that particular one was hired by Moray to assist in kidnapping your father."

Ryan slouched over to perch on the arm of the couch, right beside Sarah. She grumbled under her breath, falling silent when he spoke. "What about the other one? The *powrie* ogre thing?" Ryan's prophetic drawing of the *powrie* had warned us about the attack in time for Jack and me to save Dad and Nana. I'd accidentally made my cousin into what the *duinesidhe* called an *aislinge*—a seer or visionary whose occasional visions manifested through his art.

"All *powrie* are violent," Jack said, large eyes shadowed.

"Oh." After taking a moment to digest this uncomfortable thought, I moved on. "What does the *puca* want in exchange for helping me?"

"I have not asked him that yet."

"But you said...?"

"He is capable of investigating the packaging to try and identify the sender. I am unsure whether he would be willing. We would need to negotiate. He has agreed to speak to us about it, which is a place to start."

I pursed my lips. This was the same process we'd gone through in finding Mako, although then Jack had taken care of the initial negotiations on my behalf. *Duinesidhe* culture seemed to be driven by bargains and trades, at least when the *aosidhe* weren't nearby to boss the other races around. "Should I bring a gift or something? To thank him for meeting us?"

"He would probably find that reassuring, yes."

"Okay. Any suggestions?"

"A movie voucher?" Ryan quipped.

Jack grinned. "He is a scent hound. Any pleasant smell will do."

I stared at him. "A *smell*?"

"Yes."

"What about some perfume?" Happy with her nail polish, Sarah pulled on a pair of striped socks and then curled her feet under her. Hamish, seeing an opportunity to demand belly rubs, jumped onto her lap.

"I don't know what he likes."

"He would not necessarily wear the perfume," Jack said. "Just collect it."

"Weird," I muttered. Ryan nodded, eyebrows raised.

"You can buy sample vials pretty cheaply. A couple of millilitres for a few dollars. You could get him two or three different types of those." Sarah shrugged. "Hell, I've got a few vials I've bought and barely touched. You can have them, if you like?"

"Awesome! I can give you the money for them."

She waved her hand dismissively. "Nah, they're just taking up space on my dresser anyway. Hang on a tick." Hamish grunted in protest when Sarah shoved him off her lap and disappeared into her room. He'd barely had time to settle himself into her spot when she returned, holding a double handful of small vials, and pushed him out of the way again.

Grumbling, the dog disappeared under the coffee table.

"Here," Sarah said. "Pick a couple of these."

Most of the vials weren't in their packaging anymore. Some had labels and some didn't; I unscrewed each of the tiny lids and sniffed. "Which ones should I choose?"

I offered Jack the vials. He waved me off. "Choose whichever ones you like best, Isla."

I eventually chose two. One was refreshingly fruity, reminding me of a mango and mandarin juice I'd tried once. The other smelled of Aunt Elizabeth's garden: roses and raspberry leaves, with a hint of sweet musk, faint enough not to be overpowering.

Jack and Sarah nodded their approval when I made them smell the two perfumes I'd selected. Ryan pulled a face. "I've inhaled too much turpentine to be of any use to you."

"Shall we go now then?" Jack asked as I reached to put the chosen vials on the coffee table. Startled, I nearly dropped them.

"Now?" I squeaked.

"Why not?"

"Because it's the middle of the night?" Sarah frowned at the hob.

"Most *duinesidhe* prefer to be active at night," he replied, calm in the face of her displeasure. "We are good at hiding our differences from humans, but the darkness makes it easier."

I chewed my lip, considering. I wasn't tired. Finally being able to pursue the identity of my father's attacker filled me with relief ... although I hadn't yet considered what I would do once I knew the answer.

I'd cross that bridge when I came to it. Either way, it was better to know than be vulnerable due to ignorance.

Sarah watched my expression with narrowed eyes. "I'll come with you then."

"Ah..." Jack trailed off as her glare shifted to him. He fidgeted on the edge of the seat as he continued, "We'll be going into the *sidhe*. You would not be able to follow us there."

"The *sidhe*?" Sarah scowled. "Isn't that what you call your people?"

"No, the *sidhe* are our homes. The word roughly translates to *mounds*. The *duinesidhe* are the people of the mounds, or the faerie folk."

"And the *aosidhe* are...?"

"The rulers of the mounds." He puckered his lips as though the words left a bitter taste in his mouth. He had no love for my mother's people.

"Where are these mounds?"

He gestured expansively. "In a city like Canberra, surrounded by hills, they are all around us. But not all are occupied."

"So you live underground?" Ryan asked. I was grateful for his question, which was curious rather than overtly suspicious like his sister's.

Jack shrugged. "It is hard to explain. The *sidhe* are within the hills, and not. The doorways are in mountainsides, cliff faces and hillocks, but if a human dug into the soil they would not find us there."

"Neat trick," Ryan said. "Like a Batcave no one can ever find."

ISLA'S OATH

Jack smiled politely, probably not getting the pop culture reference. His gaze shifted to me, expectant.

"Okay, I'll come. Do I need to bring anything? Or dress for spelunking, maybe?" My voice cracked a little. I'd gone cave diving once, on a school excursion to the Jenolan Caves in the Blue Mountains. I was okay in the bigger caves, but the smaller ones felt like they were squashing the breath out of me. All I'd been able to think about was of thousands of tons of rock crashing down on my head and smearing me into red paste. I'd ended up sitting part of the trip out with my friend Natalie and one of the teachers.

Also, I owned neither overalls nor helmet with headlights.

Jack laughed. "What you are wearing is fine. Although for shoes, I would suggest sneakers rather than something tall and impractical. We will be crossing uneven ground to get to the nearest entrance."

Despite Jack's suggestion, I decided to put on fresh clothes before we left, changing out of denim shorts and into my favourite pair of navy jeans. That way my legs would have some protection if I fell over a rock in the dark. I added a black tank top with a loose, silvery-grey shirt over it. Formal enough that I hoped not to offend; not so formal I looked stuffy.

Although who knew how a scent hound would regard clothing choices?

When I got back to the lounge, Ryan was commiserating with Jack about "girls and their constant need to fuss with clothes", and Sarah was sitting back with her arms folded across her chest, regarding them with narrowed eyes. They all stood when I came in, a backpack over my shoulder. Along with my phone, purse and a bottle of water, I'd packed the wrapping from the elf shot parcel—safely ensconced in its zipper-sealed sandwich bag. Sarah handed me the vials and I put them in my pocket.

"Ready?"

"Yes."

"Be careful." Sarah hugged me. "Call if you need anything."

I wasn't sure if I would be able to get a signal in the *sidhe*, but I nodded anyway. There was no sense in worrying her further.

Squaring her jaw, she gave Jack a flinty-eyed stare. "You look after her, you hear?"

"Always," he replied earnestly.

CHAPTER FIVE

*J*ack and I walked through the quiet suburban evening for twenty minutes, heading towards the dark silhouette of Mount Taylor that loomed to our north. Since our nighttime walks down the coast, the moon had slimmed down from a perfect disc to a fat crescent. A few clouds raced by, playing hide-and-seek with the stars, pushed along by a high wind that was no more than a breath to us on the ground.

Despite the clouds, visibility wasn't bad while we walked beside the asphalt roads, which were easy to navigate and lined with streetlights that shed a mellow orange light. Our trail became more precarious once we reached the edge of the reserve that draped the mountain like a blanket.

The hob strode beside me, confident of his footing. When I grumbled, he explained the door he was taking me to, which led into the *sidhe* where he lived, was the closest entrance to Aunt Elizabeth's house. He walked this path regularly.

We followed a gravel track past the horse paddocks. A pair of eyes, black in the moonlight, watched us with vague interest, waiting to see whether we had a carrot or a lump of sugar. When we continued on, the horse sighed and dropped his head, returning to his nap.

The track intersected with an equestrian trail—which headed north along the edge of the reserve—and the walking trail. Jack veered left onto the latter, and up the slope of the mountain.

Why didn't I bring a torch? I thought, following Jack along the winding path. Our shoes crunched with each step as we ascended through the dry summer scrub, past towering eucalypts whose trunks glowed silver and grey in the shifting moonlight. The path itself was clear, so the light from above was enough to illuminate our steps, but to either side of us the shadows were thick and tangled. Even knowing there was nothing more dangerous than a kangaroo in the reserve, I shivered as I glanced into the gloom. It was easy to imagine something keeping pace with us—something silent and fierce.

Jack stopped when the path hooked right, climbing more steeply up the flank of the mountain. "We leave the track here."

I frowned at the mess of fallen branches and scrubby grass ahead of us. Rocks peeked out from beneath the undergrowth, and a tree trunk leaned drunkenly across the entrance to a black gully that stretched down the slope, its depths impenetrable to my gaze.

Jack took a few steps off the walking trail before he realised I wasn't following. He looked back at me. "What is the matter?"

ISLA'S OATH

"I can't see in the dark, Jack." I put my hands on my hips, exasperated. It was easy to imagine spraining an ankle crossing the uneven and shadowy terrain.

"Oh." He seemed surprised.

"Can you?"

"Not exactly," he answered, "but I do have quite good night vision. Here, give me your hand. It is not far."

I reached for his outstretched palm, butterflies fluttering in my stomach. The sensation made me hesitate, and Jack raised an eyebrow. "Are you okay?"

"I'm fine."

The hob steadied me with a firm grip as I eased my way over branches and past half-hidden rocks, steering me to the least-treacherous path. Together we picked our way down into the gully. Now I was closer, it wasn't as oppressively black as I'd first thought. Trees leaned over it, filtering out most of the moonlight, but a flicker of silver worked its way to the ground here and there, giving me enough light to see by as we followed it. My eyes must be adjusting to the darkness.

Or so I thought—until I saw a faint glow ahead of us. I stopped, staring.

"You see it." Jack smiled, his teeth a brief flash in the gloom.

"I see something. What is it?"

"Come."

It turned out to be a doorway-shaped ripple of opaque, greenish-blue light that emerged from between two great grey rocks. The rocks, sentinel-like, leaned up against the earthy northern embankment of the gully, forming the sides of a crude frame. The top edge was an overhang covered with thick grass that hung down like a bushy fringe.

"That's the door to the *sidhe*?" I breathed. He nodded, golden hair gleaming in the doorway's fey glow. The light caressed his features, highlighting all that was *other* about him: his large, gentle eyes, which missed nothing; the fine nose and pointed chin; the preternatural smoothness of his marble skin.

I realised I was staring and looked away, biting my lip for a moment before saying, "It's not that well hidden. You must have people wandering in all the time."

"You can only see it because of your *duinesidhe* blood," Jack pointed out. "That was one of the reasons Sarah could not come with us. She would be unable to see the gate."

"Could we have steered her to it?" I smiled at the thought. She'd hate that.

He hesitated before nodding again. "But humans ... do not always thrive in the *sidhe*."

"Why?" I felt my eyes widen as my stomach trembled with nerves. Despite everything, I thought of myself as human. The habit of a lifetime, I suppose.

"Some are enthralled by it and become unwilling to leave. Others go mad. Many are unaffected, but it is impossible to know how a person will react beforehand. It is a great risk to a human, bringing them into the *sidhe*."

"How do you know I won't react like that?"

"You will not."

"How can you be sure?"

"You can see the doorway," he responded with a shrug.

"What if I hadn't?"

"Isla, you were able to save your father from the elf shot," Jack said, voice earnest. "You made Ryan into an *aislinge* and have *aosidhe* power flowing through your veins. I never doubted you would be able to see the door, and I do not doubt now that you will be safe within the *sidhe*."

I thought about that for a moment, biting my lip. I would feel like an idiot, backing out now—and if this was the only way to meet the *puca* scent hound who could help me protect my father, running wasn't an option. I squared my shoulders, even as the tremble in my stomach turned into full-blown somersaults. "Right then. Let's do it."

Jack led me through the shimmering door.

Stepping into the portal was like diving into an icy lake on a hot day. Spinning in a dance, dizzy, until you fell. Listening to the soaring, intricate harmonies of a choir. Patting the soft belly of a kitten and feeling the vibrations of its purr through each fine hair. Taking a bite of something hot and sweet, fresh from the oven, and savouring it in your mouth.

It was like coming home.

I opened my eyes. When had I closed them? Jack and I stood on a path maybe six feet wide. The rough cobblestones were fashioned from rock native to the mountain—the cooled remains of volcanic explosions millions of years ago, if my half-remembered geology lessons were correct. We were in a circular tunnel, similar to a vast stormwater pipe where someone had flattened the floor. The sides of the tunnel were a smooth brown. Heart in my throat, I touched the wall next to me. The surface was scratchy under my fingers: solid, compacted earth. The roof, which arched six-and-a-half feet from the surface of the path, was the same substance. Staring up, I gasped—tiny dots of quartz studded the ceiling. Each of them glowed faintly from within, providing the same diffuse illumination as the stars outside.

Feeling like a gawping tourist but unable to stop myself, I turned back to the doorway we'd just come through. I could still see the gully, although it wavered and shimmered as though I was looking through a heat haze.

Jack guessed the train of my thoughts. "We can see out so that we know if the doorway is being observed before we emerge. It always pays to take caution when leaving the *sidhe*."

"That makes sense," I whispered. The sight of people, many of them strange looking, stepping out the side of mountains would startle anyone. Although, given how many stories there'd been of fairies and goblins and other beasties over the years, I suspected passage to and from the *sidhe* wasn't always managed as discreetly as it should be.

"You do not have to whisper," Jack said with a smile. "No one on the other side can hear you."

I cleared my throat and spoke normally. "That wasn't why I was whispering." I'd just passed through a mountainside into an alternate reality! I brushed my hair back from my face, trying to act as though I did this every day. "Shall we?"

He nodded. I took a deep breath and turned my back on the world I knew.

Jack led me down the corridor. As we moved away from the doorway and its ambient light faded, the chips of stone above us looked even more like stars. Despite the lack of moonlight, we were able to walk more swiftly than we had outside the mountain, striding along the even path. To my intense relief, the tunnel wasn't causing me any claustrophobia. It felt like walking down an oddly shaped corridor—although the air was still and felt charged, like it does before a big electrical storm hits. The tunnel didn't deviate either left or right, and the curve of the walls around us was an almost perfect arc from one edge of the path to the other. It was eerie to be in something that felt simultaneously natural and yet so ... the only description I could think of for it was *mass-produced*. My gaze ran along the sides of the tunnel, looking for the seams that joined the pieces together.

"Who made the *sidhe*? It's amazing."

Jack shrugged. "We do not know who made the original tunnels. The paving stones and stargems were added by the local *duinesidhe* over many years."

"So when you arrived here there were just..."

"Tunnels. Yes. It is the same in the Old World, of course, but the *sidhe* there are much more developed. The *duinesidhe* have had many hundreds or even thousands of years to shape what they found to their liking. Here, things are much ... simpler." His aura flickered with faint embarrassment.

I tried to reassure him. "I've never seen the Old World *sidhe*, remember, so you don't have to worry about me being all judgemental about your home."

"True." He smiled.

"Do you have any theories about who dug the tunnels?"

"There are stories of giant worms or serpents burrowing beneath the ground millennia ago. No one knows for sure if it is true."

How big would a creature need to be to dig a passage this wide? The tunnel, from wall to wall, was about eight feet in diameter. The roof was closer because, in the course of creating an even path, the *duinesidhe* had filled in the bottom of the cylinder.

I stopped, heart thumping. A worm that big would swallow me as easily as I ate a strawberry.

Jack returned to my side, his voice reassuring. "No one has ever seen one, either alive or dead. Odds are that they are long gone, like your dinosaurs. If they ever were."

"Odds are." My voice cracked, obviously still dwelling on the idea of a giant worm with long teeth, chewing through the earth.

I made my feet move again.

After a time—my wristwatch said fifteen minutes—it grew lighter ahead of us. The passage widened abruptly, and we came out into the cavernous home of the *duine-sidhe* of Canberra.

The tunnel emerged high in the wall of a terraced valley that ran as far as the eye could see. Structures—houses?—dotted the valley, some clustered close together, others standing apart from the rest: pariahs or recluses. Lights glittered all around the structures like earthbound stars. Stands of trees hemmed the valley, tall and slender. The trees strongly resembled the eucalypts we'd left in my world, except their trunks glowed silver and gold, and their leaves shimmered and whispered despite the still air.

Something drew my eyes upwards. The edges of the valley peaked in what looked like hilltops ... but where you'd expect a stretch of sky to be, there was only a giant blackness so vast it seemed to stare down like an enormous eye. Was it a huge, curved roof, or the inside of the top of a mountain? I couldn't tell.

Vertigo gripped me, and I lowered my gaze.

"Nice," I told Jack, my tone even this time. Go me!

He didn't respond. He was staring at me, his expression—and emotions—a mixture of satisfaction and awe

ISLA'S OATH

… with the tiniest thread of fear woven through it. Seeing that glimmer of fear in his eyes hurt more than I would have imagined. "What is it, Jack?"

"Nothing," he lied, his voice constricted. He turned from me, beginning the walk down the path into the valley.

"Don't *nothing* me! I get that enough from Sarah." I reached out and caught his shoulder, turning him back to me.

That was when I saw why he was staring.

The skin on my outstretched arm was luminescent, glowing faintly like the stargems in the roof of the tunnel. Heart in my throat, I examined my arms and hands, then ran my fingers over my face. My skin felt normal. Was my face glowing too? "Jack?" I couldn't keep the panic out of my voice. "What the hell is going on?"

He hesitated. "It was to be expected. It will not harm you."

"Expected by *you*, maybe! How come you're not glowing like a firefly?"

"It is an *aosidhe* thing."

"To glow inside the *sidhe*?" He nodded. "And will it turn off when I leave again?" Another nod. My panic segued into exasperation. "You knew this was going to happen!"

"Not for certain. But it was likely."

"And you thought you wouldn't mention it and I might not notice?"

He stared at his shoes, mumbling something I couldn't hear. The fear was gone, replaced by a flush of embarrassment.

"Well, that's just great, Jack." I stuffed my glowing hands in my pockets and took several breaths, trying to calm down. When I thought I could speak without yelling,

I added, "Is there anything else you're not telling me?"

He hesitated and I scowled. He spoke hastily. "There is one other thing. The *sidhe* may … change in response to you."

"Change? How?"

"I do not know."

"Jack!"

He held up his hands as if to ward off a blow. "I really do not know, Isla. I told you once that the *aosidhe* are the rulers of the *sidhe* by virtue of their power, remember?"

"You told me that it could sustain the hob outside the *sidhe*. That was all." When I'd first met Jack, his face—and probably the rest of him, although I had no firsthand evidence of that—was covered in a fine network of wrinkles. They'd filled out as he started to help me. Now his skin was smoother and finer than my own.

"They can also reshape the insides of the *sidhe* to their will. And those within them. The mounds will also sometimes respond to their desires even if they do not consciously will it. It gives them tremendous power over the ones who live here."

My eyes widened. "They can reshape the *duinesidhe*? The *people*?"

"Yes."

"How?"

"By willing it. They can change everything from their skin, hair and eyes to their skeletal structure." He lowered his voice, looked away. "It is very painful."

"That's awful!" I felt sick. That shadow of fear on Jack's face suddenly made sense, as did the *puca*'s reluctance to help. Were all the *duinesidhe* going to have the same reaction when they saw me? I stared down at my glowing hands. I wasn't going to be able to conceal my heritage from anyone I met tonight. "No wonder the rest of you hate them so much."

"It does not have to be that way." He took one of my hands and smiled. "You are not cruel or arrogant. Once the others learn that, they will grow to trust you. As I do."

Before I could say anything else, the hob turned away, leading me into the valley.

Feeling awkward and more than a little nervous at the welcome I might encounter, I followed Jack down the path towards the first of the terraces. Although the buildings in the valley might be houses in the sense that people lived in them, many bore little resemblance to what I'd always thought of as a house. Some had familiar architectural styles, although I didn't know of anywhere you could see a small, Greek home—gleaming white and speckled with blue, aquamarine and turquoise tiles like ocean spray— leaning up against an American ranch-style house with a gabled roof. Farther away, separated from our path by a large, reed-filled pond, a row of English terraced houses sat opposite a single Australian bush shack. The shack looked odd, the roof made of wooden shingles rather than the traditional, rusty corrugated iron.

More-outlandish structures included a building made from the hollowed-out trunk of a huge tree; a small door, no higher than my shoulders, provided access, and windows peeked out from under bark awnings. A door to another residence nestled unobtrusively between two of the uprights holding the terrace in place; it was barely two feet tall. A third house, woven entirely from dried grass, reminded me of the story of the three little pigs. In the distance hulked a building with the structure of a Mongolian yurt, sewn together from scraps of fabric—tie-dyed denim, shimmering blue satin, unbleached calico, a stretch of white brocade that may have once been the train of a wedding dress. Not waterproof ... but inside a mountain I guess it didn't rain.

At least, not often.

Did the hodgepodge of structures reflect the personalities of their owners, or was there some other reason for their curious designs? Most of them, even the most outlandish ones, were built from materials I could find in the outside world. Did the *duinesidhe* have to scavenge the pieces for their homes from outside the mound?

One thing that was not from my world was the lighting. Stargems studded the doorframes of some houses, and the streetlights were made from glass jars filled with the small glowing stones, fixed to the tops of wooden poles.

As we reached the floor of the valley, my ears strained to hear the sounds of a village going about its evening business. The air was still. I could clearly hear the sighing of the distant trees between the rhythmic slapping of our footsteps against the cobbles. Part of it was the lack of electronic noise from the buildings we passed—no televisions, gaming consoles or radios chattered here. But it was more than that. And it couldn't be that everyone was asleep either. Jack had already made the point that the *duinesidhe* were primarily nocturnal.

"Is it normally this quiet?" I whispered.

Jack shook his head.

"They're hiding from me." It wasn't a question; I already knew the answer.

"I warned them you might be coming. They are cautious."

ISLA'S OATH

"They're afraid."

He nodded, eyes sad.

The thought made my stomach churn. "Then let's get this done so I can leave and they can get back to normal."

Jack led me through the deserted streets to a small garden cottage surrounded by bushes and climbing vines that sagged, heavy with flowers. Most of the blooms were shut for the night, except for a spray of white evening primrose near the gate. The sweet, heady scent of the blooms eased my anxiety, intermingling with the aromas of fragrant herbs—I could smell lavender, basil, lemon balm and mint—from elsewhere in the garden.

If I were a creature who collected smells, this was the sort of garden I would grow. Although given I had a black thumb I might need Aunt Elizabeth to come and tend it for me.

Jack knocked on the wooden cottage door. There was no answer. I stood patiently by his side for a minute or so before raising my eyebrows at him. He shrugged apologetically and knocked again.

Maybe the *puca* would be more likely to answer the door if I weren't standing so close? I wandered back towards the garden beds. I wasn't an avid gardener like my aunt. I knew enough to identify some of the flowers, at least those that were common Canberra varieties. But most of these plants were strange to me. One, with glossy green leaves and plump buds, caught my eye. From the wicked, curved thorns that pierced the stems like the hooked claws of a cat, it was probably a variety of rose, although not one I'd ever seen. The petals were a vivid royal purple.

I heard murmuring voices behind me and glanced

back to see Jack bent over double, head poking through a dog flap in the bottom half of the cottage door. I couldn't hear what he was saying but he sounded irritated. A muffled voice replied, "I've changed my mind. Go away!"

Pretending not to notice, I turned my attention back to the flowers with a sigh, running a luminescent finger—I didn't think I would ever get used to that—along the outside of one of the fat buds. The petal was soft as fine silk.

The flower unfurled under my fingertip.

I gasped. The sweet, distinctive aroma of roses in bloom filled the air as, one after another, radiating out from the flower I'd touched, the rest of the buds on the bush opened to the night sky.

"What have you done?" a voice cried. The door thumped open. I turned to see Jack scrabbling to retain his balance as a short, stocky figure pushed past him.

The *puca* was barely five feet tall, dressed in tracksuit pants and a plain, baggy T-shirt. His black hair was cropped close to his head, and his eyes were bright with concern. His bare feet ran silently along the ground towards me, the soles stained dark with dirt. He interposed himself between me and the rosebush, scowling. Despite his courage, his aura was awash with fear.

"I'm sorry, I didn't mean to. I just touched the bud and all the flowers opened!"

"You shouldn't go touching other people's things," the *puca* said, his voice pitched high with anxiety. His skin was as pale as mine ... except for his nose, which was a few shades darker and twitched with agitation as he scented the air.

Jack hurried forward. "Isla, this is Talbot. Talbot, Isla." I nodded. The *puca* grimaced. "You know the *sidhe* will respond to an *aosidhe* sometimes, without them willing it," Jack chastised the *puca*. "And the plant is unharmed."

Talbot muttered something under his breath that sounded like "shouldn't be *aosidhe* here anyway". Jack frowned at him.

Moving slowly so as not to startle the skittish creature, I retrieved the vials of perfume from my pocket, relieved to see that the lids remained secure. "Here," I said, holding them out. "Take these as an apology. I really didn't mean it, Talbot."

The *puca* reached out a trembling hand, hesitating for a long moment before snatching the vials away. His fingernails were long and dark, blunted at the ends; they scraped lightly against the skin of my palm. "What are they?"

"Perfumes. Go ahead, open them." I took a couple of steps back so that he would feel less threatened.

Watching me from the corner of an eye the same golden brown as Hamish's, the *puca* unscrewed the lid on each of the vials in turn, his nose quivering in a way I found fascinating. He didn't hold the perfumes up to sniff the way a human would have; his sense of smell was keen enough that he could smell them without it. Given all the competing odours, I was impressed.

Once he'd sampled each vial, Talbot slipped them into the pocket of his tracksuit pants and then looked from me to Jack and back again. "What do you want?"

Jack winced at his bluntness, but I wasn't offended—I could see the roiling anxiety in the *puca's* aura and felt sorry for him. Would it be wrong to drain a small portion of his fear from him, to help him relax? The thought made me uneasy, and I decided not to. Besides, what if Talbot could tell I'd done something? That would ruin any chance I'd have of convincing him to help me.

Willingly, at any rate. But I refused to act like my mother's people, forcing him to cooperate. Or obey.

Trying not to make any sudden moves, I explained my predicament. "My father was attacked late last year. I want to find out who did it."

He stood up straighter, meeting my gaze. "Your father is the human one?"

"Yes." Was my half-breed status obvious? Either that or the *duinesidhe* gossiped as much as humans did.

"I assume you have some trace of his attacker, or you wouldn't be talking to me."

I nodded, deciding on some judicious flattery. "I heard that you were the best." Talbot stood up a little taller and his anxiety receded, replaced by simple pride. Jack, who stood to one side, raised his eyebrows at me. There was approval in his quiet nod.

"Show me what you have."

Reaching into my backpack once more, I pulled out the plastic bag with the packaging in it. "I realise it may be a long shot, because this came through the mail, but—"

Talbot paused, hand inches from the bag. Caution rippled across his aura. "How did you say he was attacked?"

"He was elf shot."

The *puca* backpedalled, almost falling into his own rosebush in his haste. "Oh no. No-no-no!"

"What is it?"

"I won't get mixed up in a conflict between *aosidhe*," he said over his shoulder as he ran for the cottage. "I can't help you."

The door slammed closed behind him.

Feeling like an idiot, I lowered the outstretched arm that held the packaging. Jack followed Talbot to the door, knocking repeatedly and attempting to wheedle or bribe the *puca* into talking to us. There was no answer from the other side.

"Leave him be. Harassing him isn't going to make him want to help." I rubbed my eyes, suddenly weary. "Let's go."

Jack gazed at the closed door as though he wanted to break it down and drag Talbot out by the scruff of his neck. Then the hob's shoulders slumped and he walked towards me, head down. "I am very sorry, Isla. I should have realised he would react that way."

"Even if you had, it wouldn't have changed the outcome." We walked out of the garden and along the cobbled road, back towards the tunnel.

"I should have forewarned you," Jack said. "You could have lied about how your father was attacked."

"I wouldn't have wanted to." He looked surprised and I shrugged. "I'm not that good a liar. And even if I was, what if his not knowing what was in the packaging somehow meant he missed a clue we needed him to find?"

"True..."

"Plus if his sense of smell is that good, he might have figured it out anyway. Smelled the magic of the arrow or something. Then there's no chance he would trust me."

"Also true." The hob looked down at his shoes, hands in his pockets. Shame stained his aura.

"Don't worry about it," I said. "We'll figure something else out." When his mood didn't lighten, I cast around for a way to change the subject. "Um. So, which one is your place?"

He blinked at me. His pale hand pointed to the row of terraced houses. "See that one on the far left?"

"Closest to the pond?"

"Yes. That is where I live." He brightened. "Would you like to see it?"

"I'm not sure. I think your neighbours would be happier if I left."

"Please. There is someone I would like you to meet."

Something about his tone made me suspicious. "Jack! Have you got a girlfriend?" I tried to ignore the jealous rat that gnawed at my insides, reminding myself, not for the first time, that I had a boyfriend.

Jack smiled enigmatically and remained silent for long enough that I scowled at him. Then he laughed. "No. It is my sister. Come."

We turned to cut across the valley towards the silent pond. Were there no frogs in the *sidhe* to croak their nighttime songs, or had they too been scared into silence by my presence? It was a sobering thought. Away from the lit streets, the hillside sloped down, shrouded in a deeper darkness. Although the grass was short and unmarred by rocks or other obstructions, I picked my way along, envious of Jack's confident stride. I wished for some moonlight. Or a torch. The light from my exposed skin was faint: enough to see a foot in front of me, but not enough to cast a shadow or give me any confidence about where I was placing my feet.

"Is it always so dark here?" I asked peevishly.

"Yes."

"What happens during the day?"

"It remains dark."

Staring down at my footing, I wondered how the grass—or

ISLA'S OATH

Talbot's lush garden—could grow with no sunlight. But when I asked Jack, he shrugged.

When we entered the circle of light around the row of houses, the ground evened out. I sighed with relief.

The terrace houses were two storeys tall, with black-painted timber frames and white stucco walls. The common roofline was steep, slanting up towards a central beam. Above each front door hung a small glass sphere filled with stargems; their light illuminated designs carved into the timber uprights, all abstract swirls and curving lines.

Jack was smiling at me and reaching for the door handle when the heavy door swung inwards.

Standing there was a hob. Shorter than Jack—and me—by an inch or two, she wore a loose-fitting cotton dress that left her arms bare. Her skin was finely wrinkled, like Jack's had been the first time I met him—the sign of a hob with no *aosidhe* master. Unlike Jack's, her ears weren't concealed by a bandana; they protruded from golden hair the exact same shade as his. She wore it loose so her long, silky fringe hung across the left side of her face, obscuring it.

The hob's visible right eye glittered with hatred. Her aura mirrored it.

Jack twisted his fingers together. "Isla, this is Evie. Evie, Isla. Evie is my sister."

"Hi." I forced a smile. My father would have wanted me to add, "pleased to meet you" but, given her glare, it would be a lie.

Besides, she clearly wasn't pleased to meet me.

"Hello," she said, voice flat. That glittering eye flicked to Jack's face. "Why is *she* here?"

"We went to see Talbot. But I wanted to introduce her

to you. So you would believe me."

"Why? It does not matter what I think," she said, low and bitter.

"Yes, it does!"

"Very well then." She looked at me again, and the intensity of her loathing made me retreat a step. "I think you are an idiot, brother, for getting involved with the *aosidhe* again. And an idiot twice over for bringing one to our home, and showing her how to find us again, should she wish to."

Jack opened his mouth to speak. I replied first, anger curling my hands into fists as I spoke through gritted teeth. "Look, I know you all hate the *aosidhe*. And from what Jack's told me, you have good reason. But I'm not like that!"

"What Jack has told you?" Her voice was quiet, the centre of a hurricane. She stepped forward, directly under the glass sphere. Her shadow puddled black beneath her feet.

"Evie," Jack said, a note of caution in his voice. He put a hand on my arm, as though to pull me back.

"Did Jack tell you about *this*?"

With a flourish, Evie brushed that fall of hair back behind one pointed ear, revealing her left eye.

Or where her left eye would be, if not for the puckered scar running down that side of her face, from her hairline to the corner of her mouth. A twisted knot of flesh nestled in the eye socket.

I gasped, a hand flying to my mouth. My stomach churned.

Her mouth curled with grim satisfaction. "An *aosidhe* did this to me. For *fun*. So you will forgive me if I choose to believe you have addled my brother's wits. I know the power you possess."

"I didn't," I whispered.

"Why should I believe you?" she spat. "Jack loathed the *aosidhe* as much as I did. Until you came along." Jealousy and grief clashed in her aura, lime green and silvery grey.

Evie felt betrayed by Jack's decision to help me.

"I'm sorry," I said, speaking more to that pain than in response to her words. I wanted to say more to her—I never meant to hurt anyone; I didn't choose this any more than she did—but what was the point? She wasn't going to believe me.

Shoulders slumped, I turned to go.

Jack hesitated on the path for several moments. Then I heard his shoes thumping on the grass as he hurried to catch up to me. The door banged shut behind us.

"Forgive her, please," he said, his voice tight with emotion.

"I don't blame her. But this was a really bad idea, Jack. You had to know how she felt." I glowered at him from the corner of my eye.

"I am sorry. I just thought..." He trailed off, defeated. Silhouetted against the glittering valley below us, he hung his head, his expression faintly lit by the illumination from my skin.

"You thought I'd win her over with my dazzling personality? Yeah, that didn't go so well." I ran my hand through my hair. I didn't know whether to laugh or cry. A thought occurred to me. "I should have sworn it to her. An oath that I hadn't used my power on you, I mean."

He stopped short, eyes wide. "*That* would have been a really bad idea."

"What? Why?"

"Because it would have been a lie."

"It would not!"

He nodded slowly. "My being in service to you has allowed your innate power to revitalise me."

The hairs stood up on the back of my neck as I realised what he was saying. "It wasn't deliberate," I said slowly. "Would it have counted?"

"Depending on how you worded the oath, yes."

"Oh." I rubbed my arms. "What would have happened if I'd done it?"

"Unless we could have persuaded Evie to release you from the oath, you would have sickened."

"Died?"

He remained silent, which was answer enough.

"Crap." I frowned as we climbed the final slope to the mouth of the tunnel. Evie wasn't exactly my biggest fan. Although I didn't know what she would do if she had the power of life and death over me, it was a safe bet it wouldn't end well for me. "Coming here was a big mistake. All I did was upset people."

He gave me a miserable look. The silver in his aura reminded me of Evie's. So sad.

"Look, Jack, I can find my own way back from here. Why don't you head back to your sister and make sure she's okay?"

"I cannot. I promised Sarah I would look after you."

I frowned, trying to remember. "It wasn't a proper oath though, was it?"

He shrugged. "A promise is a promise."

From around us, the ever-present rustling of the gleaming eucalypts grew louder, as if there was a sudden gust of wind—although no air moved against my skin. We stared at them in puzzlement, watching as they trembled, branches upswept, leaves pointing towards the sky. The movement was like a dance. Joyous.

"You did not upset *everyone*, I think," Jack breathed. He stared up into the sky.

Stars winked into life in that great black ceiling, mirroring the night sky outside. As I watched, the Southern Cross appeared: four bold stars at the points of a crucifix, the fifth, fainter star a dimple on its cheek. The only other constellation I recognised, Orion's Belt, glittered like a join-the-dots saucepan.

The fat crescent moon inched above the horizon.

"Are you saying I did this?" My voice came out in a squeak.

"Who else?" Jack smiled, the moon reflected as silver chips in his eyes. "You were complaining it was dark."

There were cries from the valley below. I couldn't tell from this distance whether they were of joy or dismay.

"Time we went. Before the lynch mob comes?"

He glanced back down the hill. "Time we went, indeed."

CHAPTER SIX

*E*xhausted, the next morning I slept in late. A loud knocking at my bedroom door dragged me from an uneasy dream where I kept trying to call Sarah but couldn't remember her number.

"Wah?" I mumbled, peering out from under my sheet.

"You almost ready to go, pumpkin?" *Dad?* The memory surfaced like a tortoise lumbering from the surf: we'd organised to go out for coffee this morning. I leapt out of bed, smoothing my rumpled hair, and pulled the door open. My father leaned against the doorframe, grinning.

"I'm so sorry, Dad! I overslept."

He glanced at his watch. "It's almost eleven. It's not like you to sleep so late."

"I know, I know. Late night."

His eyebrows shot up. "Dominic?" Although his tone was neutral, anxiety clashed in his aura, too bright for first thing in the morning.

Wincing, I glanced around, wondering where my aunt

was. "No. Other stuff." This keeping secrets thing was hard work. "I'll tell you later. Do you mind waiting while I get ready?"

"Not at all. Your cousin's out in the shed; I'll go see what he's working on."

The shed was Ryan's art studio. I didn't go out there anymore, because there were several shelves of Dad's ironwork along the back wall. I used to store his dozens of gifts to me out there, having no use for that many candleholders and coat hooks. Since my eighteenth birthday, when my *duinesidhe* heritage manifested, I had extra incentive. Proximity to that much iron made me lose my lunch.

Dad had offered to take the ironwork back. Sarah told him not to. "It might come in handy. You know, for stuff."

Probably thinking of the *duinesidhe* that attacked him, Dad had agreed.

Refreshed after a quick shower and with minty-clean teeth, I went out onto the back porch. "Dad! You ready to go?" There was no answer, and anxiety made me grip the railing in tight hands. Only a couple of months ago I'd found Ryan passed out in the shed, overwhelmed by a vision. "Dad? Ryan?"

"Here." Dad stepped into the shed doorway and beckoned me. "I think you need to see this."

I shook my head, staying where I was. "See what?"

"Ryan's latest painting."

"Can he bring it out?" I asked plaintively.

"Oh. Right."

There was a murmured conversation in the shed. I clenched my jaw with impatience. After a couple of minutes, Dad and Ryan filed out and up onto the porch.

They weren't carrying the painting. "It's too wet to move," Ryan explained. He had a smudge of paint on the side of his nose, and his face was pale. "But I took a photo on my phone."

"Clever." I smiled.

He didn't smile back as he handed me the phone.

At first the photo, small as it was, appeared to be an abstract style uncharacteristic of Ryan's work—his usual preferences were either realism or comic book. The photo was comprised of curving yellow, red and orange lines, with a black shape underlying them. I shaded the phone's screen from the sun's glare and zoomed in to get a better look.

My eyes widened. Flames encompassed the entirety of the painting, from edge to edge, licking at the black sticks of trees and rolling across familiar ground.

It was Mount Taylor.

"Do you think this is an *aislinge* vision painting?" I whispered. A cold ball settled in the pit of my stomach, tendrils of ice seeping through my body.

He nodded. "I can tell now, when I'm painting one. There's a weird feeling to it, like my hands aren't entirely under my own control. And when I'm doing one of these paintings I can't stop till it's done, even if I want to. It … grips me."

My eyes widened. "That sounds awful. I'm sorry, Ryan."

There were bags under his eyes, but the smile was genuine. "I don't mind, really. It's sort of like having an overzealous muse." He hesitated. "Do you think it'd be okay to try and sell some of the *aislinge* paintings? They're some of my best pieces."

I hesitated. As far as I knew he'd had four *aislinge* visions, and two of them were pencil sketches—one on the back of a toilet door I'd had to scrub clean the next day. "Maybe not the one of my mother, if that's all right? This one might be okay, but let's wait till we figure out what it means first."

One corner of his mouth pulled downwards with disappointment. But he didn't argue.

Dad scowled back towards the shed, his weathered face dark. His aura was anxious, an unpleasant greyish yellow with purple swirls roiling in it. "I don't like the look of that painting at all. Do you think there's going to be a bushfire?"

"I hope not," Ryan murmured fervently. "I don't want to live through that again."

I'd been eight and still living with Dad when, one scorching hot Saturday in January, a firestorm ripped out of the Brindabella Mountains like a smoke-wreathed dragon, riding on thermals generated by incinerated pine plantations and exploding eucalyptus oil. The inferno roared down on the unprepared city. We'd seen the smoke haze in the distance and struggled to get into Canberra, to find the rest of our family. The police roadblocks defeated us, and we hadn't made it to Sarah, Ryan and Aunt Elizabeth until the next day. Afterwards, Sarah spoke in a hushed voice about the eerie rain of charred eucalyptus leaves and how the sky had been as black as night at three in the afternoon—except for an angry red glow that engulfed the western horizon.

I didn't need to be a mind reader to know my father and cousin were thinking similar thoughts. Dad shook his head, casting off the unpleasant reminder of scary memories. He looked like Hamish shaking water off after a bath. "Shall we go find that coffee?"

The weather was glorious; the full hammer of summer heat hadn't yet settled in for the day, and there was a light, cool breeze. We bought ice creams and take-away coffees, before driving down to Lake Tuggeranong.

Dad parked on the eastern edge of the lake, near the dog park, and we walked until we found an empty picnic table. Nearby was a piece of public art—a circular clearing with four carved totem poles equally spaced around its edges and a bowl in the centre, painted in an Aboriginal style. The bowl contained a shallow fire pit.

Thinking about Ryan's painting, I shuddered.

We ate our ice creams before they melted into sticky sludge. Dad finished first and waited patiently until I was done before asking, "So where were you last night?"

I lowered my voice even though the nearest people were in the dog park, a couple exercising a cocker spaniel whose ears flapped as it bounded after a ball. "Jack took me into the local *sidhe*."

He whistled low in surprise. "What was it like?"

"Strange. Bits of it were magical, like you'd expect in a fairy tale, but parts of it were almost…" I hesitated.

"Mundane?"

"That's a good word for it."

"What about the people? The *duinesidhe*?"

I grimaced, staring at the surface of the lake. The still water reflected the achingly blue sky and a shimmering copy of the sun's white-hot disk; farther away, the school on the opposite shore was mirrored in vivid orange, red and white. "They weren't exactly happy to see me."

"Why?"

I glanced at him, surprised he didn't know. "The *aosidhe* aren't popular with the locals."

ISLA'S OATH

"It wasn't because of your mixed heritage?"

I shook my head. "Not exactly. I think they would have preferred me if I were totally human. It's the *aosidhe* side of things they're afraid of, not the half-breed bit. They think I'll try and enslave them or something."

"Once they get to know you they'll realise that's not true."

I raised an eyebrow at him. "Yeah, because I'm such a people person."

"Don't sell yourself short, Isla." Dad sipped his coffee and watched a duck wander towards us, looking hopeful. "You know, you could have made them more comfortable with you. With your talent. Mako showed you how."

"If I did, wouldn't that be doing exactly what they are afraid I will do? Enslaving them against their will?"

He narrowed his eyes, glancing at me. "I don't know."

"Me neither. Until I figure out where that line is, I don't want to risk it. I don't want to be like that." *Like my mother.* The words hung unsaid between us. I took a deep breath, mustering the courage to raise something I'd struggled with for months. "Dad, did you know she could manipulate emotions?"

"Melpomene?" he said. That was what my mother called herself among the *duinesidhe*, naming herself after the Greek muse of tragedy. The rest of my family knew her as Melanie.

"Yeah."

"Not at first. I found out once we were already married and she was pregnant with you."

"Did you ever wonder whether she made you love her? The day you met her?"

"No," he said with absolute certainty.

"Why not? Love at first sight doesn't happen except in the movies."

It was Dad's turn to raise an eyebrow at me. "Because you're such an expert in the ways of the heart."

"I'm not a kid."

"Of course not," he said calmly. "But didn't you know you were attracted to Dominic when you first met him?"

"I thought he was cute, sure, but that's not love, that's … uh." *Lust*. I looked down at the scarred picnic table, squirming. I so didn't want to talk to my father about Dominic. Or lust.

Dad began to chuckle.

"Stop it. I want to ask you something," I blurted. "And I want you to promise me you'll think about it and not just say no out of hand."

He stopped laughing, examining me with serious blue eyes. The cautious amber yellow in his aura was so strong that for a moment I thought he'd refuse. But, finally, he nodded. "I promise."

I spoke quickly. "I know you still love her. You always have, even though you know she might want to hurt you. Probably wants to hurt you." He started to say something and I raised my hand, talking over him. "If I could figure out how to make that love go away, would you let me do it?"

Dad sat back on the rough wooden bench, running a hand through his greying red hair. His mouth fell open and his eyes widened.

I pushed on, lowering my voice again as a cyclist whirred down the bike path nearby, slipping past us in a blur of red-and-black Lycra. "Even if you're right and it really was proper love at first sight, it's been eighteen years since you saw her. What if I could make it so you didn't love her anymore? So you could move on?" Dad never even dated after he fled my mother's wrath. There'd never been a stepmother, wicked or otherwise, in my life. I would even settle for a wicked one, if she made Dad happy.

"I ... don't know. Could you do that?"

I thought about his mother, my Nana. Before I even knew what I was doing, I'd made her remember she loved Dad under all the reproach and disappointment that had choked her affection for so long, ivy throttling the life from a tree. "I think so, yes."

He gazed across the water, blue eyes unseeing. "I'll need to think about it," he murmured.

Disappointment ached in my chest, but I told myself it was silly to think he'd agree on the spot. "Just so long as you don't dismiss it out of hand."

"I won't."

The silence stretched between us. Dad was lost in his thoughts. The duck gave up on us and launched itself into the air, heading west across the lake to see if it could find more-compliant humans near the fast food outlets. The breeze died with a final puff of surrender, and the heat settled in. A fly, the ever-present herald of Australian summers, buzzed around us. I shooed it away.

Dad stirred. "I should get you home."

As we walked back to the car, I decided to change the subject. "Did Aunt Elizabeth tell you Sarah got a job? She's at the same supermarket as Ryan."

"She mentioned it. I assume you've had no luck finding work?"

"I've put my name down at a bunch of places, but nothing yet." I raised my eyebrows at him. "Is Aunt Elizabeth scolding you yet?"

"For not pushing you harder to find a job?" I nodded, and he smiled and gave me a broad wink. "A little. I'm ignoring her. I'm quite good at it. Years of practice."

We both laughed.

Dad dropped me off at the curb, declining the offer of lunch. My question about Melpomene had shaken him, although he was trying to hide it beneath his usual jocular banter. Given I could read his emotions, the pretence was an exercise in futility. But I loved him for trying.

The offer was for his good. I told myself that repeatedly as I walked up the driveway to the front door. The guilt clung on, though, as stubborn and irritating as a bindi prickle in a sock.

The house was wonderful after the baking heat outside. The air conditioner in the entry hall exhaled a blast of frigid air down the length of the house. I stood in front of it for several minutes, letting it cool my skin. Sarah was home; I could hear her singing loudly along with the radio in her bedroom. When I went into the kitchen, I found Ryan putting a couple of dishes in the dishwasher. "I just boiled the kettle—want a cuppa?"

I shook my head, pouring myself a glass of water and cracking a couple of ice cubes into it. "You're crazy. It's an oven out there."

"Didn't you just go out for coffee?"

"That's not the point."

He snorted a laugh and then murmured, "I put the painting in the lounge room, if you want to have a better look."

ISLA'S OATH

I hurried into the next room. Ryan followed with his hot chocolate, his aura a mixture of pride and concern.

The canvas was small, about the size of a foolscap piece of paper. Ryan had propped it up against something on the coffee table. I couldn't tell what, because he'd draped everything with an old sheet. "Aunt Elizabeth will kill you if you get paint on the furniture."

"It's mostly dry. Just a bit tacky now. Besides," he winked, "she won't be home for hours."

I knelt in front of the table, studying the image more closely. Did those smaller black marks represent people? I hoped not.

"What's that?" Sarah asked from the entryway; she was wearing a baseball cap pulled low over her hair. "New pic, Ry?"

He nodded. "An *aislinge* one, I'm pretty sure."

She suppressed a twinge of jealousy—it flickered for a heartbeat and then vanished beneath curiosity and glee—and came to stand behind me. "That doesn't look good."

"No," he grunted.

"Is that Mount Taylor?"

"Looks like it."

She frowned at him. "You don't know? You painted it."

He shrugged. "It doesn't work like that."

"It's not much good then, is it?"

I refrained from pointing out how Ryan's vision paintings had given us—well, Jack—the clue we needed to wake Dad from his *aosidhe*-induced coma the previous year and had let us know when Moray and his posse attacked the farm. Sarah was still sensitive about the fact it was her brother rather than herself who received the visionary power. She understood it was an accident, but sometimes it felt like she blamed me for it.

Ryan scowled but held his tongue too. Thankfully, Sarah didn't notice. "Anyway, speaking of your paintings, I have exciting news!" she crowed. "Look what I did!" She swept the cap from her head and shook her hair so it fell free.

A streak of blond gleamed in the red of her fringe. "I just got back from the hairdresser. Isn't it great?"

I clapped and hugged her. Ryan's mouth fell open. "That's the way I did your hair in the painting I gave you for your birthday." When Sarah turned eighteen he'd given her a portrait; it depicted her as a rock goddess, standing on a stage, playing a guitar and singing into a headset microphone, surrounded by adoring fans.

Sarah rolled her eyes. "I know, doofus. I got them to make it the same."

"Why?"

"Maybe 'cause I like it?" She punched his arm lightly. "Also, remember the band that played at my party?" We nodded. I had a terrible suspicion I knew where this was going and willed the smile to stay on my face. The expression felt brittle. "Well, John—that's the lead guitarist—he asked me to join the band. And they have a gig this Saturday night. How cool is that? I'm going to play in a rock band." She almost sang the words. "Your vision's coming true, Ryan!"

Stunned silence filled the room for a moment before we mumbled something supportive. A car horn honked out front, and Sarah jammed the hat back on her head. "I've got to go. That's John. I won't be home for dinner— can you let Mum know? Thanks!"

And she was gone, the door slamming shut behind her.

"Um, Ryan?"

ISLA'S OATH

"Yes?"

"That painting you did for her birthday. It's not actually a vision painting, is it?"

He shook his head. "No. It's just something I made up."

"Ah." I bit my lip. "Should we tell her?"

He stared at me as though I'd just sprouted an extra head. "Feel free. But I want to be in the next state when you do."

"It feels wrong not to, though. What if she gets her hopes up?"

"That ship appears to have sailed." Ryan pointed at the painting on the table. "See that fire? That'll be nothing compared to Sarah's reaction if you tell her."

I grimaced. He wasn't wrong.

He picked up the painting and turned towards his bedroom. "So long as she's enjoying herself, does it matter?"

I didn't know the answer to that.

CHAPTER SEVEN

*T*he pub wasn't what I'd expected.

I sat at a sticky table in the corner closest to the low stage, minding our seats while Kim and Natalie went to the bar. The band wasn't playing yet. A recent indie single jangled over the pub's speakers, barely audible over the hum of conversation.

Sarah was on stage, talking to John. The other two members of the band—the bass guitarist, Macca, and drummer, Keith—were scuttling around them, busily repositioning speakers and fiddling with wires.

"I wish she'd worn different pants," Ryan muttered, sitting down next to me, cradling a Coke-and-something in one hand. He'd come to the pub with a couple of his mates, who sat two tables away.

I smiled; I'd helped her choose the outfit. "She looks great." Her short shorts emphasised just how long her legs were, and the bronze-and-green tank top—and some judicious eye shadow—highlighted the flecks of green in her blue eyes.

"Yeah, but all these drunk blokes are going to perv on her." He scowled.

I hid a smirk behind my hand. Now Ryan wasn't looking, his friends were gazing at Sarah with appreciative smiles. "If she wasn't your sister you would be too."

"That's disgusting." He turned faintly green.

I sighed with relief when I spotted my other friends weaving their way through the crowd.

"Hey, Ryan." Kim smiled, handing me a glass of ginger beer.

But Natalie frowned at him. "You're in my seat."

"Hi Kim. And Natalie—charming as usual," he said, standing so she could slide past him into the chair.

"Shut up." Natalie was a petite blonde with big blue eyes; I'd always thought she resembled a doll, an image enhanced by her recent pixie haircut. She reminded me of a sprite. Or what I thought sprites might look like, if they existed ... which, I realised, sipping my drink, they might. I'd have to ask Jack.

"Why are you staring at me?" she demanded.

"J-just thinking I love your haircut," I stammered.

"Thanks." Her reply was soft as she flushed pink.

Sarah bounded over to us. She was acutely nervous; her aura trembled with anxiety and her hands clenched at her sides in white-knuckled fists. But there was a strong core of confidence there too. How much of that came from her belief that she was destined for musical greatness? I felt guilty all over again. "We're about to start. Thanks so much for coming." She kissed Kim's and Natalie's cheeks. Ryan rolled his eyes at being ignored and strolled back to his table. His friends studied their drinks, as though they weren't ogling his sister moments before.

"Wouldn't miss it," Kim said, brushing her glossy black hair over her shoulders with a practiced gesture. "Your first gig with ... what's the band called?"

"Drakeford," Sarah bubbled. "After the road." Drakeford Drive was one of the arterial roads that connected southern Canberra to the centre of the city.

"I like it," I said. "It reminds me of dragons."

"And ducks," Natalie said with a sparkle in her blue eyes.

Sarah poked her tongue out and then leaned over to whisper in my ear. "I'm so nervous I think I might puke."

"Well, don't do it on me!" I hissed.

Her eyes were so wide I could see the whites all around. "Seriously, Isla—help me out?"

"Sure." I offered her a sip of my drink, speaking normally for the others, who were looking at us curiously. "Ginger's good for nerves." As she sipped at the straw, I gripped her other hand and gave it a reassuring squeeze. My ability amplified with contact, I quickly siphoned off most of her stage fright. The emotion settled like a lump in my stomach for a few nauseating seconds before being absorbed into my system. A sudden burst of energy ran along my limbs.

"Thanks." Sarah beamed at me, handing back the glass. "That's much better."

She turned to head back to the stage, but Natalie caught her arm. "Before you go, I'm making lunch tomorrow at my house. Can you come? All of you?" Her tone was casual, but a tight knot of anxiety clotted her aura. Unlike Sarah's, Natalie's emotion were much more deeply rooted. Where was the line with assisting people with their feelings? Helping Sarah was okay because she'd asked, but Natalie didn't know to ask. And I wasn't sure how she'd feel about having her emotions tampered with if she *had* known; it's not the sort of thing that comes up in general conversation.

Around the table, the others were nodding. I copied, hoping no one had noticed how distracted I was.

Sarah raised an eyebrow at me. "Tomorrow's Valentine's Day. Don't you have plans?"

"Dominic and I are going to the movies in the afternoon. It'll be fine. I can do both." I smiled reassuringly at Natalie. "We haven't caught up in ages. He'll understand."

Sarah hesitated, mouth open to speak, but John called her from the stage and she bounced away.

"Where is Dominic, anyway?" Kim glanced around as though expecting him to appear.

"Working," I sighed. "He finishes at midnight. He's going to text me and if we're still here he'll meet us."

"What about Jack?" Natalie asked archly. I frowned at her. Kim and Natalie—and the rest of our friends—had met the hob at Sarah's birthday party at the end of the previous year, although they didn't know what he was. We'd told them he was an old friend of the family. Natalie thought I had a crush on him. She'd warned that Dominic was likely to get jealous if I wasn't careful.

Remembering that conversation, I shrugged, tried to act casual. "What about him?"

"He's not coming?"

"No." I had a big mouthful of ginger beer and, hoping to end the conversation, turned to study the quietening activity on stage. Keith sat behind the drum kit, tapping the drumsticks idly into his palm. The rest of the band members picked up their instruments.

John, who owned two electric guitars, had loaned one to Sarah. He was the lead guitarist and singer. My cousin was good, but she usually played an acoustic and she'd only had a few days—minus shifts at the supermarket—to practice the band's songs. She would be playing rhythm guitar, nothing fancy, and singing basic harmonies on the choruses.

Knowing her, it wouldn't be long before she claimed a starring role. She'd already told me that the first thing she was going to save up for with her pay was her own electric guitar. Or maybe an electric acoustic guitar; she wasn't sure.

Sarah flashed us a grin and then Drakeford began to play, drumbeat pounding up through the soles of my shoes.

I'd never studied music, but I could hold a tune—and, to my untrained ear, they sounded pretty good. Feeling anxious on my cousin's behalf, I studied the other tables. Other patrons nodded their heads in time to the music or tapped fingers on the sides of beer glasses, their eyes fixed on the stage. A good sign.

Sarah played the first two songs—modern rock covers—with a tiny frown on her face, concentrating on her fingering. But slowly she relaxed, grinning at her bandmates and those of us she knew in the crowd. During the third song, an original number written by Keith, Sarah danced as she sang, earning herself a few wolf whistles from a table of drunken twenty-somethings in the back of the pub. I glanced across at Ryan. He was glaring in the whistlers' direction. They hadn't noticed.

As I turned back towards the stage, a wave caught my attention. Jack stood in the doorway, but when our gazes met, he started weaving through the crowd towards our table. He'd dressed in his own version of urban camouflage: jeans and a plain, dark grey T-shirt, with a black-and-white bandana covering his hair and ears. A canvas messenger bag hung over one shoulder. He gave me a brief smile, although even through the crowd I could see he was worried about something.

Natalie and Kim followed my gaze. "I thought he wasn't coming," Kim said, speaking loudly over the music. Natalie tightened her lips.

"So did I." I shrugged, trying to look relaxed. He reached us and I smiled a greeting at him, trying to ask the question with my eyes rather than my lips. "Hi, Jack! Great to see you."

"I could not miss Sarah's show," he said, trying to sound casual. The girls gave him an odd look, but he didn't notice.

We didn't have a spare chair, so he stood between Natalie's and my seats, leaning against the brick wall. I kept my gaze on the stage, pretending to be interested in John's guitar solo. I was acutely conscious of the hob's motionless presence behind me and of Natalie's speculative gaze flickering between us as though she was trying to pluck a secret from our minds.

John and Sarah launched into the final repetition of the chorus with gusto. My cousin, when she glanced across at us, had a similar, vague air of disapproval on her face as she looked from me to Jack and back again. Shakespeare they were not, but I couldn't help but feel the lyrics were being aimed pointedly in my direction—which was silly, because Drakeford had been performing this song for months. I'd heard it at Sarah's birthday party.

Guilty conscience? Me? I gnawed my lip.

"Oh baby, I can't decide
What you're tryin' to hide.
But I knew it when you lied
And a part of my heart diiiiiiied."

I did my best to look attentive and innocent for the next two songs, until intermission. When the band set their instruments down to a smattering of applause and a few more wolf whistles, I made a show of patting my pockets, looking for my mobile phone. Then I rifled through my purse. "Crap."

"What?" Kim asked.

"I left my phone in the car," I lied, glad the pub was gloomy and my phone was hidden in the shadowy recesses behind my makeup compact and keys. "I'll have to duck out and get it in case Dominic texts." I stood.

"I will come for the walk," Jack volunteered instantly.

"Okay."

Kim didn't say anything, but Natalie raised a single, sceptical eyebrow at me. I wanted to be indignant, but she was right to be suspicious. I *was* lying to them, and I *did* want a chance to talk to Jack alone.

She was just wrong about why.

We paused at the foot of the stage on our way to the exit. "You were wonderful," I enthused, embracing Sarah. Her cheeks were flushed and her eyes glowed with pleasure.

"I was, wasn't I?" she said with a wink. "Hey, Jack. Wasn't expecting to see you here."

He spoke quietly. "I needed to have a word with your cousin."

"Duh." She rolled her eyes, taking a swig of water from a plastic bottle. "I didn't imagine you were here for the gig."

ISLA'S OATH

He shrugged. "Isla is correct though. You were very good." His expression was earnest, and she beamed at him.

"Are you leaving?" she asked me.

I glanced at Jack. "Just ducking out for a minute. I left my phone in the car."

"Okay," she said brightly, glancing at my purse. She knew my phone was there. I'd texted Dominic on it before Kim and Natalie arrived. "We're back on in fifteen. Try and be back then. Please?"

"I'll try."

The air outside the pub was fresh and cool after the stifling, close pub air, which stank of aftershave, sweat and beer. We hurried through the haze of cigarette smoke just outside the door and into Garema Place, a paved square fronted by shops, restaurants and cafes with outdoor dining. Some of the cafes were closing; others still served coffees and desserts to their more tenacious customers. Conversation and snatches of music blended into a background hum punctuated by the occasional burst of laughter. A busker sat on the concrete with crossed legs, playing the two small bongo drums wedged between his knees. He was towards one end of the square, back against a tree, staying away from the pair of fire twirlers that danced on the huge chessboard up the other end. They smelled faintly of kerosene.

"Do you really need to go to your car?" Jack asked as we passed the drummer.

"No." I glanced at him out of the corner of my eye, hands in my pockets, as we strolled slowly down City Walk towards the carousel. "I figured you came looking for me for a reason. Was I wrong?"

"No," he said, subdued.

"What's up?"

"I think there is an *aosidhe* in the city. Other than you."

A chill raced up my spine, propelling my heart into my throat. "You're sure?"

"Yes." His expression was solemn.

"How come?" I said.

"How come I am sure?" I nodded, and he led me to one side of the walkway, to stand against the window of a bank. After looking around to make sure we weren't being watched, he reached into his messenger bag and pulled something out to show me.

Cupped in his hand was a creature the size of a large mouse. It—no, he—was dressed in ragged, miniature clothes; his hair was a tangled mass of gold and his eyes were little blue flecks of summer sky. On his back, a pair of diaphanous wings like a dragonfly's beat slowly, only visible because of the tracery of veins. Around his neck, strung on a piece of cotton, was a glossy pink bead.

The creature resembled Tinker Bell, if she were down on her luck and had grown sharp around the edges. A fairy made from mosquitos rather than butterflies.

"Isla, this is Welkin. He is a *piskie*."

"Uh. Hi!" I said brightly, trying to pretend I'd heard of a *piskie* before now.

"Hello," Welkin piped. Jack held his hand up so that the tiny fairy was at eye level with me. Welkin bobbed his head in gratitude.

"Please tell Isla what you told me," the hob said.

Welkin looked me up and down, a gesture that only took in my face. He pursed his lips, eyes narrowed. "Okay," he said after a moment, putting his hands on his hips. The gesture was adorable ... but also reminded me of my year seven science teacher. "Do you know about energy flows?"

"Pretend I don't."

He craned his neck to frown at Jack before looking back at me. "Right. Every living thing in the world sheds energy. It's a lot like air. Sometimes it pools, still, and sometimes it flows and you get a breeze or a storm."

"Like water?"

Welkin scowled. "Like *air*. This is my metaphor, lady."

I bit my lip so I didn't laugh, nodding to indicate he should continue.

"Well, some *aosidhe* are like mountains. The air bends around them and continues on, but becomes more turbulent. And if there are a bunch of them together you can get wind tunnels and it gets really tricky to fly..." He trailed off, staring distractedly through Jack's fingers at a passing couple, absorbed in their conversation.

"And other *aosidhe*?" I reminded him gently.

"Oh, yes. Other *aosidhe* are more like cyclones, throwing everything around and making a mess." He sniffed in disapproval.

I wondered which type I was, but decided not to ask. "So you can sense the presence of *aosidhe* based on this energy movement."

"Yes. There was one here—" he narrowed his eyes at me "—and now there are two."

"When did the other one arrive?"

"Today."

"Could you figure out where they are?" I asked, pulse racing in my ears.

"I could, but I won't. Are you crazy? I only came to talk to you because Jack swore you wouldn't harm me. And because I wanted to see the half-breed *aosidhe*."

"Welkin!" Jack protested.

"What? It's true. Anyway, as soon as we're done here, I'm leaving. Going to find somewhere less crowded."

"Is there anything else you can tell me?" I asked. *Is it her? My mother?*

"Plenty." He giggled shrilly.

"About the other *aosidhe*, I mean."

"Oh. Not specifically. But *aosidhe* are trouble. This one will be too. No offence."

"None taken," I replied dryly. "Thanks for the warning. Is there anything I can do to repay you?"

The *piskie* narrowed his eyes and licked his lips with a tiny pink tongue. "I wouldn't mind a taste of that half-breed *aosidhe* blood."

I blinked. "Pardon?"

"Just a drop. The tiniest thing. You won't even notice it's gone," he assured me hastily.

I glanced at Jack and he shrugged. "It is up to you. But do not let him bite you." He wrinkled his nose. "Their teeth are not clean. The wound could fester."

The *piskie* drew himself up, hands on his hips. "I wouldn't. So can I?"

"Okay," I said reluctantly, holding out my hand. "Just one drop."

The tiny fairy jumped onto my palm, his feet barely dimpling my skin as he tripped lightly over to the soft webbing between my index finger and thumb. Before I could flinch, he pulled a copper pin from his belt, wielding it as though it were a rapier. And stabbed me.

"Ouch!"

"Sorry," Welkin trilled, not at all sorry. He dropped to his hands and knees and lapped up the welling blood with his tongue. "Uhm. That's good. Piquant, like fear."

I remembered the feeling of Sarah's stage fright as I'd absorbed it. Was that what he tasted? Shuddering, I resisted the urge to bat the drinking *piskie* away with my other hand.

"That is enough, Welkin," Jack said sternly. "You have had your drop."

"Yes," the tiny creature said sadly. He stood and bowed to me, then licked the needle clean and slid it back through the loop on his belt. His wings flexed more slowly, soporific after a good meal. "If you get rid of the other *aosidhe* and need my services, let me know. I'd happily work for a little more of that ruby wine."

"I'll keep it in mind." I was probably going to have nightmares about his contented predator's smile tonight. At least he wasn't taller.

He grinned, tiny white teeth stained pink with blood, and flew into the sky as though launched from a slingshot. I looked up after him, but he was gone, invisible through the leafy boughs of the tree above us.

"Ow," I muttered, pressing my thumb to the tiny pin-prick on my other hand. The blood was already slowing.

"Would you like me to heal it for you?"

Jack was able to take injuries from others, but they appeared on his own flesh, like stigmata. He argued that it was worth it because hobs heal faster than other *dui-nesidhe*, but I didn't like the idea. "It's nothing, really. I just hope that pin was sanitary." Given how he'd cleaned it, I didn't like my chances. "Let's head back. I want to wash my hands before Drakeford comes back on."

"Did you want me to look for the *aosidhe* for you?" Jack said as we started back to the pub.

"You can do that?"

"Now I know there is one out there, yes. The same way I found you."

"Smell him out, you mean? Would it be dangerous?" I remembered my first encounter with Jack. He'd rushed out of the bushes that bordered Aunt Elizabeth's lawn and sniffed me. I'd tripped over, and he'd fled.

"That depends on the *aosidhe's* intent," said Jack.

"So yes, then."

"Probably," he admitted, avoiding my gaze.

"Then no. Please don't go looking for trouble."

"As you wish."

I gave voice to the idea that had bothered me since Jack had first said there was another *aosidhe* here. "Do you think it's her?" I lowered my voice to a whisper. "Melpomene?"

"It is impossible to say."

I frowned, pulling my phone from my purse and flicking through my contacts for my father's number at the farm. "I'd better call Dad. If she's tracked him down, he'll be in trouble. And he'd walk straight into her arms. He's still…"

"Besotted? Ensorcelled?"

"Those are good words for it, yes." The phone was ringing now, and I held a finger to my lips.

"Hello?" Dad answered after a dozen rings.

I breathed a sigh of relief. "Hey, it's me."

"What's the matter, pumpkin?"

"Why would something be the matter?" I was aiming for guileless, but my voice sounded tight to my own ears.

"You don't usually ring this late."

I glanced at my watch and grimaced when I saw it was after ten. "Oh crap. I'm sorry, Dad; I didn't realise the time."

ISLA'S OATH

"It's okay, I was just brushing my teeth. What's up?"

"Um." I tried to think of the best way to urge Dad to stay safe without raising the hope that his estranged wife might be in town. "Jack's here. He said there might be something going on. Can you stay at the farm for the rest of the weekend?" Iron surrounded Dad's farm. He'd be safe there.

"Are you okay? Do you need my help?" His voice was anxious.

"I'm fine. I just need to know you're going to be safe, in case it's related to the attack on you last December. Promise me you'll stay home."

"I don't have anywhere to be till Monday. I'll stay home, but only if you agree to call if you need help and let me know what's going on."

"I will," I agreed. We were nearing the pub entrance now. The rhythmic drumbeat told me we were late. "I've got to go."

"Love you, Isla Rose. Stay safe."

"You too."

I dropped my phone back into my purse and walked towards the pub's door, Jack at my side.

"Going somewhere?"

A tall woman stepped out of the shadows and into our path. She was about Sarah's height—a couple of inches shy of six feet—and looked like she'd been dipped in honey, with sun-bleached golden hair, golden brown eyes and gold-tanned skin. Even her aura matched. The amber of caution was stippled with golden flecks whose significance I didn't recognise, although they looked vaguely familiar. Where was Mako when I needed him? She had dressed to break up her monochrome appearance, in black slacks and a jade silk shirt with a mandarin collar. A silver torc with a twisting design nestled against her collarbones, at the small of her throat.

"My name is Shannon. I'm here on behalf of my master," she said coolly, with a faint Irish accent. She studied me for several seconds. Beside her, I felt shabby and immature in my shorts, sneakers and baby doll T-shirt.

"Let me guess. Your master's an *aosidhe*?"

She nodded. "His name is Everest and he bids me invite you to visit him."

"Now?"

"Now."

Trouble had found us.

CHAPTER EIGHT

*J*ack regarded Shannon for a long moment, lips pressed together so hard they were white. He drew me aside and whispered, "We do not have to go with her." His fingers wound tight around my forearm, conveying his urgency. "She is human. She cannot force you."

"She found us once. If this Everest means us harm, won't he just find us again?"

He glanced away as though wanting to deny the truth of my words. Then he sighed. "Probably."

"It'd be better for us to meet him when we're expecting it," I said, although the idea of running for the hills had a certain appeal. I lifted his hand from my arm and turned back to the woman. "I just need to duck inside and let my friends know I'm going," I told her.

"Very well. Shall I wait here with your hob?"

The question annoyed me. "He's not sworn to me. I don't own him." Jack had sworn, several months ago, that he only served me. But he wasn't bound by that now, because he'd sworn it in the present tense. As my Nana told me at the time, oaths were tricky things.

Shannon's eyes flickered to Jack's smooth face and back to me. "His skin...?"

"He does me favours sometimes. It's good for his complexion."

"Then he is yours," she said with a faint curl of her lip. "Don't you need to speak to your friends?"

I still wasn't comfortable with Shannon's choice of words—*your* hob—but, from an *aosidhe* perspective, the term was probably correct. Grimacing, I let it go.

"Okay. I won't be long."

Thoughts whirling, I hurried through the pub. Sarah and the others were on stage; her gaze picked me out instantly when I hurried back in. She gave me a broad smile that faded as I shook my head.

"Where's Jack?" Natalie asked as soon as I reached the table.

"Waiting outside." I bit my lip as I scrambled for an excuse that wouldn't prompt more insinuating comments. "He got a call—his aunt is really sick. I'm going to drive him to her place."

"That's terrible!" Kim said, standing to hug me tightly. "Do you know her well?"

"A bit. But poor Jack's pretty upset." I hung my head, my hair falling in front of my face, so they wouldn't see the lie in my eyes.

"Will you be able to make lunch tomorrow?" Natalie said, her expression still as an empty pool, though nowhere near as transparent.

"Definitely." I hoped. "Can you let Sarah know I'm sorry and that I'll send her a text to explain?"

ISLA'S OATH

"Of course. Tell Jack we're sorry about his aunt."

"I will. Thanks." I gave each of them a kiss on the cheek and waved goodbye to Sarah. Her eyes widened, disappointed and concerned in equal measure; my face burned with shame as I hurried from the pub.

At first, I didn't see Jack and Shannon, and my heart constricted with panic. But there they were, standing a few metres away and watching the fire twirlers. Their hair was almost the same colour, I noticed, although Shannon's was streaked with paler blond on the top. She must spend a lot of time in the sun—or at the hairdresser—to get that look.

"Are you ready?" she asked me.

I nodded, doubting she was referring to whether I was psychologically prepared for meeting one of the *aosidhe*—a race everyone told me was cruel, self-centred and egotistical. I didn't think I'd ever be ready for that.

To my surprise, she led us through the city, down past the carousel and towards the cluster of hotels by the lake. I hadn't really considered *aosidhe* accommodation requirements before but I supposed, if the local *sidhe* were off limits for whatever reason, human accommodation would be the next best thing. Especially swanky human accommodation. We weren't heading towards the budget motels—those chains couldn't afford lakefront real estate, separated from the water only by the leafy green expanse of Commonwealth Park.

Soon the silence between the three of us began to grate on my already tense nerves. I blurted, "So ... been in Australia long?"

"Not long, no." Shannon raised an eyebrow at me and kept striding along, almost at a jog. Her longer legs left

Jack and me scurrying to match her stride.

After a couple of minutes of trying to keep up, her deliberate pace irritated me. I grabbed Jack's hand and slowed down to a normal walking pace. "She can wait," I murmured to him. "What a cow."

He grinned at me, although, the closer we drew to the hotels, the more anxious he became. "You don't have to come," I whispered. "I know you don't like the *aosidhe*."

He paled. "Then who will keep you out of trouble, Isla? I am *your* hob, remember?"

"That wasn't my choice of words."

"I know." He patted my hand. "That is why I do not mind."

The label? Or being mine? I decided not to ask.

Shannon stopped to wait for us at a pedestrian crossing. "Forgive me," she said, her aura seething with irritation.

"No worries." I smiled brightly. The hotels loomed. She steered us to the most expensive chain hotel on the strip. "What's he like? Everest?"

The look on her face then was the first true reflection of her emotions since we'd met: sheer, blissful adoration. "Magnificent," she breathed, gaze distant and a slight smile on her face. Smiling, she was beautiful.

"Oh."

Her expression shut down again, falling back into deliberately neutral lines. She led us through the hotel's revolving doors, which were big enough that all three of us could have fit into one segment—although Jack and I held back, letting her go first.

I'd stayed in a handful of hotels and motels with Dad on family holidays: everything from a bed and breakfast in the Blue Mountains to cheap motel chains in Sydney and a motor inn in outback New South Wales. But I'd never set foot in a hotel like this one. A huge expanse of timber parquetry, polished to a high sheen, stretched between us and an imposing reception desk. The ornately patterned floor was dotted with rugs that looked like they were worth more than my car. To one side, a bored-looking waiter stood in the middle of a waiting area outfitted with lounge chairs. On the other side, a baby grand piano dominated the space; a pianist wearing a tuxedo played a classical piece I vaguely recognised. A vase of roses sat on the piano's lid. Everything glittered under strategically placed down lights.

"I can see why he would want to stay here," Jack observed as Shannon led us to the elevators, pulling a plastic key card out of her pocket. My lack of understanding must have shown on my face, because he added, "Brass fittings."

I gazed around with new eyes. There was presumably steel hidden behind the walls—I doubted you could build a high-rise building without it—but all the exposed metal surfaces glowed golden yellow. "Good point."

I'd thought the hotel foyer was impressive. It had nothing on the sumptuous décor of the hotel suite Shannon let us into, on one of the highest floors of the hotel. She hustled us through the foyer, with its slate-tiled floor and built-in wardrobe. We passed the open door to the bathroom, through which I caught a brief glimpse of white-veined black marble, glowing brass fittings and enough down lighting to stun a wayward kangaroo.

The suite's main sitting area was lavishly decorated. The thick powder-blue carpet gave under my feet with every step, even through the soles of my shoes. Cream fabric covered the wing chairs and matching loveseat;

the chairs sat at right angles to a coffee table with curved legs. On the other side, opposite the entrance, a floor-to-ceiling glass door was rendered opaque by the interior's reflection. A television dominated another wall of the room, its huge screen black. Opposite it, an alcove held a small office.

Movement in the alcove startled me, and I realised I was gaping like a tourist. The movement turned out to be a hob, dressed in tight black slacks and a flowing grass-green tunic the same colour as his eyes. Celtic designs adorned the tunic's cuffs and collar. The hob stood from the desk and glided across the carpet, bowing before me.

"Greetings," he said, meeting my gaze, ignoring both Jack and Shannon. "I am Ariel. If you would wait here, I shall fetch my master for you."

"Sure, okay." I pulled a face at Jack as Ariel padded silently up the corridor.

"Would you like a drink?" Shannon asked stiffly.

"Just a glass of water. Thanks." As soon as she was out of the room, I turned to Jack. His hands were curled into fists, his jaw clenched. "Are you okay?"

He gave a barely perceptible shrug, gaze fixed on the direction the other hob had gone. I rubbed my hands along my arms—the air conditioning in the suite was obviously set to refrigerator, because after thirty seconds I began to shiver.

Although maybe that was nerves.

Ariel returned, followed by what I was sure was a *puca*: he was of a similar height, build and colouring to Talbot, although he wore his black hair in a ponytail at the base of his neck and, instead of scruffy tracksuit pants, he wore tight leather. A black muscle shirt revealed that his pale arms prickled with goosebumps. At least I wasn't the only one feeling the cold.

Behind the *puca* was the most attractive man I'd ever seen.

Everest—it couldn't be anyone else—was the same height as Shannon but vibrated with such energy that he towered over everyone else in the room. His hair flowed straight down his back in an inky waterfall streaked with platinum; his eyes were the bright silver of a newly minted twenty-cent piece, framed by a profusion of dark lashes that made me green with envy. His high cheekbones narrowed to a strong, tapered jaw.

Shannon was right. Everest was magnificent.

His full lips quirked into a smile as he watched me stare at him, his aura shining with amusement. I flushed to the roots of my hair, feeling even more awkward in my casual summer clothes. He, on the other hand, was dressed for winter: his calf-length, sable fur coat hung open at the front to reveal tailored black slacks clinging to his narrow waist, and a grey turtleneck jumper hugging his muscled torso.

"Aren't you hot?" I blurted. He raised one elegant black eyebrow, and I wished I could sink into the floor. "I mean, it's pretty warm outside," I stammered.

"No, I am not hot." He smiled. His voice was a sensual baritone that thrilled along my skin. "I have my coat." He ran a hand along the lustrous fur. My hands itched to stroke it, to see how soft it was.

I took a breath. Maybe he'd cranked the air conditioning so he could show off the expensive fur. The idea he might be that vain steadied me a little, made his perfection slightly less intimidating. I gave him a bright smile. "I'm Isla and this is Jack. You wanted to see me?"

"Indeed. Shall we?" He sat on the loveseat and indicated the empty spot beside him with an inviting gesture. I pretended not to notice, sitting in one of the single seats. He was overpowering my senses; caution told me not to get to close. Was that his brand of *aosidhe* magic?

The flicker of irritation in Everest's aura told me I'd made the right decision. I didn't know what he was after, but he wanted to set me at my ease … which made me even more nervous.

Jack stood at my side, hands behind his back like a bodyguard. Everest stared at him for a long, uncomfortable moment, silver eyes narrowed, speculative. My throat constricted. Was I a fool, agreeing to meet with the *aosidhe*?

Shannon returned, handing me a tall glass of water. Condensation beaded the sides of the glass, making it slick under my fingers. I wished I'd thought to ask for tea instead.

"So," I said, taking a polite sip of the water before setting it down on the coffee table, "it must have been exhausting for you to get all the way to Australia from…?"

"Ireland," Everest said, arranging his coat around him with unconscious ease. His answer surprised me—I hadn't detected much of an accent. "It was not the easiest voyage. You understand we cannot fly."

"Of course," I agreed, although the thought hadn't occurred to me until that moment. "So you sailed?"

He nodded. Well, that explained Shannon's hearty tan. "We heard rumours of *aosidhe* activity in this city, which surprised us. We had not believed any of our brethren had travelled to such an isolated continent. I came to investigate, and here you are."

His smile warmed me to my toes. I shifted in my seat. "Yes. But I'm only half *aosidhe*, I'm afraid. Sorry you wasted your trip." My fingers nervously brushed the velvety couch fabric as I babbled.

"Nonsense." Everest leaned forward, resting his elbows on his knees, to gaze at me. I leaned back slightly. "A child sprung from a human and an *aosidhe* parent is something even more marvellous and wonderful. I thought to find a flower growing in a strange place. However, I never expected the flower to be so ... unique."

My heart skipped a beat. I told myself it was because his gaze was too intent, like a predator's, not because of his overt flattery. My irritation at my own foolishness sharpened my tone. "And what are you going to do now you've found me?"

Jack gasped.

Everest blinked slowly. "Pardon?" Standing behind him, Shannon gave me a look that made me glad she wasn't holding anything sharp.

Mentally cursing myself, I tried to soften my words. "Sorry, but a few months ago some *duinesidhe* tried to abduct my father. They were working for an *aosidhe*. I guess I have trust issues."

"Your father would be your human parent?" he asked, voice gentle.

I nodded, biting my lip. Why had I mentioned Dad?

"How do you know they were working for one of us?" The *aosidhe* gave Jack a disappointed look, as though he had badmouthed Everest's people. Which, of course, he had.

"He was elf shot."

"Ah." Everest steepled his fingers, his gaze intense.

My breath caught in my throat. "Then yes, your father has an *aosidhe* enemy. Do you know who it is?"

I shook my head.

"You haven't attempted to investigate?" Another reproachful look at Jack irritated me all over again.

"Of course we have. We just haven't had much success. But we will."

"Would you like me to assist you? I have resources you may not." He indicated the two attendant *duine-sidhe*—the unctuous Ariel and the leather-clad *puca*. "Ariel is an exceptionally fine investigator, with a keen mind, and Fintan there is one of the best trackers in all of Europe. Are you not, Fintan?"

The *puca* stepped forward and bowed from the waist. "My lord is too kind," he murmured, his emotions indicating only grateful pleasure at the praise. I realised with widening eyes that he was wearing a studded dog collar around his throat.

I glanced at Ariel to see whether he was wearing something around his throat as well. He wasn't.

"What do you say?"

I looked at Jack, wishing—not for the first time—that I had telepathy rather than empathy. His aura was primarily the deep blue of suspicion, but a slow tendril of sickly yellow fear curled there too. He saw my gaze and shrugged slightly. He seemed to be doing his damnedest not to move. I suspected if he could have stopped breathing he would have.

I turned back to Everest. "Would you want something in exchange?"

"Of course not." Outrage stiffened his tone, although it didn't reach as far as his aura. "Clearly you do not trust me, Isla, and I can understand why that would be. Let me do this thing for you, to prove that the *aosidhe* are not all monsters. And once you know you can trust me, we can talk again."

"Okay. Right. Thanks." I shivered, wondering if I'd just made a deal with the devil.

"What can you tell me about the attempted abductors?"

"There were three: a hob named Moray, a *puca* and a *powrie*," I said. "The *puca* and *powrie* were working for Moray. They both got away."

"And what happened to this Moray?" he asked.

"He didn't make it."

Everest raised his eyebrows. "He was killed?"

I nodded, refusing to elaborate. Mentioning my father was stupid; I wasn't going to make that mistake with my nana too. Especially since she'd gone back to England and was more easily within reach of the bulk of the *aosidhe* population.

Standing directly behind Everest, Ariel's expression stayed carefully neutral even as his aura flashed blood red with rage. After one startled glance, I kept my eyes fixed on his master. The hair on the back of my neck prickled as I felt the hob's glare bore into me.

Wringing my hands, I decided it was time to make our escape. "Well, if you don't mind, I have places to be. You'll get in touch if you find anything out?"

"Indeed. My *aislinge*—" he gestured to Shannon "—will find you. And if you need me in the meantime, I will be staying here."

That's what the gold flecks in her aura meant. That's where I'd seen them before: in Ryan's aura after a vision.

Everest was waiting for a response. "Okay. Thanks."

I didn't breathe easy until Jack and I reached the hotel foyer. I rubbed my forearms vigorously to warm myself up. "That was different," I said, keeping my voice low so the staff didn't overhear. "Are all *aosidhe* like that?"

"Some are worse," he muttered as we shuffled through the revolving door.

"He definitely had a sort of … energy about him. I don't know how he could possibly pass for human."

Jack shrugged. "That may not be a particular concern of his. Besides, people will remember him afterwards as a particularly beautiful man. They are likely to attribute his energy, as you put it, to that fact. Humans are very fond of beauty."

I wanted to defend the race I'd grown up with, but found I couldn't—particularly as, at that moment, we entered a crowd of girls my age, who were waiting at the lights to cross the road. They wore short dresses and tall heels and leaned against one another drunkenly, giggling. With Jack's words in mind, I tried to look at them objectively. They were dressed up to show off their physical assets as best they could: long legs; curved bodies; pretty faces; long, glossy hair. This late in the evening—it was almost midnight—their efforts were fading, eroded by alcohol and dancing, mascara smudged and bodies smelling of cigarette smoke and perspiration.

When the lights changed, we crossed, branching off towards the car park.

"Are you saying the *duinesidhe* don't value beauty?" I said pointedly when the nearest people were out of hearing distance. "Everest clearly took great care with his appearance. His servants did too."

"Some of us do. The *aosidhe* are usually extremely

vain. Others of us care to a greater or lesser extent, but if one is in service to a vain *aosidhe*, one does not get a great deal of personal choice about how one dresses."

I thought about the collar Fintan wore—and Shannon's more ornate torc, which was definitely collar-like—and grimaced. "Do you know what his special brand of *aosidhe* magic is?"

"No. I have not heard of him before. All I can tell you is that he is not one of the most powerful *aosidhe*. Them I know."

"I suppose that's something." Another idea occurred to me. "Do you think he knows what mine is?"

"It is unlikely, unless he also knows that you are Melpomene's daughter. In that case, he may guess you share her gift. What was his emotional state?"

"Mostly pleased. Almost smug. I don't know what he was so happy about though." I wrinkled my nose. "I really wish I hadn't mentioned the attack on Dad. Ariel was angry when he found out Moray was killed. Really angry. Do you think maybe they knew each other?"

"Possibly," Jack admitted. "His reaction could also be outrage at the notion a hob was killed in service to its master. It is not unheard of, but it is unusual." He looked at me for a long moment, sapphire eyes troubled. "You know they probably assume you killed Moray."

"Maybe that's a good thing," I suggested, although the waver in my voice wasn't so sure. "They might think I'm tougher than I really am."

"That is true. Although, in that case, you had best hope that Ariel did not actually know him. Otherwise, you have just made yourself an enemy."

Oh goody.

CHAPTER NINE

The next day, I texted Dominic and asked him to pick me up from Natalie's place after lunch. Sarah agreed to give me a lift there beforehand, even though she radiated resentment all morning. Aunt Elizabeth hummed around the house doing chores, which made private conversations difficult and meant I hadn't had a chance to explain to her why I'd left the pub so precipitately the night before. Ryan also gave me several curious looks, mercifully free of any bitterness. Given he wasn't the one I'd skipped out on, he didn't really have any reason to be angry with me—but I regretted not taking a minute to tell him why I was leaving the night before, so he could pass the message on to Sarah. I'd been so flustered I hadn't thought of it at the time. And I'd forgotten to text her like I'd promised.

By the time we got into Sarah's battered hatchback, my stomach was a knot of nerves. Her silence as we pulled out of the driveway reminded me of the chilly air in Everest's hotel room the night before. I wished I could modify my own emotions as well as others', so that I wouldn't have to feel so anxious.

Sarah didn't speak. When she turned the corner, the indicator seemed loud.

"I'm sorry I had to go last night," I said, my words a tentative peace offering. "How did the second half go?"

"Fine."

I took a deep breath, swallowing the flare of irritation. "Did you want to know what it was about?"

"Well, it obviously wasn't a sick aunt," she muttered, gaze fixed out the window.

"Jack got word that there was an *aosidhe* in town. I was worried it might be her. My mother."

Sarah glanced at me, eyes wide. "Was it?" I breathed a quiet sigh of relief as the irritation faded from her aura, replaced with curiosity and concern.

"It turns out no. Just after we found out about him, the *aosidhe* sent his minion to come and collect us."

"Minion?" Her lips quirked with a faint smile. "How very dark ages."

"No kidding, but she totally was. Anyway, his name is Everest and he claims he got wind of the fact I was here and came to investigate."

"Do you believe him?"

"I don't know. He's from Ireland. It's a long way to travel when you can't fly—"

"It's a long way to travel when you *can*..."

"—and I can't imagine that a half-breed like me is worth that amount of effort."

Sarah frowned, drumming her fingers on the steering wheel. "Didn't Jack say the *aosidhe* are über-political? If they don't make babies with humans, maybe Melpomene's enemies can use you to embarrass her." Although there was no spite in Sarah's tone, I winced as she continued. "I mean, whoever wanted to kidnap your dad probably planned to use him against her somehow. If it wasn't her behind it."

"Moray said he was working for someone else. He could have been lying, though."

"Assume he wasn't. If she cares about your dad, they could have used him as a hostage."

I stared out the window at the passing traffic, fidgeting with the strap of my purse. "I know Dad wants to believe it could be true, but even he admits it's unlikely. He didn't flee across the world and surround himself with iron for no reason. He thought she wanted to hurt him. Or worse."

"That's the other option then," Sarah said as we pulled onto the gravelled strip out the front of Natalie's house. When I gave my cousin a puzzled look, she elaborated. "If Melpomene wants to get her hands on your dad, maybe another *aosidhe* wanted to beat her to it, to use him as leverage. Trade him for something they want from her."

I considered that as we got out of the car. "Maybe Everest came out here for the same reason. Thinking to use me against her in some way."

She shrugged. "If he knows who your mum is, sure. If he doesn't, you can bet those cute sandals he's trying to find out. There's Kim. Smile!"

I turned with a bright grin to wave at our friend, who had parked on the curb in front of the neighbour's house. She smiled back, picking her way across the uneven ground to where we stood. She held a cake box in one arm, resting the corner of the box against her hip for balance.

ISLA'S OATH

"Were we meant to bring dessert?" Sarah asked, aghast.

"No. Natalie rang this morning and asked me to pick one up," Kim said.

"What is it?"

"A bee sting cake." At our blank expressions, she rolled her eyes. "A German honey cake. Honestly, I thought *I* was the immigrant." Kim had no trace of an accent, having grown up in Canberra, but her family spoke Vietnamese at home.

"We're both immigrants too, you know," I pointed out.

"Emigrating from England barely counts," Kim said with a sniff.

Sarah led the way up the path to the door. "Neither of us are from Germany—"

"And I am?"

"—so why would we know about German cakes? Anyway, can I see?" Sarah turned and tried to prise the box's lid open. Kim held it firmly closed, laughing.

The smell of roasting chicken was clearly detectable—and delectable—from the porch of the house. The front door was open, and the screen door did nothing to diminish the delicious aroma.

"Knock, knock!" Sarah called, rattling the screen door lightly.

After a few moments, during which we listened to the sounds of a console racing game from the living room, Natalie answered the door. She was dressed in a girly fashion that was unusual for her: a white floral dress that came to her knees, printed with bold crimson poppies, and red, high-heeled sandals. She was even wearing lipstick. I was grateful I had dressed up too, although I'd done it for my date with Dominic afterwards. I hadn't realised lunch was a dressy affair.

From the sheepish look on Sarah's face, she hadn't either.

"Come in," Natalie smiled at us. "The food's almost ready. I hope you're hungry."

I followed the others into the dining room, frowning at Natalie's back. Anxiety knotted her aura, more acute now than the night before.

Natalie's mother, a petite woman with silver-streaked blond hair tied back in a bun at the nape of her neck, was putting the last touches on the table. She gave each of us a pat on the cheek as we entered the room. "Good afternoon, girls."

"Good afternoon, Mrs Brandt," we chorused. "This looks great," Kim added, gesturing to the table. Porcelain crockery and glittering silverware adorned a burgundy damask tablecloth and, in the centre of the table, a crystal vase held an artfully arranged bunch of gerberas. Everything gleamed in the bright sun streaming in through the broad windows, the colours glowing.

"Natalie did most of the work," she said with a proud, slightly bemused, look at her daughter.

Natalie blushed and took the cake box from Kim. "Thanks for grabbing this. It's Dad's favourite. I was going to bake one but ran out of time."

"No probs. Did you need help dishing up?"

"Sure, okay."

We weren't all able to fit into the tiny kitchen, so Natalie and Sarah dished up the food while I ferried plates to the table and Kim poured drinks. Mrs Brandt slipped away to tell her husband and Natalie's brother, Ethan, that it was time to eat.

Ethan arrived promptly—the revving engine noises

stopped—and grunted a greeting at us. A scowl from his mother kept him from digging in, so instead he slumped in his chair, eyeing the contents of his plate. He was thirteen and had hit puberty unevenly; he was a tangle of arms and legs but still had a baby face and no trace of facial hair. He reminded me of a long-limbed, awkward puppy who hadn't quite figured out how to make all four feet head in the same direction.

Mr Brandt, when he arrived, was impeccably dressed in slacks and a blue polo shirt. He looked like he'd just stepped off the golf course. For all I knew, he had. He was a tall man, dwarfing the rest of his family, his eyes obscured by the light glimmering off the thick lenses in his glasses.

He sat at the head of the table, his wife to his right and his son to his left. Natalie sat opposite her father, at the other end of the table. I ended up between Sarah and Ethan, hoping the latter kept his bony elbows to himself.

Mr Brandt said a quick grace and we began to eat.

Natalie had outdone herself, preparing the sort of meal I'd expect for Christmas lunch, not a regular Sunday afternoon. Roasted chicken, potatoes, carrot and pumpkin, served with beans, corn and minted peas. My plate overflowed with food. How was I going to eat it all?

Glancing around the table while Sarah enthused about her gig the night before, I noticed that I wasn't the only one struggling to finish their meal. Natalie was only picking at her food. Her mother kept looking at her up the length of the table with an expression of increasing concern. And the more the dinner progressed, the more miserable Natalie became. Every time she glanced at her father, who was eating with oblivious efficiency, her nervous aura flared.

By the time we'd cleared the table and served dessert, I'd concluded she was planning a big announcement. And it was something her father, in particular, wasn't going to like. Glancing at the old-fashioned Mr Brandt, I could think of any number of options.

Natalie didn't touch her cake; instead, she cleared her throat and looked around the table. Her hands curled around her napkin, twisting it as though she was wringing water from a dishrag. "I guess you're all wondering why I went to such an effort with lunch today."

Everyone nodded except Ethan, who put a huge mouthful of cake into his mouth and began chewing. His father gave him a dark look, which he either didn't notice or studiously ignored.

"I have something important I want to tell you. You're my family and closest friends, so I wanted you all to hear it at once." Natalie took a deep breath, as though preparing for a plunge into deep water.

Then she said, "I'm gay."

There was a moment of complete silence; even Ethan stopped chewing and stared at his older sister, eyes like dinner plates and mouth hanging open. Opposite me, Mrs Brandt paled, looking from her daughter to her husband. Her aura flooded with dread. Sarah was as astonished as I felt, eyes wide. Kim also looked surprised, although her aura was less so—as though Natalie's announcement was confirmation of something she'd suspected for a while.

Mr Brandt's fist slammed down onto the dining table, rattling the spoon on his plate. We all jumped. "No. I forbid it." His aura was a burning furnace of anger, mottled with disgust.

ISLA'S OATH

"Dad, I—"

"No child of mine will turn into a, a..." He clenched his jaws and ground his teeth. His face was flushed, nostrils flared.

"A lesbian?" Natalie said softly.

Mrs Brandt spoke quickly, before her husband could explode. "Honey, are you sure?"

"Yes, Mum. I'm sure."

"You've dated boys!" Mrs Brand said, hands clutching the edge of the tablecloth. "What about that Tommy? The one who took you to your year ten formal? You seemed sweet on him."

"He's a nice guy. But that's it. That's always been it. This isn't something I chose." Her eyes begged for understanding. "It's just how I am."

"Well, we're proud of you," Kim said stoutly.

"*Proud*?" Mr Brandt roared. Beside me, Ethan pushed his chair back. He was afraid of his father's temper. I'd know that sickly yellow colour anywhere. His mother cringed too.

But Kim wasn't daunted. She lifted her chin and stared at Natalie's father, dark eyes flashing with indignation. "Yes. I'm proud that she was brave enough to come out to us. It can't be easy." *With you for a father.* She didn't say the final words, but, looking around at the shocked faces, I wasn't the only one at the table to guess what she was implying.

Natalie's father started yelling at Kim then, accusing her of being the one who had led his daughter astray, the two of them indulging in a wanton and immoral university lifestyle. Never mind the fact they'd only done orientation. I opened my mouth to say something when

I felt a hand on my upper arm. Sarah stared at me. I frowned, confused, and she leaned towards me.

"Do something!" she whispered.

My eyes widened as I realised what she meant. Calm Mr Brandt's rage. Remind him he loved his daughter, the way I'd reminded my Nana of her long-buried feelings for her son. *Fix it.*

I hesitated. I wanted to help Natalie, who sat beside Sarah with unshed tears glittering in her eyes. I wanted to fix this. But my mind returned to the same Gordian knot it always did. Was it wrong to change how someone felt about something—especially something they held strong views on? Even if I didn't agree with them? Was I changing who they were?

I wasn't comfortable playing God.

Sarah's fingers tightened on my arm. There would be bruises tomorrow. Her emotions were almost as hot as Mr Brandt's: anger when she looked at him entwined with frustration when her gaze returned to mine.

Mrs Brandt tried to pacify her raging husband, who was on his feet, clenched fists braced on the table on either side of his plate as he glowered down the table at my friends. "Please calm down, Leon," she pleaded, placing a hand on his arm. He threw her off, and she fell back with a cry. Her chair almost toppled over, balancing precariously on two legs. Kim reached out to steady her before she fell back into the wall.

Hell with it.

I reached past Ethan to place my hand lightly on Mr Brandt's fist. "Stop it."

Trying to affect someone's emotions remotely was like wrestling smoke. With the physical contact, I had a direct connection to the maelstrom of his emotions: fury, revulsion, fear, shame. I thrust my power into him, needle-like, lancing the boil so the poisons could drain; they flowed into me, filling my mouth with a sour, oily taste. I fed him back his shame, reworked so that the focus was on his own behaviour, intertwining it with the thread of love for his family—for Natalie; for his wife and son.

For a moment, everything hung motionless, breathless. Then, with a wordless cry of remorse, Mr Brandt embraced his wife. Weeping, she clutched at him.

"Dad?" Natalie's voice was low and rough, struggling from a throat caught in a chokehold of grief and hurt. "I know I've let you down. But this is just how I am."

He looked up at her, eyes filled with disappointment. He loved her. I knew he loved her. But you wouldn't have known it from the chill in his voice when he replied. "So you say, Natalie Anne. I hope you change your mind. You can come back when you do."

Mrs Brandt murmured a low protest. Her husband ignored her. Natalie looked stunned. "Come back?"

"Yes. Until then, you aren't welcome under this roof."

"What happened?" Sarah demanded as soon as we were in her car. Behind us, Natalie started her own silver sedan, ready to follow us back to our place. After a frantic phone call, Aunt Elizabeth had agreed our friend could stay with us for a few days, until she figured out what to do next. I think my aunt was hoping Mr Brandt would cool down and change his mind.

He wouldn't. He'd been perfectly calm when he evicted his daughter.

"I don't know." I leaned back against the headrest. A headache was blooming behind my eyes; jittery bursts of the raw energy I'd absorbed from Mr Brandt made my fingers tremble in time with my heartbeat.

"You did it, right? I saw you."

"Yes."

"So what happened?" she asked again.

I gritted my teeth, willing myself to patience. "Nearest I can figure is his dislike of gay people isn't just an emotional thing."

She exhaled in frustration. "That doesn't make sense. He was pretty much crazy with rage."

"I know. But if you strip the emotion away, he believes homosexuals are … I don't know, wrong, or sinful, or whatever. He loves Natalie. For all I know he thinks booting her out will give her the incentive to get over it. Like kicking her out is for her own good."

Sarah's lip curled with disgust. "She can't just change whether she's gay or not."

"I'm not saying I agree with him," I said, pressing my fingers to my temples to try to still the throbbing. "I'm just telling you what I think happened. I don't know what he was thinking. It's not like I can read his mind. I can just see how he's feeling about whatever it is he's thinking."

"That's not much bloody good, is it?"

"You don't have to tell me that," I snapped back.

Neither of us spoke for the rest of the drive home. When we arrived, Sarah locked her car without speaking and went to help Natalie get her bags from the boot of her car. The petite blonde's eyes were puffy and raw from crying;

her mascara ran in sooty black streaks down her cheeks.

I briefly contemplated helping Natalie with her grief, but if I took any more emotions right now, my head might fly apart like a watermelon dropped from a second-storey balcony. So instead, I gave her a brief hug and shouldered her university backpack. The strap cut into my shoulder—the bag was full of textbooks and her laptop, and weighed about a tonne.

We set Natalie up on a mattress in Sarah's room. Our friend was oblivious to the tension, thanking us profusely and with no little embarrassment for our help. Hamish, excited at having a new occupant in the house to sniff, promptly set himself up in her lap, soliciting cuddles and distracting her with his antics.

When I went to fetch Natalie a pillow from the linen cupboard, Sarah followed me out to the corridor. "Sorry for snapping at you," she said, looking down at her hand, which fidgeted with the watch I'd bought her for her eighteenth birthday.

"It's okay." I handed her a pillowslip. "I was pissy too. And Sarah? I really am sorry about last night."

She opened her mouth to reply. My phone beeped a message alert. It was from Dominic. *You ready to go?*

I texted him back, asking him to collect me from home rather than Natalie's. *I'll explain when you get here.* I gave Sarah the pillow and went into the kitchen to get a couple of painkillers before he arrived. I was determined to try to enjoy the rest of my Valentine's Day.

CHAPTER TEN

"*Y*ou want to break up with me? On *Valentine's Day*?"
My voice was louder than I'd intended, drawing speculative and pitying looks from nearby tables.

Dominic shuffled on his chair, blushing. I wanted to sink into the floor.

Garema Place was busy. Couples were more prominent than usual, many of the women—and a few of the men—carrying flowers or heart-shaped balloons and expression that, when I was single, I would've described as smug. This year, with a cute pink teddy bear and a helium balloon of my own, I'd found myself feeling charitable towards the overt displays of affection between others.

Now tears prickled my eyes and I bit my lip to stop it from trembling.

"I'm not saying that," Dominic mumbled. He shifted, and his seat's metal legs creaked on the pavement. He wouldn't make eye contact, and embarrassment streaked his aura at the attention I'd drawn. "I'm just saying you're difficult to get close to. You don't open up to me."

An older woman at the next table snorted into her muffin. I could guess what she was thinking: *that's a euphemism for her refusing to sleep with him.* Maybe it was my guilty conscience, but I was sure that wasn't what he meant. Because Dominic was right. There was part of my life that I didn't talk to him about.

A major one.

I lowered my voice too. "I try to." My voice wavered. "I'm not good at this."

"You could be. You just need to tell me stuff."

"I do!"

"Well, okay," he replied, looking up with narrowed eyes. "Tell me why you're so jumpy."

"Lunch freaked me out." I'd already given him the abridged version of Natalie's coming out, omitting my involvement.

He narrowed his eyes a little. "I know, but that's not the whole reason, is it? You got more agitated after we sat down to order."

My stomach flipped. I tried to hide it by having a sip of juice.

The café Dominic had chosen for our pre-movie date was on the same square as the pub Sarah had played at the night before, right near where Shannon had found me and Jack. I felt exposed in the hot afternoon sunshine, as if Everest were going to swoop down on us at any moment, fur-bedecked, gorgeous and as out of place in an Australian summer as the Abominable Snowman. I imagined Bruce Wayne might feel the same way if he went out on a date in the Joker's main hangout. Except Bruce Wayne had a secret identity, so the Joker may not recognise him—whereas Everest knew exactly what I looked like.

Maybe I needed a secret identity.

"Are you going to answer me?" Dominic snapped.

I looked down at my hands and took a wavering breath before meeting his angry gaze. "I don't know what to say. I feel a bit headachy, and it's making me feel like I had too much coffee. If I'm jumpy, that's why."

"Maybe you should have just stayed home. We could have done this another time." Although his voice was neutral, his aura flared with bitterness and distrust. The intensity of it shocked me.

"But it's Valentine's Day," I whispered. Why was he so angry? Not because I kept looking over my shoulder for Everest and his flunkies.

"So?" he muttered. "It's just commercial rubbish any-way, to get us to buy cards and chocolates. It's been two months since Christmas—the shops need *something* to sell us."

That annoyed me. "Hang on. The date was your idea."

"Yeah, well, that was before."

I narrowed my eyes. "Before what?"

He took a deep breath and matched my suspicious glare with one of his own. "Where did you go last night?"

I blinked. "What do you mean?"

"You left the pub with Jack. Sarah told me."

The penny dropped. "You went to the pub?"

"Obviously."

Sarah hadn't mentioned it. Was that the other reason she'd been angry with me this morning? My hand balled into a fist around my napkin. "You didn't text me. I assumed you went home after your shift."

"I didn't."

"Did Sarah also tell you Jack's aunt was sick?"

He frowned, dark eyes intent on my face. "She said that's what you told Kim and Natalie."

"And you didn't believe her?"

"I got the impression *she* didn't believe *you.*"

I could have strangled my cousin just then. "You think Jack and I are, what, sleeping together?" My voice was shrill.

"Are you?"

"No!" People were looking at us again. I didn't care. "How could you even *think* that?"

He sat back in his chair, folding his arms across his chest. "Because you don't talk to me. You disappear with him and, when I offer to help you, you accept his help instead."

He was referring to Sarah's birthday party the previous year, when I'd found out Dad was under attack. I'd taken Jack with me because the attackers were *duine-sidhe*—something my human boyfriend was unequipped to deal with. But, like so many other elements of my life, I couldn't explain it to Dominic without telling him the whole truth. And I definitely didn't feel like opening up to him now, in a public café, when he was yelling at me. Although it wasn't logical, his accusations that I didn't share things with him made me want to share even less.

"That only happened once. And I apologised, like, a thousand times."

"What about last night? We were meant to meet. And Sarah said you left halfway through her gig. She was pretty cut about it."

"It was an emergency. You think I wanted to leave?"

"Did you?"

"No. Besides, we're not talking about Sarah. We're

talking about us."

He didn't reply. His emotions were a tumble of irritation and doubt.

I held out my hand to his. After a moment, he took it. "Please," I said softly. "I would never cheat on you. You have to trust me."

And, with the physical contact between us, I changed him so that he did.

By the time Dominic dropped me home my head pounded like a bass drum. I took a couple of strong painkillers and crawled into bed, muffling my tears in my pillow until the medication dragged me under.

The next morning I overslept. When I finally crawled out of bed, I felt fuzzy, as though I'd slept too deeply to dream.

Part of me was thankful for that.

By the time I got out of the shower, my aunt had left for work and Natalie was packing her backpack, ready to head out the door to university. She looked grim. Her plain black shorts and charcoal-grey shirt were funereal compared to the floral dress she'd worn the day before.

She looked, in fact, as grim as I felt.

"No news?" I asked her. Sarah, visible through the open door to the kitchen, smiled a greeting at me. Remembering my fight with Dominic, I ignored her. Seeing her brought back my resentment from the afternoon before, tangled up with remorse so overwhelming I felt as though I might vomit.

Natalie shook her head and sighed. She wasn't wearing

makeup, and her face was pinched. "There won't be. Dad's stubborn as a mule."

"Maybe your mum will get through to him," I said hopefully.

She sighed again and gave each of us a forlorn wave. "I'll see you guys tonight."

"Have a good day. Learn stuff."

After she'd gone, it felt like the temperature in the house dropped ten degrees. Squaring my shoulders, I went into the kitchen to make a cup of tea—my stomach felt too fragile for coffee. Sarah was pouring milk into a bowl of brightly coloured cereal with no nutritional value.

"How's your head?" my cousin asked.

I shrugged. "Can you pass the milk?"

She handed me the carton with an odd look. "And the date?" I clenched my jaw, not saying anything. "Isla, talk to me. What happened?"

"Like you don't know, after what you told Dominic," I muttered.

"What? I didn't even see him yesterday." Guilt flickered in her aura, grey tinged with pink, like a faint blush. She knew what I was talking about.

I narrowed my eyes. "Are you sure? He wouldn't have showed up to the pub till close to midnight, so maybe it *was* technically yesterday."

It was her turn to shrug, reaching for her cereal. The guilt remained.

"You didn't tell me he arrived after I left."

"I forgot." She sat at the dining table, not meeting my gaze.

I leaned back against the kitchen bench, arms folded. "There's something I need to know, Sarah."

"What?" she asked, before putting a rainbow spoonful of cereal in her mouth.

"Did you suggest to Dominic that I was sleeping with Jack?"

She choked, reaching for her glass of water. After several long moments of coughing, she croaked, "No."

"He seems to think you did."

"What did he say?" She dropped her spoon into the cereal and sat back, frowning.

"He said you didn't believe I took Jack to see a sick aunt."

"Well, that's true. You hadn't." She brushed her hair back from her eyes impatiently. "Does Jack even *have* an aunt?"

"Sarah!" I protested, a catch in my voice. "Dom nearly dumped me!"

Her emotions were a curious mix of remorse and resentment—but when she spoke, resentment won out. "I'm sick of lying for you, Isla. Just tell your boyfriend the truth. Besides," she added, "I'm not the only one who had my doubts. Natalie didn't believe you either."

I turned my back on her and began making my tea, not trusting myself to speak. Tears burned my eyes.

After a long moment of silence, Sarah asked softly, "Did he? Break up with you?"

"No." I pressed my lips together and didn't say anything else. Shame roiled in my gut. I'd taken away Dominic's free will—and not because he was threatening others, like Mr Brandt, or for his own good, like the boy on the beach. I'd done it purely for my own selfish reasons. I was as bad as my mother.

Was my headache the night before a result of overusing my power or due to unadulterated self-loathing?

"Well, that's good then," Sarah said, unaware of my thoughts.

He didn't break up with me. But he should have.

CHAPTER ELEVEN

I spent the next two days staying away from everyone I cared about. Dominic and I spoke on the phone on Monday night. He apologised for upsetting me on Valentine's Day and assured me he trusted me. I knew it was true—he no longer had a choice—and couldn't keep the strain out of my voice. If he noticed, he didn't say anything. Was he even able to notice the signs of my guilt now I'd removed his capacity to doubt me?

I particularly avoided being alone in Sarah's company, not sure I could bear another lecture about honesty. At least when we were around Natalie and our family, my cousin kept her opinions to herself. Natalie, whose perceptiveness was usually only eclipsed by her bluntness, was so caught up in her own misery she didn't notice the tension.

Ryan did, but didn't say anything.

Avoiding the common areas of the house, I hid in my room, surfing the internet between half-heartedly looking at employment agency websites. Driven by guilt over Dominic and ambivalence over Mr Brandt, I researched what a lack of emotion could mean. A *Wikipedia* article on schizophrenia unnerved me—could I create mental illness?

The article on psychopathy gave me nightmares.

When, on the second day, Jack dropped by, wanting to talk, I was relieved. We drove down to the eastern shore of Lake Tuggeranong, near where I'd come with Dad the week before. The sun dipped low in the sky, casting long shadows behind us. We were alone except for the occasional jogger on the bike path, which was far enough behind us that we wouldn't be overheard unless we shouted.

As soon as we sank down in the long grass, I launched into my concerns, explaining what I'd done to both men on Valentine's Day.

I didn't tell him why Dominic was about to break up with me. Because awkward.

He listened patiently until I talked myself out. When I stopped, exhausted and ashamed, he tipped his head to the side and frowned. A few strands of hair had escaped the ponytail and broad-brimmed hat keeping the points of his ears concealed; the strands floated around his face in the breeze like threads of golden silk.

"You seem anxious about all this," he said.

I choked back a hysterical laugh. "No kidding."

"Why?"

"Because it's wrong!"

"From what you say, Natalie's father was about to hurt someone. Why would you be worried about preventing that?"

"I'm more worried about what happened with Dominic," I admitted. "Mr Brandt was the slippery slope. Dominic is the terrifying plummet off the edge of a cliff."

He raised an eyebrow. "Well, as for that, you say Dominic was beginning to distrust you because he knows you are keeping a secret life from him. Revealing that secret could put him in danger and is something that should not be divulged lightly in any case. Correct?"

"Well, yes, but—"

"But nothing," Jack interrupted, sounding remarkably like Sarah. "You have a secret you must preserve. In doing so, you have caused the boy no harm."

"How do you know that? What if I damaged him somehow? Did you know that psychopaths don't have remorse, guilt or empathy? They're emotionally shallow. What if I did that to him? *Broke* him?"

He blinked. "Did you?"

"I don't think so, but—"

"Isla, you are worrying about nothing."

"I'm really not." Frustrated, I threw myself back onto the grass, staring up at the canopy of eucalyptus leaves silhouetted against the deepening blue sky. "I don't want to turn into my mother, making someone love me just because it's convenient at the time. She only did it to Dad because she was fleeing some other *aosidhe* and she wanted his help, did you know that? And it backfired on her because he trapped her with an oath."

"You would not do that to someone." His voice was certain. "You are not that type of person." He let me consider his reassurance for a few seconds before adding, "Besides, what is the alternative?"

I turned my head to frown at him; his eyes, illuminated by the setting sun, were the same light blue as his aura. Serene. "What do you mean?"

He ticked his points off on his fingers. "You cannot tell your secret to someone unless you know you can trust them. For a relationship to develop to that point, they need to forgive the fact you are keeping a secret without knowing what it is. You can help them grant you the time you need to learn whether they are worthy of your trust and reduce anxiety for both of you in the meantime. Would you prefer to be alone?"

Self-pity made tears well in my eyes. "Maybe that would be better for everyone."

He snorted derisively. The reaction was so at odds with his normal demeanour that I sat up, staring at him in surprise and annoyance.

When I saw the twinkle in his eye, I laughed, feeling sheepish.

A feeling like spiders crawling up my spine made me look around. Shannon stood on the cycle path, watching us with wide eyes. She met my gaze and her expression swiftly shifted to her usual polite disdain. She still wore long slacks and another long-sleeved shirt that only partly concealed her silver torc—although this time the shirt was carmine instead of jade. Her only concession to the heat was that she had neatly rolled up the sleeves to reveal her golden tan.

"We've got company," I murmured to Jack. He helped me stand and we walked over together.

"Hi, Shannon."

"Isla." She nodded her head stiffly in greeting. "My master bid me find you."

"I figured. What does he want?" I wasn't in the mood to be diplomatic. Jack pressed his lips together, glancing at me.

"He has some news on the *duinesidhe* you requested he locate for you," Shannon said. "The ones that attacked your father."

"That was fast. It's only been four days."

"Yes." Shannon lifted her chin. "Everest demands the best from those that serve him."

"So what's the news?"

"I don't know." The *aislinge* was telling the truth, if her brief flash of irritation was anything to go by. She didn't like not knowing. "He wants to tell you in person and requests the honour of your company."

I frowned at her for a long moment before taking Jack's arm. "Excuse me for a sec." She watched, baffled, as I led the hob out of hearing distance for a hushed conversation.

"You're thinking of going?" Jack asked. His anxiety was back. The sickly yellow fear I was getting to know pretty well jarred against purple whorls, giving me sympathetic jitters.

"I'm wondering if we should," I whispered. "If he knows anything that could lead us to Dad's attackers it would be worth it. Wouldn't it?"

He shrugged, watching Shannon cautiously. She stared back, not bothering to try to hide it. "He may have offered to investigate without cost," the hob observed, "but I am worried about what you would call the fine print."

"So what do we do?"

"If we go, do not agree to anything, especially anything binding. And ask him to swear an oath to be truthful with you so that you know he is not lying."

I thought about it for a moment, watching a butterfly wing its lazy way between the dandelions dotting the grass. "Would he agree to that?"

ISLA'S OATH

"If you limited the oath to today, perhaps. He is clearly trying to win your trust and, if he wishes to continue doing so, I do not see how he can refuse."

"Okay. Let's do it." We began the walk back to where Shannon waited with barely concealed impatience. "Why do I get the feeling I'm walking back into the lion's den?" I murmured.

"Because you are not foolish?" Jack smiled grimly.

We took my car—it turned out the *aislinge* had used a taxi to get to the lake. I called shotgun on Jack's behalf so I could buckle him in. He watched the stainless steel buckle in my hand the way Aunt Elizabeth would a hairy spider, while Shannon observed from the back seat with an odd expression. When I pulled out of the dirt parking lot and into traffic, she said, "I'd assumed we would take the *sidhe* paths to get back to the hotel."

I glanced at Jack, wondering what she was talking about. Were the tunnels under Mount Taylor extensive enough that we could get halfway across town without coming out into the human world?

"Isla thought it was best not to show the servant of a new *aosidhe* how to get into the local mound," Jack lied, shaking his head faintly at me.

In the rear vision mirror, I saw Shannon cross her arms, radiating offence. I couldn't see her emotions in the reflection, I realised with surprise.

"No insult intended to Everest," I said to cover my confusion. "He's nice enough, but we only just met. A girl doesn't reveal all her secrets on the first date, know what I mean?"

That won me a flicker of a smile. "Quite."

We drove in silence for fifteen minutes; when Civic

was in sight, Shannon spoke again. "We can park at the hotel. The room key gives us access to the underground parking."

I didn't like the idea of only being able to leave at the *aislinge's*—and therefore Everest's—whim. I couldn't think of a polite way to refuse. On the other hand, I'd already annoyed her, so what was one more lapse of good manners? "I might just park across the road, actually. To save you having to let us out afterwards."

She pressed her lips together, keeping her thoughts to herself until we parked the car and were walking towards the hotel. "If you don't mind me saying, you're quite the enigma, Isla."

I blinked. "What do you mean?"

"When I first saw you this afternoon you seemed friendly with your hob." She indicated Jack with a wave of her hand as we walked three abreast across the pedestrian crossing. Everest's hotel towered above us; I wondered for a moment if he was looking down at us before recalling that his hotel room faced the lake, not the city. "But then you forced him to ride in a car to protect the secret of your *sidhe*. Not many *aosidhe* would be so cruel."

I stared from her to Jack in consternation. I knew Jack found it uncomfortable riding in the car, a cause for nervousness and a little queasiness given the proximity of all that upholstered steel. He'd always told me it was unpleasant but tolerable.

Anger flushed the pale skin of Jack's cheeks. "I do not mind. In fact, it was my idea."

"Was it?" She raised her eyebrows faintly. "I'd always thought being enclosed inside that much steel wracked a hob with nausea and even pain. You are indeed a loyal servant to your master."

"Yes," he growled through gritted teeth. "And I would protect the local *sidhe* from *yours*."

Her expression cold, she stalked into the hotel.

"Was that a good idea?" I whispered as we shuffled into the same segment of the revolving door.

"Probably not, but she annoyed me."

"Jack, why didn't you say being in the car bothered you so much? We could have found another way."

"Because I am capable of managing my own weaknesses," he replied stiffly. I hung my head. As we emerged into the reception, Jack gave my hand a brief squeeze. "Do not worry about it," he murmured, barely audible beneath the tinkling piano.

Shannon stood by the elevator doors, tapping her foot. Apparently, her snit hadn't extended to returning to Everest's room without us. What would the *aosidhe* have done to her if she had? Better not to dwell on it. This was the same *aosidhe* we were about to pay a call on.

After our last meeting with Everest, I'd wondered whether I'd imagined how chilly his room was. As soon as Jack and I entered the suite the second time I realised, if anything, the reality was worse than the memory. Or maybe it was because this time we'd come in from a hot summer evening rather than a cooler summer night. Either way, goosebumps stood to immediate attention on my arms and legs.

Everest waited for us in the sitting area, artfully arranged in one of the wing chairs. Shannon fell in behind him. The other *duinesidhe* were absent.

The *aosidhe* wore a different fur coat, one the colour of untrampled snow. His hair seemed blacker by comparison, as dark as the space between stars. I'd forgotten how beautiful he was. Magnetic. I dug my fingernails into my palms, a physical reminder to keep alert.

"Isla. So good to see you." He smiled, his aura so happy it was almost gleeful. My stomach tightened. Nothing that pleased him that much could bode well for us. "Please, take a seat. Your hob, too." He indicated the free loveseat with a wave.

Exchanging a look, Jack and I sat. The seat was small. Barely a finger's width separated us. After declining an offer of refreshments—I wouldn't have minded a coffee but didn't want to prolong the visit—we waited for Everest to speak.

"First of all," he began, pursing his lips, "I feel it is important that you trust what I am about to tell you. You're aware that oaths sworn by our kind are binding?"

I nodded.

"Well, know I swear to only speak the truth to you during this meeting."

The oath took force, brushing along my skin like the light touch of a goose down feather. If Everest lied to me, he would suffer, wasting away. Jack and I shared an astonished look. Neither of us had expected Everest to *volunteer* such a promise.

I noticed, however, that the wording of the oath didn't require him to tell the truth to anyone else.

"As promised, I had Fintan and Ariel pursue the *duinesidhe* who attacked your father," the *aosidhe* said, brushing his hair back behind pointed ears much like Jack's. "Today they captured the guilty *puca*. Unhappily, the *powrie* remains at large." He scowled, his aura flashing with anger, and I felt a moment's pity for Fintan and Ariel.

ISLA'S OATH

As though summoned by my thought—although more likely summoned by their master's words—the hob and *puca* entered the room. The former wore a calf-length jacket over neat jeans, while the latter was dressed in leather pants identical to those he'd worn last time we'd met, with a white muscle shirt and his dog collar. He also carried a bowling ball bag so new the price tag dangled from one of the straps.

Beside me, Jack stiffened. I was a little slower on the uptake so, when Fintan unzipped the bag to show me its contents, I leaned forward to peer inside.

A head stared up at me with glassy, dull eyes. Its—his—face was bruised, as though he'd been beaten before his neck was severed from its body. A hint of spine peaked out whitely from the mass of blood and meat below the jawline.

I gasped, my gorge rising at the coppery stench of blood, and buried my face in Jack's shoulder. He put an arm around me. "Please put that away." His anger leant heat to the polite words.

The sounds of the zipper closing and someone leaving the room seemed overly loud. The blood stink faded, although I was unable to shake the mental image of that staring face. Tears prickled my eyes. A minute later, someone pressed a cool glass of water into my hands. I looked up and saw Fintan. The bowling bag was gone.

I took the glass carefully so I didn't brush his hand with my fingertips—as though the horror of what I had just seen was something that could be caught from a touch. In my case, maybe it could.

The water was sweet after the taste of bile. "Thank you," I croaked.

The *puca* bowed. Strangely, given he was Everest's hunter, his eyes were sad.

Ariel and Shannon, on the other hand, took pleasure in my discomfort. The *aislinge*, who was in sight of her master, tried to keep her expression neutral. The hob's face on the other hand was alight with malicious joy.

"I apologise," Everest said smoothly. "I had thought to make you a gift of the criminal's head. I had not realised your, ah, human sensibilities were so strong."

I wasn't sure what to say to that, although I really wanted to tell him what he could do with his "gift". I took another sip of water.

"It is a shame the *puca* was killed," Jack said, his voice sharp. "Now we cannot question him to confirm his involvement." When the *puca* had attacked us, we'd only seen him in the form of a large, black dog. Jack was right—this could be anyone.

Everest didn't hide his disdain. His lip curled. "I did so myself, before putting him to the sword for his offence against Isla."

"What did he say?" I asked, my voice raspy. As much as I didn't want the *aosidhe's* attention right then—or ever—I didn't like the look in his silver eyes when he stared at Jack.

And if he wasn't talking directly to me, I couldn't be sure he was being honest.

"He confessed he was one of the two who attacked the farm that night. He said after the hob Moray was killed, he and the *powrie* fled. He had not seen the *powrie*, whose name is Aghi, since."

"How was Moray killed?" I asked, probing for a hole in the story.

ISLA'S OATH

"An old woman slew him with iron."

I hadn't told Everest that my grandmother killed Moray. The *aosidhe* must be telling the truth—as suspicious as the callous murder of the witness made me.

"Did he know who Moray was working for?"

"He did not say. However, he did confirm that he and Aghi were hired in Australia for the job. They were from a *sidhe* north of Sydney, apparently."

I frowned. "Is that all he said?"

"No. He also begged for mercy," Everest said dryly.

My fingers curled into fists on the velvety fabric of the chair. I hated him right then. A lot.

Oblivious, he continued, "We will keep looking for the *powrie*. My hound will find him eventually, no matter where he has fled." He indicated Fintan with possessive pride.

Despite Aghi's part in the attack—his broken-toothed snarl was a regular feature in my nightmares—I hoped the *powrie* was far, far away. Unfortunately, Fintan's quite competence didn't fill me with hope that any distance would save him.

"What was his name?" I asked softly, thinking of those staring eyes and wishing I'd had the presence of mind to close them. Knowing the name of someone I'd —unintentionally—had killed seemed important.

"Whose?"

"The *puca's*."

Everest was genuinely surprised that I'd asked; although his expression didn't show it, his aura was easy to read. "Cavall."

Jack's arm was still around my shoulder. The skin of his forearm was a warm counterpoint to the chill of the room, which seeped into me until even the marrow in my bones felt like shards of ice. Everest's gaze dropped from my face to that arm. A tiny frown marred his perfect brow. I guessed he didn't let Ariel touch him.

There was an awkward silence. I cleared my throat. "If that's all, we really should be going."

"There is something else," Everest said. His gaze flicked from my face to Jack's and back again, so quickly I wouldn't have noticed it if I weren't studying him as closely as he studied us. "Perhaps we should speak privately?"

Jack's anxiety purified into raw fear, shivering from his skin to mine. I wanted to look at him, to read his aura more clearly, but kept my gaze fixed on the *aosidhe*, trying to imitate Shannon's neutral expression. "Anything you want to say to me you can say in front of Jack," I said. "I trust him."

"Are you sure that is a good idea?" Everest asked.

I stood. "I'm not going to sit here and listen to you insult my friend."

"Your friend?" His eyebrows arched in surprise, and he sat forward to catch my hand. His touch was as unnaturally warm as Jack's, despite the frosty air, and as soft as satin sheets under moonlight. My thoughts turned of their own accord to what those fingers would feel like, running though my hair or down the length of my spine.

"Please stay," Everest said. "I am sorry if I caused offence."

"You did," I said bluntly, freeing myself from his grip with reluctance and resuming my seat. My hand tingled with cold. I didn't like the way a brief touch from him made me think thoughts I more commonly associated with Dominic. Was that an *aosidhe* talent or uniquely Everest's own? Suddenly I understood Shannon's blind adoration of her master and pitied her.

Although, from her expression, she wanted to strangle me.

"I am sorry. You may not like what I am about to tell you," Everest said. I dragged my attention back to the conversation. "Do you know the secrets of Jack's past?"

"I know he wasn't a fan of serving the *aosidhe*," I said.

"That is something of an understatement, I am afraid. Jack fled to Australia after he murdered his *aosidhe* master. And he has been sentenced to death."

CHAPTER TWELVE

*F*or a heartbeat, nobody moved. Then Everest's *duine-sidhe* servants descended on us.

With shocking swiftness, Ariel drew a short, silvery sword from beneath the folds of his coat and levelled it at us. Fintan stepped forward with liquid grace to the other side of the couch, placing a firm hand on Jack's shoulder.

"Let go of him," I hissed, mentally shoving the *puca* with the force of my panic and rage. His eyes opened wide and he recoiled, nearly tripping over Shannon, who had placed herself between us and the suite's main door.

The hob—my hob—was paralysed with fear and a terrible resignation. I didn't want to believe what Everest had said, wanted to find a way for it not to be true. But Jack's gaze, when it met mine, was apologetic. My heart sank.

"Everybody stop," Everest said calmly. His servants froze—although Ariel's blade hovered at Jack's pale throat.

I turned to the *aosidhe*. "I need to talk to Jack."

ISLA'S OATH

"I cannot let you leave with him. He is unsworn and dangerous."

Between panic and rage, the former wouldn't help. I decided to embrace the latter and see where it got me. "Fine." I gestured to the glass door behind me. "We'll go out on the balcony." When he didn't reply, I scowled. "We're ten floors up. Do you imagine he's going to sprout wings and fly away?"

"Of course not." He nodded as though it was his idea. "The balcony is all yours."

"I'd take it as a kindness if you'd stop your people from listening in and refrain from doing so yourself."

He blinked slowly, cat-like, his silver eyes speculative. "I shall do so."

Given he still couldn't lie to me, that was probably the best guarantee of privacy I was going to get.

Despite the situation, I breathed a sigh of relief when we emerged through the glass sliding door onto the balcony. After the frigid hotel room, the summer air was a hot caress across my frozen skin. Given enough time, I might defrost.

I leaned on the railing, back to the glass, staring at the view with unappreciative eyes. The setting sun painted the white marble and concrete buildings beyond the lake with pink and orange, while gold flecked the water spouting from the memorial jet. I didn't care. Jack stood stiffy beside me. "Tell me," I murmured.

"His name was Cacodaemon," he said. I raised an eyebrow, and he twisted his mouth wryly, as though he had bitten into a lemon. "I agree it is pretentious. But have you met our current host, who named himself after the tallest mountain in the world?"

"Fair point."

"Cacodaemon chose the name deliberately. It means evil spirit, and he was one of those *aosidhe* who is not just arrogant and self-centred—although he was those things too—but who takes delight in being deliberately, maliciously evil. And Evie and I were sworn into his service."

My stomach swooped. Although I didn't want to hear the rest of the story anymore, I gripped the balustrade and remained silent. To protest would be selfish. I hadn't had to live through it.

"He liked to torture girls," Jack continued in a mono-tone. His skin was pale as a hospital shroud, his eyes so dark with remembered pain that they seemed black. "Once a month, at the dark of the moon, he would choose a candidate and have her brought to him, to receive his … attentions. This particular month he wanted a specific girl, a human child, and sent one of his *puca* out to collect her. The *puca* was successful but the child, in trying to escape, fell into a river within the *sidhe* and drowned. Cacodaemon slew the *puca* in a rage but still did not have a girl. So he took Evie."

Jack's voice wavered and broke. His aura was the deep silver of sadness, a colour that reminded me of Everest's cool gaze. I took Jack's hand, remorseful that I'd asked him to relive this. His fingers closed slowly over my own and, after a few moments, he drew a breath and continued.

"He tortured her for hours. I tried to fight my way in, and his *powrie* thugs beat me. Even near unconsciousness, I could hear her screams. When I recovered from the beating, it was two days later and Cacodaemon was done. He came to the room where the *powrie* had left me and threw her body down, told me to make sure she was

fit to serve the next day. Her clothes were torn, her body…"
He looked across the lake. "Most of her wounds had
healed in that time, as had my own, except for one."

"Her face," I breathed.

"Yes. Cacodaemon had used iron to inflict that wound.
Not personally, of course. He had a human man, a creature with a soul as black as Cacodaemon's own, who
wielded the knife on his behalf. A hob's preternatural
healing is not as effective on wounds made of iron. I tried
to take the damage onto myself, but it had been more
than a day since it was inflicted, so I could not." His aura
shifted to darker, charcoal grey, regret so deep-seated I
knew he would carry it always.

"So you killed him."

"I killed them both. The human and Cacodaemon."

"How? I thought *aosidhe* within their domains were
unstoppable."

"Nearly, yes. So when next he was intoxicated after a
feast, his senses dulled, I gave him a small glass of a
rare *piskie*-brewed spirit. I had filled it with iron shav-
ings. The effect was … dramatic."

I remembered the ease with which Nana's iron pro-
jectile had melted through Moray's skull. Cacodaemon
would have dissolved from the inside out, as though he'd
consumed industrial-strength acid. I swallowed hard,
my hands shaking. "Why did he let you serve him after
he'd tortured your sister? That seems stupid."

"We were bound by oaths to serve and protect him."

"But you—"

"I broke the oath. As soon as I handed the glass to
Cacodaemon a wave of dizziness shook me, and pain
stabbed through my chest. I managed to hide it until he

had swallowed the drink. At that point, it became a matter of who died first. I knew if I outlasted him, I would be freed from the oath by his death. And if I had died first, well…" He shrugged. "At least Evie would have escaped."

I could imagine the scene too well—Jack and the *aosidhe* falling to the ground together, one gasping for breath and clutching at his failing heart, the other uttering a burbling scream, cut short as his vocal cords were ravaged, melted away by the iron. I bit my lip.

"After he was dead I recovered swiftly." Jack continued, looking down at my hand wrapped around his. "I found the human torturer and slew him before the alarm was raised. Then Evie and I fled as far as we could from the *aosidhe* courts. We ended up here, although I always suspected it was not far enough. I would have gone to Antarctica if it were possible."

We fell silent. I struggled to shake the mental images Jack's tale had conjured, struggled with the notion my friend was not just a killer but had killed someone in such a painful, cruel way.

He didn't need to be an empath to see how I felt. "You are disappointed with me. But I had to kill him. It was the only way to free us of our oaths. We could not fled, otherwise."

"I know. It's not that, exactly." I struggled to explain my feelings. "It's just, the way you did it—"

He looked away from me. "It was cruel. I know that. And I could tell you that I could not have overwhelmed him with physical force, that I could not wield an iron blade and give him a quick death. All of that would be true. It would not be the whole truth, however." His gaze returned to mine, his expression—and aura—a curious mix of defiance and a plea for understanding. "I had little choice in the method of his demise. However, I *am* glad that he suffered as he died. He did not just torture Evie. He tortured, to death, hundreds of human girls. And those are just the ones I know of. I am ashamed it took me so long to act."

I nodded slowly. "I'd be lying if I said I was happy about it, but I think we can at least agree you were provoked and he was an arsehole." *And the award for understatement of the century goes to Isla Blackman.* "Just how much trouble are we in here?" I glanced over my shoulder, peering through the glass door. Shannon remained in the room, standing by the suite's exit. Her expression was neutral, but her aura was one of longing as she watched how closely we stood together. Again, I felt that unwelcome surge of pity for her.

"How much trouble am *I* in," Jack corrected me. "You are in no kind of trouble."

I gave him a scornful look. "Whatever. Everest said you were sentenced to death. So there's some sort of *duinesidhe* court, with laws?"

He smiled slightly, pleased at my support despite his reservations. "After a fashion. You must understand, the *aosidhe* often kill each other, and send their sworn *duinesidhe* and human servants to kill one another as well. That is no crime."

"I don't know about that," I muttered.

"However, for a *duinesidhe* to kill the *aosidhe* he is sworn to is punishable by death. They cannot chance their slaves getting any ideas about rebelling." He clenched his jaw.

"Right," I said, giving his hand a final squeeze before

releasing it. "Well, let's go see what he wants to let you off the hook."

The cold air in the hotel was a slap in the face. Although it was trivial by comparison to what we were facing, it annoyed me. I left the sliding door open behind us so the hot breeze outside could flow into the suite.

Shannon remained on guard at the suite's exit, eyeing us distrustfully. "Ariel!" she called. After a moment, the faint sound of classical music grew louder before falling silent. Footsteps padded down the corridor. I frowned. What were they all doing in Everest's bedroom?

Jack, guessing my thoughts, murmured, "They all have good hearing. The only way Everest could guarantee they would not overhear us would be for them to remove themselves from this room. The music is a nice touch, although possibly unnecessary."

"Not true," Everest said as he swept into the room, his *duinesidhe* twin shadows behind him. "Fintan's ears in particular are especially keen. As you see, Isla, *I* keep my oaths." He gave Jack a pointed look and sat in his wing chair, pressing his fingertips together. Jack and I remained standing, while Fintan and Ariel stood close by, eyes fixed on Jack as though he was a dangerous criminal. Which I suppose he was. "I presume he outlined for you the details of his crime?"

"He did."

"He murdered the great *aosidhe* Cacodaemon."

"I think you and I define 'great' differently." The words left my mouth before I thought about them. I winced, unsure whether irritating the *aosidhe* was the wisest strategy at this point.

"Cacodaemon was not humane, I grant you. I certainly

did not like him or approve of his lifestyle. But, Isla, we are not human, so why must we be humane? Why must we live up to mortal standards of political correctness and mediocrity when we can be so much more?" His silver eyes gleamed as he stared at my face.

"Morality. Ethics. Compassion." My words sounded hollow to my own ears. I struggled to think of a more elegant way to express something I knew in my heart was a basic truth. Unfortunately I wasn't a poet. "Because it's right."

"Morals are humanity's herd instinct."

"I disagree," I said curtly, folding my arms.

He smiled, revealing no trace of the irritation that flashed in his aura like distant lightening. I would have given my pinkie finger for a poker face as good as his. "I could discuss philosophy with you all day, my dear, but we are here to talk about Jack's moral failings, not Cacodaemon's. Whatever you think of the latter, he was tortured to death by the former."

I nodded. "Because Jack wanted to save his sister."

Everest narrowed his eyes. "Because he wanted revenge for what was done to his sister."

"Do his motivations matter?"

"They do to you."

His words struck a dissonant note in my heart, raising a truth I'd rather not consider just then. I shifted from foot to foot, trying to conceal how much he'd bothered me. "What do we need to do to get this verdict overturned?"

"There is no court such as you understand it," Everest replied. "There are simply crimes, the committing of which will result in every *aosidhe* seeking your destruction. He committed one of them and, without the protection of a master of his own, he must—"

"Isla." Jack spoke softly, interrupting the *aosidhe* mid-sentence. Something about the intensity of his tone made me turn to him. He took both of my hands in his, and I realised what he was about to do.

"Jack, don't."

"This is the only way. Please. I want to."

I glanced at Everest, saw his thunderous look. That, as much as anything else, decided me. I swallowed, heart in my throat. "Okay."

Jack locked gazes with me. His sapphire eyes were as earnest as I had ever seen them. "I am Jack, and I swear that I will speak only the truth to you, and devote myself to serving and protecting you, Isla Half-Blood, for all of my life."

The feeling as his oath settled over the two of us was different from anything I'd experienced before. The other oaths had been temporary undertakings; this was an enduring promise, the committing of one life to another in a lopsided wedding vow. The sensation was like standing inside a carillon while someone struck a grand chord. The notes reverberated through me, every particle of my being vibrating in response. After a time—seconds or an eternity—the notes trailed away into silence.

Incredibly, there was no sound. How could there be no sound when something so momentous had just happened? Every cell in my body felt energised.

There was a muffled gasp from one of the observers. I didn't know who—my gaze was locked on Jack's. He seemed equally moved by the impact of the oath, although his expression was less surprised than I felt. I guess he'd done it before. Or had it done to him.

ISLA'S OATH

"I wish you had not done that," Everest said.

Jack lifted his chin, breaking eye contact with me. "Because now you may not slay me out of hand?"

"No, you miserable, self-centred creature," the *aosidhe* growled back. The hair on the back of my neck stood on end at the snarl in his voice. "Because Isla's protection is imperfect."

"Oh, that's nice," I said sarcastically.

"I am sorry." Everest stood, attempting to take my hand in his. I refolded my arms, hoping I seemed irritated rather than afraid of his touch. The memory of the uncomfortable reaction I'd had last time he touched me was too fresh.

Beneath Everest's politely concerned expression, his aura flashed again with that lightening strobe of irritation. "When I speak of imperfection I refer only to your standing among the *aosidhe*. Some will argue that, because you are half human, you are not a true member of our race, and that therefore Jack is still an unsworn murderer. By swearing his oath to you, he has mired you in the peril resulting from his own, foul deed."

Everest was definitely a fan of emotive language.

"And what will you argue?" I was acutely aware that we were outnumbered. If Everest decided to take justice into his own hands, we were indeed *mired in peril*. I glanced at Ariel and Fintan. The former's hand rested on the hilt of his sword, visible now he'd removed his coat, while the latter stood with an easy, loose-limbed grace that spoke of a capacity for swift and deadly action.

Everest sighed, sitting back in his chair as though weary. "I am unsure. It depends whether you are able to maintain control of Jack's behaviour."

"He has to do what I say, right?" I glanced at Jack.

"Don't kill anyone, okay?"

The hob nodded, his expression grave even as his aura sparkled with amusement.

"I would caution against flippancy," Everest said with a frown. "He already killed one master he had sworn to protect. How can you be sure he will not do the same to you?"

"I don't plan on torturing anyone."

"Still, as you are now his master, I would suggest that you order Jack to submit to the punishment he has earned. We can carry out the sentence immediately."

I imagined Jack's head staring up at me from a leather bag. Would it be Ariel's sword that did the deed? Would they beat him first, as they had Cavall? My stomach twisted with revulsion, and my chest ached. "No thanks," I said, my voice hoarse.

The *aosidhe* shook his head with a sad smile. "I thought you might say that. Your humanity is charming, if entirely unsuited to *aosidhe* politics."

"Uh. Thank you?"

We stood in silence for almost a minute as Everest looked from me to Jack and back again, eyes narrowed and lips pursed. Finally, he nodded to himself and stood. "I have an offer for you, Isla—one that will see you protected from Jack's crime."

"And him?"

"He will be protected too," he said, not bothering to conceal his disappointment.

I could feel Jack's alarm without even glancing his way … or maybe I was just projecting my own feelings onto him. "What's the offer?" I asked, not bothering to hide my reluctance.

"Swear an oath to me."

ISLA'S OATH

I stared at him. "What?"

"Swear to serve me, as Jack just swore to serve you. With you as part of my court, Jack will come under *my* protection. No *aosidhe* will be able to harm him without declaring war on me."

My mind whirling, I gasped the first thought that came to mind. "*You* could."

"I would be willing to make your oath conditional on me not seeking to punish him for Cacodaemon's murder," he offered. "He would effectively be absolved of his crime for as long as you both remained in my service."

I studied Everest intently. He seemed sincere in his offer—although, given he was bound to tell me the truth, he didn't have much choice in the matter. His aura was content, the expression on his beautiful face open and calm.

"What would you require of me?"

"Isla, no," Jack choked out. Everest ignored him.

"You will come back to Ireland and be the treasure of my court. I will introduce you to the bright, glittering world of the *aosidhe*. Perhaps even to your mother."

I couldn't help it. My heart lifted at his final words, despite everything—that she'd used me for her own ends before I was even born; that she'd walked out of the hospital and my life immediately after my birth. To meet my mother. What would that be like?

Jack took my hand and squeezed it, bringing me back to myself. "Do you know who she is?" I said.

"I could discover it easily," Everest said, trying to sound reassuring, although his silver-eyed stare was unnerving. He hadn't directly answered the question. Did he know? And if not, did he suspect I knew? If I swore service to him, he could order me to tell him and I would have to.

Or he could capture my father and interrogate him. I'd be helpless to protect Dad if Everest owned me. Because ownership was what we were discussing. Me agreeing that he owned me, as though I were a prized pet.

Thinking of Shannon's collar, I glanced over to where she was standing, still in the doorway. Tears glittered in her golden eyes and her hands were clenched at her sides. Her aura burned so brightly with the nauseating lime green of jealousy—speckled through with scarlet rage as though someone had splattered it with paint, or blood— that I had to look away.

Had Everest promised Shannon she'd be the treasure of his court when he'd made her his *aislinge*?

I hung my head. "Can you give me a couple of days to sort everything out? And say goodbye to my family?"

"Of course," Everest smiled. "That should give us time to locate the *powrie*, Aghi. I would not have you troubled by the notion he is still at large if you are leaving your loved ones."

"Thank you." I turned to Jack, whose expression was anguished. "Let's go."

"Isla, I cannot let you do this," the hob groaned as we turned for the door.

"Quiet," I ordered.

Jack fell silent. He had to.

Shannon stood to one side. I didn't know what form her *aislinge* talent took, but I was glad the power to kill me with her thoughts wasn't on the list. Her hatred was palpable, hands hooked at her sides as though she wanted to launch herself at me, rake at my face with her nails. Her master's gaze kept her quiet.

By the time Jack and I reached my car, he was quivering

with anxiety. I waited until we were both inside and the doors were closed before I said, "Okay, you can talk now."

"You cannot swear to him!" The words burst from his mouth. He reached across and took my hands, his grip desperate. "Please. I would rather die than see you bound to an *aosidhe*. Any *aosidhe*."

"I have no intention of it," I said with a lopsided smile. "Although if you believed me, then hopefully he does too. I've bought us two days to figure a way out of this mess. Better get thinking."

"Isla!" Jack laughed, delighted.

Then he leaned over and kissed me.

The gesture was impulsive, a peck on the lips. But an unexpected thrill of desire rippled through me. His lips had the same preternatural warmth as his hands, and were, if anything, even softer. My desire was immediate, and even more intense than it had been when Everest took my hand. My eyes fluttered closed as I leaned into the kiss and his lips opened. His tongue brushed my lips, tentative as a butterfly. I shivered.

And then I remembered where I was, who I was with, and pulled away.

"Sorry." I blushed. Flustered, I straightened in my seat and started the car.

"Do not be," Jack said, turning to look out his window.

I barely heard him over the sound of the radio as he added, "I am yours."

CHAPTER THIRTEEN

*J*ack and I left Civic in an awkward silence. Flustered, I'd driven halfway home before noticing I hadn't buckled up his seatbelt. I pulled over on the side of the parkway to help him with it.

We were careful not to touch.

After I dropped Jack off at the foot of Mount Taylor, close to the *sidhe* entrance, I drove the short distance home, my mind a fog of uncertainty. I was looking forward to a quiet evening alone so I could sort through my thoughts and those traitorous emotions that had roared so loudly when Jack and I had kissed.

I really liked Dominic. Out of panic that he might break up with me, I'd done something to him of which I was deeply ashamed. But I really liked Jack too. Was it just because of how devoted he'd been to helping me these past few months? Was I that shallow? Or was there something more to my feelings? I remembered my jealousy at Sarah's party, when other girls had shown such obvious interest in the hob. Had Natalie been right all along when she told me I had a crush on him? I wasn't sure of anything, and I needed some space to figure it out before I committed an even greater wrong. To either of them.

Also, I still had to come up with a way to get Jack and myself out of lifelong servitude to the magnificent and terrifying Everest. That wasn't asking too much of my evening, was it?

My heart jumped like a startled kangaroo when I saw Dominic's car out the front of our house. I nearly kept driving, but chided myself for cowardice and pulled in behind it, taking a couple of deep breaths to slow the pulse that skittered in my throat before heading into the house.

Dominic, Sarah and Natalie sat in the lounge room. Empty tumblers were scattered across the table, near a half-empty bowl of corn chips.

"Isla! I'm so glad to see you." Dominic leapt to his feet and gave me a warm hug. I hugged him back awkwardly, feeling a brief flare of panic that he'd be able to smell Jack on me. I bit my lip, feeling stupid. He wasn't a bloodhound, and it wasn't like I'd been *rolling around* in Jack.

Not exactly.

"Hi," I smiled as brightly as I could. It felt painted on. "I wasn't expecting to see you here."

"Surprise!" he said, pulling me by the hand towards the kitchen. "I bought you a gift."

"What? Why did you—oh!"

On the dining table, wrapped in green-and-white tissue paper and bound with a matching ribbon, was a bouquet of long-stemmed roses. Their petals were a deep pink. Dominic scooped them up and pressed them into my arms.

"Do you like them?"

"Yes, of course, but—"

"I wanted to say sorry," he said in a rush. "For Valentine's Day. For not trusting you. I feel like I ruined it. I almost threw away one of the best things that's ever happened to me." When I stared at him, open-mouthed, he smiled lopsidedly.

"I… Thank you." I blushed and stared down at the roses, hoping he read my reaction for embarrassment instead of the truth. Black shame gnawed at my spine like a rat with a carcass. I'd been thinking about breaking up with him. I still was. The flowers must have cost him at least a hundred dollars.

"They're beautiful," Sarah said from behind us. I turned, grateful for the interruption. She was leaning on the doorframe, arms folded. Natalie stood behind her, expression soft and wistful.

"I should put them in water before they wilt." I busied myself with finding the vase, filling it with water and adding half a teaspoon of sugar, something Aunt Elizabeth insisted increased the longevity of cut flowers. Dominic watched me with a contented look that under other circumstances I would have found charming.

I was the worst person in the whole world.

Sarah and Natalie surrendered their spots on the couch so Dominic and I could sit together. My cousin draped herself across a single-seater chair. She picked up a magazine from the side table and flicked through it, pretending she wasn't eavesdropping. Dominic sighed. I guessed he'd hoped there'd be kissing. The idea made me squirm inside, and I was grateful Sarah had stayed, even though I dreaded what she might say.

ISLA'S OATH

Natalie excused herself and went out to sit on the porch to, in her words, listen to the crickets.

Dominic took my hand. I couldn't help comparing his touch to Jack's—his fingers were cooler, a regular, human temperature, and his skin had the nicks and calluses of everyday wear and tear. Jack's were as smooth as a newborn's. Despite my guilt about the kiss, I found Dominic's hands comforting in their normalcy after the strangeness of my day.

"Have you had dinner?" I asked after a silence that felt way too long—although Dominic hadn't seemed to notice. He gazed at me with a small smile.

"I haven't, but I have to leave in for work in fifteen minutes. I'll eat at the pub."

"Were you waiting long?"

"A while." He shrugged.

"An hour," Sarah corrected, nose buried in the magazine.

"Why didn't you text me? I would've come home." That wasn't entirely true. I would've come home if I weren't in the middle of life-or-death negotiations with a callous, beautiful *aosidhe*, though … so it was close enough.

"I wanted it to be a surprise," he said with a rueful smile.

"Well, that part worked," I said with a laugh that felt brittle.

"Sarah suggested next time I text her, so she can let me know when you're home," Dominic admitted sheepishly.

"Good idea."

Another awkward silence. Hamish trotted into the room and eyed the table, nose twitching, before jumping onto the couch and wedging himself between Dominic and me. His tail wagged as I gave him a scratch between the ears.

Sarah looked up at us. Then she closed the magazine, rolling it and tapping it on the arm of the chair. "So, Isla, how is Jack?"

"He's fine," I said shortly. All of the irritation I'd felt during our last argument returned in full force. She was trying to prompt me to tell Dominic about the *duinesidhe* parts of my life. That wasn't going to happen, especially right now.

"How's his aunt?" Dominic asked.

"She's okay. Getting better."

"I forgot to ask the other day. What's wrong with her? Is it serious?"

Damn. I struggled to think of an answer. "Pneumonia," I blurted after a too-long pause.

Sarah threw the magazine onto the table and stalked from the room. Her bedroom door slammed moments later.

Dominic frowned but didn't seem to connect her response with our conversation. How could he? I'd programmed him not to doubt me, even when the fact something was wrong was staring him in the face.

When he left for work a few minutes later, I walked him to his car and embraced him fiercely, burying my face in his shirt. He smelled of fresh pine deodorant and, underlying that like rich soil under thick grass, of soap and shampoo. The smell was a comforting, Dominic scent. When he kissed me goodbye, tears burned my eyes.

After he left I thought about returning inside, but I didn't want to face Sarah's wrath, which was no doubt lurking to ambush me in the corridor to my room. Feeling cowardly, I slunk around to the side gate and let myself into the yard.

The soft sound of weeping came from the back porch. I hesitated, not wanting to intrude. Natalie's voice mumbled, "You might as well come over. I can see you."

She sat on the porch, imperfectly lit by the rectangle of yellow light falling through the glass door from inside. Her feet curled under her on the outdoor chair, emphasising how petite she was. As I climbed the stairs, she wiped her eyes on the collar of her T-shirt. "Do you want me to turn the outside light on?" I asked, hesitating.

She shook her head, looking out over the garden.

"Want me to leave you alone?"

"It's okay. You can sit if you like. Has Dominic gone?"

"To work." I sat next to her at the glass-topped table.

"He's a good guy. I'd be jealous if I was, you know, into guys."

He *was* a good guy. The thought burned. "There's no one … no lady in your life?"

She shrugged. "A few I like to hang out with. Nothing that's going anywhere right now."

"Anyone I know?" The idea crept into my mind, slow as dawn after a thunderstorm, that maybe she was interested in one of our friends. Sarah or Kim. Not me—I was sure of that. Being able to see people's emotions did have some advantages.

Natalie gave me a sideways look, lips twitching with faint amusement. "No. Girls from uni. Not Kim."

"I assumed not Kim if it's no one I know," I teased gently.

She shrugged. Even in the poor light, I could see circles like bruises under her eyes. I was sure they weren't just from sleeping on the thin mattress on Sarah's floor. Despite that and her red nose, she was still pretty.

I hesitated. "Have you heard from your family?"

She ran a hand through her hair. Spikes of blond poked up in her fingers' wake. "Ethan sent me a couple of texts. Nothing from my folks."

"How is he dealing with everything?"

"He's shaken up. But he asked if he can have my stereo." Natalie forced a smile, although her aura was still the colour of a lake's surface on a gloomy day.

I tried to sound cheerful. "Cheeky bugger! What did you say?"

"I said he can borrow it till I find somewhere more permanent to live. I'm going to look at share houses this weekend, if you want to come."

"I will if I can," I promised. The weekend was three days away; right now, that seemed like a lifetime. On the other hand, if I went I'd be useful in identifying the crazy houses— even if she didn't know that was what I was doing.

She fell silent, slumping back in the chair. Her sadness made my heart ache.

I spoke before thinking it through. "Hey, Natalie, can I ask a question that may sound a little ... crazy?"

She raised her eyebrows, her stare sharpening to something closer to her usual piercing gaze. "Sure."

My brain caught up with my mouth and started muttering warnings. "Um. Hypothetically, if there was a way to make you less sad about your dad's reaction, would you take it?"

"Hypothetically?"

"Yeah."

"By using drugs? Like, antidepressants?"

I shook my head.

She stared unseeingly through the trees. I waited, fidgeting with the hem of my shorts. Why had I asked such a stupid question?

Finally, she turned back to me, blue eyes glittering with unshed tears. "It's hard," she said. "If I didn't care about what they thought of me, would that mean I didn't love them anymore? Because I do, you know. Love them. Even though Dad is a jackass." She muttered that last part under her breath.

"That's why their reaction hurts so badly," I said, before biting my lip. *Way to make it worse, Isla.*

"Yes." A tear slid down her cheek; she brushed it away with the back of her hand.

"What if you still loved them, but the immediate pain of their reaction had passed?"

She laughed shakily. "That would be awesome. At least I'd be able to get on with stuff, you know? Studying, finding a place to live—"

"Give me your hand."

Natalie gave me another, longer look before she placed her slender hand in mine, palm up as though I was going to read her fortune. Instead, I wove my fingers through hers and, slowly and carefully, tapped into that seemingly bottomless pool of sadness inside her, pulling it into myself until I felt sympathetic tears welling in my own eyes. I was careful not to take it all—I barely took half. Enough so the sadness would be noticeable, but not debilitating.

Her blue eyes were staring at me, almost perfectly round, when I blinked and released her.

"What did you do?" she breathed, stunned.

"I took some of the sadness away." There seemed no point in lying to her about it—I'd as much as told her what I was going to do before I did it, so she was acutely aware of the change.

She laughed a little. "Not so much a hypothetical question then. When did you learn to do that?"

"Before Christmas." I stared down at my hands, fiddling with my charm bracelet. "Sarah and Ryan know, but please don't tell anyone else, okay? I don't want to be, I don't know, carted off to a government lab and made to help politicians with their anger management." Although as far as community service went, that wasn't such a bad idea.

"How do you do it? Could anyone learn?"

"It's something I inherited from my mother." I didn't elaborate. The *duinesidhe* world didn't seem that safe right now.

"Oh." Natalie's eyes narrowed. "You did something to Dad last Sunday, didn't you?" I winced and then nodded. "I wondered why he calmed down so suddenly. Thank you."

"I wish I could've done more. There are limits."

"Well, thank you for trying." She leaned over and kissed me on the cheek. Then she stood. "I'm going to bed. Hopefully I'll be able to sleep through for once."

"Me too."

I followed her inside, waiting in the lounge while she padded quietly up to the bathroom to brush her teeth and splash some water on her face. My stomach churned with anxiety about what had just happened. I'd been friends with Natalie for years; I trusted her and cared about her. Suddenly, watching her mourn when I could help her through it seemed unbearable. At the same time, I could've aided her discreetly like I had her father, rather than playing all my cards beforehand so she would figure out what I was doing. Although if I hadn't asked, I'd have never received permission either.

Had I *wanted* her to figure it out? And did helping Natalie go some way to absolving my guilt about Dominic?

No, it didn't. Nothing would.

Gnawing on a hangnail, I walked over to close the open blinds and saw Jack standing in the park across the road, the place we'd always met before I revealed my secret, and his, to my cousins. When he saw me silhouetted in the window, he waved: he was wearing his usual shorts and a hooded sweatshirt that cast his face into shadow and hid his protruding ears.

Wondering what he wanted, I slipped out the front door, telling myself the reason I was excited to see him was curiosity, not anything kiss-related. My heart pounded in my ears; it didn't believe me.

It was only when I entered the playground that I realised the waiting hob wasn't Jack.

"Look out!" a tiny voice cried.

There was *pop* and the faint tinkle of glass as the streetlight behind me exploded, throwing the park into deep gloom. Panic shot through me. I spun towards the broken light.

A huge, lumbering form emerged from the trees to my left. A slingshot tumbled to the ground, crushed under a giant foot as the figure's hands stretched out towards me.

The dirty, unwashed—and frighteningly familiar— stench of a *powrie* washed over me. Had Aghi come for me before Everest's servants could find him?

I ran. The hob darted forward, swift as a striking lioness, and grabbed my arm. The momentum spun me around, leaving me staring into the shadows of the hood at the scarred, furious face of Evie. Jack's sister.

"Surprise," she hissed.

As I'd done to Fintan earlier that evening, I plunged my raw panic into Evie like a sword, using her hand on my arm as a conduit. Her fingers clenched convulsively as though I'd jolted her with electricity. She held on for a couple of seconds before releasing me with a sob.

Those seconds were enough time for the *powrie* to wrap two huge arms around me and lift my body from the ground. I struggled to free my arms but it was as if steel cords bound me.

Trembling, Evie pulled a small, very sharp knife from her pocket. The blade gathered what little light there was, gleaming like a brittle splinter of starlight.

"I will not let you enslave Jack," she said, her voice high and terrified. Her single eye glittered with mad terror and her hand shook.

"He only swore to me to stop Everest from killing him," I gasped.

"I. Do. Not. Care," she growled.

The *powrie*'s grip around my ribs tightened, bruising my sides. My lungs burned. If Evie didn't kill me, he would. I tried to focus my thoughts, to push the same fear into the *powrie* that I had into Evie, via the great filthy arms surrounding me. My efforts were feeble by comparison. If my power were a muscle, I'd already exhausted it when I'd used it on her.

Although my captor whimpered, childlike, he didn't release his grip.

Mustering her courage, Evie took a step towards me, clutching the knife like a lifeline. Her face twisted as she fought the panic. How many steps before she reached me? Two? Three? Spots danced before my gaze.

I'd never see Jack again. Never get to say sorry to Dominic. A tear ran down my cheek.

Sadness.

Closing my eyes, I tapped into the well of sorrow I'd drawn from Natalie, her grief at being rejected by those she loved. I poured that into the *powrie*, on the heels of that small dose of bitter fear. The emotion flowed freely, as though it came from a different place inside me. I drained that red-hot rage from him at the same time, giving energy to my limbs.

With a sob, the *powrie* released me. I fell to the tan-bark, gasping.

Squealing with terror, Evie darted forward. The knife slashed. My shoulder shrieked with agony. I scuttled back, bumping into the weeping *powrie*, and tried to stand. The pain made my head spin.

"Drop the knife, bitch."

Movement in the shadows snagged my gaze, and then Sarah appeared, holding something in her hands like a weapon.

An iron candlestick.

If Evie weren't so afraid, her hob reflexes would have easily won the day. But she hesitated. Sarah moved swiftly, smashing the candlestick down across the back of the other girl's outstretched hand.

There was a stomach-turning sizzle of flesh. Evie dropped the blade, screaming. Sarah pushed her backwards; the hob stumbled into the swing set and fell to the ground. My cousin kicked the knife away. She stood over Evie, pointing the candlestick at her head like a gun.

To Evie, it might as well have been. She stared at the end of the iron stick as though looking down the barrel of her own doom and began to cry, covering her face with her hands. The skin where Sarah had hit her was scarlet, already blistering, as though she'd held her hand in a fire.

"Isla?" Sarah said, her voice tight. "You okay?"

"Yeah." I touched the cut on my shoulder tentatively, hissing my breath through my teeth. The blood on my fingertips looked black in the poor light. "Bleeding."

"Want to tell me what the hell is going on?"

I scrambled to my feet and walked over to Sarah, making sure to keep the *powrie* in sight in case it recovered. Even though the iron's proximity made me want to vomit, I still felt safer next to my cousin. "That's Evie. Jack's sister."

"I guess she's not a fan of yours?"

"I guess not." I gazed down at the weeping hob with reluctant sympathy. "She doesn't like me because I'm half *aosidhe*."

"Doesn't like you? She tried to kill you." Sarah's voice was outraged. Evie flinched as the candlestick wavered in my cousin's clenched fist.

"She thinks I'm going to make Jack my slave." Blood dripped from my elbow to the tanbark. The wound throbbed. I tried to keep my shoulder still.

Sarah raised a sardonic eyebrow. "Are you?"

My reply was sharp. "No."

"He swore an oath of service to her today!" Evie wailed. She dropped her hands to glare at me. Sarah, seeing her face for the first time, gasped. Evie lifted her chin. "An *aosidhe* did this to my face. Someone like her." She spat at me.

174

ISLA'S OATH

"Hey," Sarah said, lowering the candlestick warningly. Evie squeaked a protest, pressing her shoulders into the dirt. She looked as though she wished she could seep into the ground like rainwater. "Unlike you, Isla doesn't cut people. And no one gets to be pissed at her except me."

A flicker of movement over near the seesaw caught my eye. A *piskie* alighted on the top of the wooden plank. He weighed so little that the board didn't shift. It was Welkin.

So that was who had cried the warning, just before the *powrie* broke the light bulb.

Realising I owed him, I beckoned him over. He eyed Sarah and the candlestick and shook his head.

Sarah kept her gaze fixed on Evie. Probably a good idea, given the loathing on the hob's face. "So what do we do now?" she asked me without glancing over.

"We get them to swear they won't try to harm me again. Or you."

"You trust them to do what they promise?"

"They have to, remember?"

Evie's dismayed cry convinced my cousin more than my assurances; she supervised, candlestick in hand, as first Evie and then the *powrie*—it was not Aghi but one I'd never met before, named Gall—uttered reluctant oaths.

Afterwards, Sarah stepped back and let Evie up. Gall stayed seated, wiping the stream of tears away with large, dirty hands. Natalie's sorrow still held him in its inexorable grip. What did he think he was crying about?

"Gall?"

He looked up.

"Why did you attack me?"

"The sun," he muttered, grief-stricken. "You made the

sun come to our *sidhe*. I don't like the sun. Also, Evie said please."

I tightened my jaw. I hadn't been back to the *sidhe* since that first time, and Jack hadn't mentioned that the addition of moon and stars had extended to a sun as well. I should have asked.

Sarah scowled at the hob. "At least she has good manners," she muttered. We turned to go.

"Please," Evie whispered. "Do not tell Jack what I did."

Sarah barked a laugh. "You're kidding, right?"

She shook her head, miserable. "He will never forgive me."

I bit my lip. Jack would be mortified. Knowing what his beloved sister had done would deeply upset him, even though she had done it out of love for him. No, *because* she'd acted on his behalf, however unwanted. He'd feel responsible.

I didn't want to tell him. "Okay."

My cousin turned her incredulous gaze on me. "Are you for real?" I shrugged and then hissed with pain as the wound in my shoulder gaped. "At least make her give you something for it," Sarah said, exasperated. "A wish or a favour or a magical Band-Aid or something. Didn't you say Jack could heal? Can Evie do it?"

I gazed down at Evie, who hunched on the ground in misery. She shivered with fear, but her determination to maintain Jack's faith in her was stronger. "I will heal your shoulder," she said.

"And you'll owe Isla a favour as well," Sarah added. "For destroying her T-shirt."

I examined my shirt. The sleeve was shredded. Even if I could sew it up—and I'd almost failed my term of home economics—I doubted the bloodstain would come out.

ISLA'S OATH

"Agreed," Evie sighed. She tensed, struggling with her emotions. That artificial terror still coursed through her. "I ... cannot."

"Give me your hand." The words echoed those I'd said to Natalie. Evie also hesitated, although in her case it was to rein in her panic. Her hand, when she extended it, shook so violently that her fingers rattled together. I brushed my hand across hers, taking back some—not all—of the fear I had injected into her like poison. Enough for her to take control of herself; not so much she forgot to be cautious of me.

Leaving any at all felt cruel. On the other hand, she *had* tried to kill me.

Evie's eye narrowed. She knew my powers, and what I had done. Able to move, she stepped forward. Sarah raised the candlestick defensively and she flinched.

I nodded at both of them reassuringly. "It's okay. This is how they do it."

I wasn't sure what was more discomforting, the feeling of Evie's hot tongue as it rasped painfully across the knife wound, leaving clean, healthy flesh in its wake—or the look of dawning comprehension on Sarah's face as she recalled that Jack had healed my wounds at least twice.

"Damn," she muttered. "You let Jack *lick* you?"

"Not all the time," I replied, exasperated.

Evie stepped back as soon as she was done, running her tongue over her lips. When she spoke, blood stained her teeth. She placed one hand on her now-bleeding shoulder, holding the fabric of the shirt over the wound. "I have an offer for you, to fulfil the rest of the debt."

"What?" My voice was curt with exhaustion.

"Talbot owes me a favour."

"That's the *puca* we tried to get to investigate the packaging Nana found," I murmured to Sarah. "He didn't want to help."

"He owes me a debt. I owe you one," Evie said. "I can call in my favour from him to repay my debt to you."

"Sounds good," I said. I really didn't want to have any more long-term ties to Evie than I had to. "How about you have him go to Jack tomorrow morning, tell him he had a change of heart about helping? That way Jack doesn't have to know you were involved."

Evie nodded, her mouth twisting. Her emotions were a tangle of hatred and gratitude, bound together with fear. "I will go now."

"Take Gall with you." The *powrie* had shown no inclination to move. I shuddered, imagining the reaction of the local children when they discovered a weeping ogre in the park come morning.

Evie, with a gentleness that reminded me of her brother, coaxed Gall to his feet. With a backwards glance at me, she led him into the darkness, only stopping to retrieve her little silver knife.

"Let's go home," Sarah said, her look promising more questions when we got there. Would she use the candlestick on me?

As we turned to leave, Welkin flew over to the site of the battle, apparently eager to taste my blood once again.

The thought didn't even bother me.

CHAPTER FOURTEEN

*W*hen we got back to the house, I stripped off the ruined shirt, bundling it into a plastic bag. Sarah threw it in the outside bin while I went into the bathroom to wash off the blood drying on my arm. In the shower, I watched numbly as the pink-stained water streamed down my arm. Even having experienced hob healing before, I braced myself for the soap to sting when I scrubbed myself, but it didn't. The only sign of the fight was the colour of the water spiralling down the drain.

My pyjamas felt good after that. Clean and safe.

Sarah waited in my bedroom, sitting at the foot of my bed. She was silent while I towelled my hair dry and brushed out the knots. Then she handed me a cup of hot chocolate, its surface smothered with marshmallows.

"It's time we had a talk."

I nodded, slipping my legs under the blanket and cuddling my childhood toy, Mister Monkey. The hot chocolate was good, warming me to my core—which had been frozen since the moment I'd realised my attacker was Evie.

Speaking haltingly, I explained the events of the evening: Everest finding and killing Cavall, his revelation about Jack, Jack's subsequent oath and Everest's "offer"—although it was really more of a threat: I swear to Everest or he kills Jack. Not much of a choice, really.

She listened quietly, hugging her knees with one arm and holding a kitten mug in the other hand. When I finished she added, "And you showed your power to Natalie."

Oh, yeah. "She told you about that?"

"Obviously." Sarah rolled her eyes. "She was so happy she was practically singing when she came to bed. She said you'd worked some magic for her, and she was looking forward to a good night's sleep. I figured it out. That's why I came looking for you."

"With a candlestick? You must have been pissed." I raised my eyebrows. I didn't know where the candlestick had ended up. It wasn't in my room. Maybe Sarah had put it in the rubbish with the bloody shirt.

"I grabbed it when I saw you leave the house. I don't often go outside without a bit of iron these days."

We exchanged a long look. Shame blossomed inside me like a dandelion turning to seed. My life wasn't the only one that had changed dramatically these past few months. "I'm sorry."

She shrugged. "Why did you decide to help Natalie?"

"I asked her if she'd want me to, if I could. She said yes. She didn't want to be so sad anymore."

"Did you tell her about the *duinesidhe*?"

I shook my head.

ISLA'S OATH

She hesitated, giving me a narrow-eyed look, and I knew what she was going to ask next. "What about Dominic? If you're going to reveal part of your dark secret to Natalie, why not to your boyfriend?" To her credit, she managed to keep her voice neutral.

"It's a bit more complicated than that now," I muttered, studying the pattern the last mouthful of hot chocolate made in the bottom of my mug as I swirled it around.

"You did something to him, didn't you?" Her tone hardened when I flinched. "You did!"

I nodded, not making eye contact with her. "On Valentine's Day. He was going to break up with me. I freaked."

"Oh, Isla." Sarah sighed, putting her own empty mug onto the floor at her feet. "I thought he seemed a bit off when he was here earlier."

"He was."

Disappointment is a pale bluish-grey. Her aura swirled with it, a dense fog on an overcast day. "You know you have to fix this, right?"

"I do. I will. Next time I see him. I just need to sort out this mess with Everest first."

"Promise?" She set her jaw, an expression of stubborn determination.

"I promise. No, I swear it—I'll undo the emotional changes to Dominic as soon as Everest is gone." I felt the oath settle over me. Sarah twitched. Did she feel it too? Even if she didn't, her expression told me she understood what I'd done.

Having made the oath gave me a cowardly sense of relief. If I released Dominic, maybe he would break up with me. No, he probably would. The idea made my throat tighten with grief, but—and I knew how selfish this was—I'd be freed from having to choose between him and Jack.

Thinking about it made me feel an inch high.

The doorbell rang mid-morning the next day. Hamish followed me up the hallway to the front door, barking furiously when he caught the scent of those on the other side. I exchanged a look with Sarah, who was in the lounge pretending to read a magazine—the same one she'd pretended to read the night before, when Dominic visited.

When I opened the door, I saw the reason for Hamish's excitement. Jack stood beside a large, heavy-boned black dog.

"This is Talbot," Jack said casually, introducing the dog as though it were his pet. I gazed for a long moment at the hob, heart in my throat as I remembered my lips on his, before forcing myself to turn my attention to the dog. Long, hanging ears framed a face like that of a foxhound or a large beagle, with its wide skull, long muzzle and curiously twitching nostrils. His eyes were full of intelligence.

He wasn't, I noticed with a faint sense of relief, wearing a collar.

I'd always thought Hamish, like many terriers, had more courage than sense. He proved me wrong, locking gazes with the *puca* and falling silent mid-bark. There was a moment of tension before Hamish backed away, heading unerringly for Sarah's legs. She picked him up and patted him reassuringly; he yapped at Talbot, having the last word, and fell silent.

"Can we come in?" Jack asked.

"I dunno," Sarah drawled from the couch. "Is your dog toilet trained?"

Jack's eyes widened. Talbot looked up at him, waiting for his answer.

Sarah and I laughed. "It's okay," I said. "We're the only ones here, and if Talbot needs to pee I'm sure he'll be a gentleman about it." Remembering I wasn't supposed to know he was coming, I turned to the *puca*. "I'm surprised to see you here. I hope it's good news."

He gave me a dry look. Anxiety, resentment and resignation clashed in his aura. I felt a twinge of guilt at forcing him to be here. But it was better than Jack finding out about Evie.

"He has decided to help us," Jack said with a relieved smile. If he suspected anything from Talbot's change of heart, I couldn't tell. "Someone else has, too."

I blinked, surprised. "Who?"

"Welkin." Jack lifted the tiny *piskie* out of his pocket.

"Oh!" Sarah gasped, hand flying to her mouth.

Welkin had taken some care with his appearance. He'd neatly brushed his golden hair, which gleamed in the sun spilling through the window. His clothes were still rough with hard use, but cleaner than when I first met him. Even his face was dirt-free, and the copper pin he used as a sword gleamed brightly at his waist.

He stood up straight on Jack's hand as though standing to attention. "You clearly need someone to look out for you," he piped. "Someone competent, I mean."

"Hey," Jack protested mildly.

Welkin jutted his chin out and narrowed his eyes.

"I'm right! After last night—"

"Never mind that," I interrupted quickly. "I thought you didn't want to pit yourself against an *aosidhe*."

"I'm not planning on taking him on myself or anything. I'm neither crazy nor stupid. But I can be useful."

"I have no doubt of that." I couldn't help smiling.

Sarah stood, eyes wide. Putting Hamish on the couch, she walked over to Jack, staring at the tiny creature on his palm. "Who's the girl?" Welkin asked, doing a remarkably good job of looking Sarah up and down given his limited vantage point.

"My cousin Sarah."

"On the human side?"

"Yes."

"A shame," he said. Sarah looked offended until he gave her a tiny wink. "Love the hair. It's like sunset."

"Uh. Thanks." She blushed, running her fingers through her fiery locks.

"What do you want in exchange for all this ... help?" I had a feeling I knew the answer, but wanted to see what the *piskie* would ask for before offering anything myself.

"Your blood," he said. Sarah squeaked. Welkin ignored her, continuing, "Just a couple of drops a week."

Jack's expression darkened. He obviously hadn't asked what the *piskie* was after before agreeing to bring him here.

"And what would you offer in return?"

"I won't fight anything for you. Or do anything that would get me killed. Otherwise, whatever." He shrugged

I regarded him for a moment. "Is it really that good? My blood, I mean?" My cousin looked a little green now. I guess a tiny vampiric fairy was much less enchanting.

ISLA'S OATH

"Lady, you have *no* idea. It's like ... sunlight in honey. Like sex with a—"

"Enough," Jack snapped, dropping his hand to his side. Dislodged, the *piskie* landed on the back of the couch, glaring at the hob. Hamish, startled, hid under the coffee table.

"Isla, you do not have to agree to this," Jack said. "*Piskies* are not even that useful."

"Useful enough." Welkin puffed out his chest.

"Please stop it, both of you," I said. Jack fell silent, pressing his lips together so tightly they turned white. Welkin bowed.

I considered Welkin's offer. A couple drops of blood, gross as it was, weren't really much to pay for the open-ended assistance he was offering. But the idea of gathering servants around me like Everest made me squirm, even though the *piskie* was volunteering. And if I paid him, he wasn't a slave. I doubted the same applied to any of Everest's *duinesidhe*.

The same can't be said for Jack, either, a mutinous voice—my conscience?—whispered.

Several pairs of eyes watched me expectantly. The only ones who weren't belonged to Hamish—who looked between Welkin and Talbot warily—and Talbot, who gazed around the room, nose twitching. Had he ever been in a human house before?

"Okay," I said. Welkin's fist pumped the air, startling a laugh from Sarah and making me smile. "I have some conditions, though."

"What are those?" His eyes narrowed. No matter what Jack thought, Welkin wasn't stupid.

"I need you to swear an oath not to reveal anything

about me or my family to anyone without my permission. Not where I live, or where I'm going. Anything. No matter what. If you decide after a while you don't want to continue with our arrangement, that's fine—but the oath about not telling others will be forever."

Jack relaxed, beaming at me. My heart skipped a beat.

"Done," Welkin said. "Anything else?"

I glanced at the hob, who shrugged slightly. "No, I think that's it," I said.

"Okay." He took a breath. "I, Welkin of the Southern Skies, swear not to reveal anything about Isla Half-Blood or her relatives to anyone without her permission, for as long as I live."

The oath didn't have that same bell-like quality as Jack's oath to me had the day before; the sensation was more like the oaths I'd received from Evie and Gall. I was starting to get a sense for the relative power of oaths based on how they felt when they shivered across my skin. Jack's was a lifelong oath of service. It made sense that it was more intense than a lifelong oath *not* to do something.

After the sensation faded, Welkin gave me a mischievous grin, sitting down on the back of the couch. "Any chance I could get my first payment now?"

"Don't be greedy," I chided him, though I couldn't help smiling back. His glee was contagious. "You can have it in a week."

"Valid," he said, not at all crestfallen. He patted his stomach and licked his lips.

Jack tipped his head to the side, puzzled. I hastily turned to Talbot, who sat near the door that led out to the entryway, ears back as though he wished he could sneak out without us noticing. "Sorry about all that. So you're ready to have a look at the packaging?"

He nodded. It was a curious gesture for a dog, even if the dog did have brightly intelligent eyes. I fetched the sandwich bag containing the—now extremely battered—brown wrapping paper, tangled around with string. I held it out for the *puca*.

Talbot buried his furred nose in the bag and inhaled deeply.

"Can you get any scents from it?" The *puca* made a complicated gesture with his forelegs and shoulders, which I didn't know how to interpret. I looked at Jack. "Can you understand him?"

Jack shook his head.

"Me neither," Welkin added. "Another *puca* could."

"Can you change forms so we can talk?" I asked the dog.

Talbot hesitated and then shook his head.

"Is it because he's going to get goop everywhere?" Sarah asked, sitting back down on the couch. Hamish scurried back onto her lap and wormed his head under her arm. "I saw that in a werewolf movie once. When they changed shape, they left fur and body fluids all over the place. Messy." She wrinkled her nose. "Don't do that on Mum's carpet, okay? She'll lose her mind."

"That is not the reason," Jack said, a twinkle in his eye. "He is not wearing any clothes."

"Oh." Sarah blushed.

"I can get a pair of pants from Ryan's room," I offered. The *puca* nodded. "Follow me. I'll show you where the bathroom is."

Talbot emerged a couple of minutes later in his human form, walking carefully to avoid tripping over the long legs of the tracksuit pants. The black T-shirt I'd scrounged from the basket of clean, unfolded laundry sitting on the end of Ryan's bed fit the *puca*'s stocky torso better. Sarah studied him, fascinated.

"The scents are faint," Talbot said without preamble. "The package went through many hands."

"Duh," Welkin muttered.

He gave the *piskie* an irritated look. "It was almost certainly addressed by a hob," he continued. "I could probably identify them if I met them."

Jack and I exchanged a look. "If it was Moray, that's pretty much a dead end," I said and then cringed at my choice of words. It had definitely been a dead end for Moray.

"There's more, but not much," Talbot said. "I got the faint scent of the elf shot itself. A vibration, almost. I may be able to identify the *aosidhe* who made it if I meet them. It was hard to get much else under the smell of lavender." He rubbed his nose with the back of his hand.

Sarah laughed. "That'd be Nana. She was the one who gave Isla the packaging. I think she showered in the stuff."

"I can tell," Talbot said dryly.

There was an awkward silence, filled only by the rumble of a neighbour mowing his lawn. Talbot looked down at his bare feet then back up again. "Are we done?"

Welkin spoke before I could. He'd heard the conversation with Evie the night before and knew Talbot had to do me a favour. "I expect there's something else that you could do for her. Right, Isla?"

"Uh. Right." I frowned, thinking. "Actually, there is one thing. The packaging was used to send the elf shot that hurt Dad. Then three *duinesidhe* attacked him. Two of them are dead. The third is a *powrie* named Aghi."

Talbot paled. "How did they die?"

"I didn't do it, if that's what you're worried about." I grimaced. "In fact, if we find Aghi quickly, we may be able to keep him from being killed by the overzealous *aosidhe* chasing him. Well, by his *puca* servant," I said. "I doubt Everest is doing much of the actual work."

"They never do," Talbot sniffed. I hid a smile behind my hand. "Do you have anything of his I could use to track him?"

"Um. No," I said, crestfallen.

"You could go out to Uncle David's farm. See if you could pick up anything there?" Sarah suggested.

"It has been months," Jack said regretfully. "And it has rained a number of times."

"Damn."

Talbot hung his head with disappointment. I suppose he'd hoped he could discharge the favour quickly, so he didn't have to deal with me anymore. Not that I blamed him. Having Evie appear at his door in the middle of the night, bleeding and distressed, and tell him about our deal must have been a shock.

"Ahem." Welkin's voice chirped like a hatchling in its nest as he cleared his throat. He preened as we all looked at him. "I might be able to help there. If it turns out I can, I want Jack to admit that I'm useful. And say sorry for hurting my feelings."

Jack clenched his jaw for a moment. I gazed at him pleadingly and he relented, shoulders slumping. "Agreed."

Welkin fluttered into the air, hovering in front of me like an overgrown mosquito. "I heard a rumour of a *powrie* hiding out in a national park between here and Sydney. There's a *piskie* swarm there, and they said he's not there as part of a *sidhe*, because there isn't one in the area. It might be your guy. If we go there, Talbot should be able to track him by scent from there. My understanding is that *powrie* are pretty, um, fragrant."

The *puca* barked a laugh.

"Sounds like we're doing a road trip," Sarah said, rubbing her hands together. "Where's he hiding?"

Welkin explained that the swarm lived in a national park called Tarlo River, a couple of hours' drive northeast of Canberra. A quick internet search told us that it was surrounded by private properties and difficult to get to by road. "It's a pretty good place to hide," I said with a sigh, putting my laptop on the coffee table.

"We could go via the *sidhe* tunnels," Welkin suggested. He had resumed his perch on the back of the couch, by Sarah's head.

"I thought there wasn't one in that area?" Sarah said, eyes bright. She was enjoying herself, I realised. She'd always expressed far more interest in the supernatural than me. If anyone was suited to being half fae, it was her.

"There isn't," Welkin said.

"What's the difference?"

"A *sidhe* is an open place where a lot of *duinesidhe* live," Jack told her. He'd sat next to me on the couch when I'd been using my laptop, carefully keeping several inches between us. "Think of it as a town or a city."

"In a huge cave," I added.

"But there are always tunnels." Welkin stretched, wings quivering. "Those things go everywhere."

"Almost," Talbot said. He'd begun to relax when we hadn't hurt him or asked him to directly confront an *aosidhe*. Maybe he'd resigned himself to having to help.

ISLA'S OATH

"They don't go under large bodies of water. But you can get pretty much anywhere on the mainland via the tunnels without coming out into the world."

"Wow." I was impressed.

"The tunnels further away from inhabited *sidhe* can be dangerous, as can the open spaces, the untenanted caves," Jack cautioned me. "They are unlit and unclaimed, but not always empty. Are you sure you want to do this?"

Finding Aghi wasn't my first priority—that much was true. The forty-eight hours I'd bought us were already down to thirty-six. But if Aghi knew who Moray was working for, maybe I'd be able to take steps to protect Dad from another attack before I decided what to do about Everest. I didn't like the fact I had an enemy I was blind to. What if it was Everest, and he'd come all the way to Australia to find out what had happened to Moray? The notion was more plausible than the idea he'd turned up here looking for magical ol' me—that was certain. And it would explain why he was so keen to find the two attackers and made sure I couldn't talk to Cavall.

"If we can get it done today, then I think we should do it," I said finally, looking at Jack. "Maybe we'll learn something useful."

"Right. Let's do this." Sarah leaped to her feet.

I looked at her in consternation. "I don't think you should come," I blurted and then bit my lip, wishing I hadn't spoken.

"Like hell," Sarah growled, a sound more suited to Talbot in his dog form. "You heard Jack. It might be dangerous."

"That's why you should stay here."

"I will if you do." Hands on hips, she glared down at me.

I glanced around at the *duinesidhe.* Welkin watched the exchange avidly, resting his chin on his hands, while Talbot, who remained near the door, fidgeted with the cord on the tracksuit pants. He reminded me of a dog Kim's family had adopted from a rescue foundation years before—it had been abused by a previous owner and grew anxious when there were raised voices, even when it wasn't the focus of conversation.

Jack met my gaze and turned to Sarah. "The journey will be more dangerous for you than even for Isla. The *sidhe* can disorient and confuse unprotected human minds."

"Are you saying I'm a non-human?" I teased.

"Well … yes," Jack said sheepishly. I wondered briefly whether I should be worried about that—but, on a scale from one to eternal enslavement in a foreign country, loss of my human identity only rated about a three.

"So protect me," Sarah said, jaw set stubbornly.

"I do not know how," he admitted. *"Aislinges* are protected by the power bestowed on them, but most *aosidhe* can create only one. And Isla's is—"

"Ryan." Resignation flattened Sarah's tone and her aura flared green with jealousy. She knew I hadn't deliberately given the power to Ryan. If I'd known what I was doing, I would have chosen Sarah. But she still wished she'd been the one.

"What if she took something made of iron in with her?" I asked, guilt motivating me to seek a solution. Although I didn't want Sarah to come if it would put her in danger, we'd only just reached an uneasy balance in our relationship. I didn't want to jeopardise that by deliberately excluding her. "Would that work?"

The *piskie* fluttered his wings with alarm and Talbot

flinched as though I'd raised a hand to strike him.

"It might," Jack said, his voice cautious. "But it would have other, unintended consequences. The *sidhe* do not like iron any more than the *duinesidhe* do. It acts like a … slow poison. A corruption of the power of the place."

"You took iron into a *sidhe* once," I murmured.

"In that instance I did not care," Jack replied just as quietly.

Sarah wasn't listening; she stared at her bare feet, scowling.

"What about steel then?" I persisted. "Or haematite? That's iron oxide, and it doesn't burn me like iron does. It might be okay."

"Haematite doesn't bother me to be around, so long as I don't touch it," Welkin offered. Talbot nodded reluctantly.

Jack looked dubious. "We could try it."

That was all Sarah needed. In a few short minutes, she was ready to leave. The haematite necklace Nana had given me for my birthday gleamed a dark, silvery grey against her throat although, out of consideration for the *duinesidhe*, she'd tucked as much as she could under her shirt.

Talbot changed back into a hound before we left, and I stuffed Ryan's clothes into my backpack, just in case. Welkin settled himself into the bag on top of the clothes, declaring he'd prefer to ride with me than a hob any day.

I blushed. Jack gritted his teeth and said nothing.

"Should we drive most of the way there and find a tunnel entrance?" Sarah asked as I locked the front door behind us.

Jack shook his head. "We can walk."

"That would take—"

"—no greater time than if we drove. The tunnels take a shorter path to cross the same distance."

My cousin frowned briefly and then grinned. "Let's go then."

CHAPTER FIFTEEN

*J*ack led us back to the same door in the side of Mount Taylor that we'd used the first time he'd taken me to the *sidhe*. Talbot ranged ahead of us up the slope of the mountain, a black outline slipping between patches of dappled sunlight. His nose was to the ground. What was he sniffing for? A human presence that might see us entering the mountain? Other *duinesidhe*? Rabbits?

Sarah muttered under her breath about snakes as we picked our way down into the gully. Jack kept glancing back at us, but this time he didn't offer me his arm.

When we stopped at the doorway, Sarah gazed around, cheeks flushed from the walk. "Where is it?"

My eyes widened. Jack had told me humans couldn't see the rippling light hanging vertical between the tall rocks, but I hadn't really believed him. Until now. To my eyes, the shaded sunlight filtering through the trees twinkled with a gentle illumination the colour of a tropical sea; Sarah's features were limned with light and her hair gleamed.

"It's right here, Sar," I murmured.

She cocked her head and approached the mountain-side, palm outstretched. Her hand stopped millimetres away from the light. Her fingers' shadows stretched back across her face. "It's solid dirt. Is there some way to open it? A magic password or something?"

"You just walk through. The dirt's an illusion."

She stared at me. "No way."

Jack and Talbot exchanged a look, worry dulling their auras.

"Are you sure you want to do this?" I had to ask.

"Hell yes."

"Then I want you to promise me something. If you start feeling at all weird in there, you tell us straight away."

"Weird how?" Lines creased her brow.

"Jack said some people go crazy."

She grinned. "Then how will I tell the difference?"

"I mean it, Sarah. Promise."

"Okay. I promise. Can we go?" Her tone was dismissive, though one hand rose of its own accord and wrapped around the haematite necklace. She was taking me seriously. Good.

"Let me go first," Jack said, slipping past us to stand in front of the door. Talbot hung back to follow us through, a furry rear guard. "Sarah can watch."

"I like to watch," she quipped, nervousness pitching her voice higher than normal.

He stepped through the doorway, the light swallowing him. She inhaled sharply, eyes wide. "It's like he melted into the mountain!"

I took her free hand. "Are you ready? Close your eyes and I'll lead you through."

ISLA'S OATH

She nodded, nibbling her bottom lip, and scrunched her eyes shut.

And I led her through the portal.

I felt her hand clench around mine as I experienced that brief moment of disorientation. I gripped it back, nerves thrilling with the rush of entering the *sidhe*, of its magic thrumming through my veins as it reclaimed me. One of its own.

Sarah appeared behind me, her skin blanched so pale she looked bloodless. She clenched the necklace. I'd be able to count the number of beads from the indentations in her palm.

I drew her away from the entrance so Talbot could glide in behind us like a shadow. Her steps were unsteady.

"I'll get you some water." I opened my backpack to get the bottle.

Welkin flew out of the bag. He took one look at my cousin and darted over to her shoulder, landing lightly, keeping a cautious few centimetres between himself and the haematite necklace. "Hey, Red. You look like you've seen a ghost."

"Leave her alone." I opened the lid and handed the bottle to my cousin. She took a mouthful, her hand shaking enough that the water trembled against her lips.

"Oh, I'm not making fun," the *piskie* said earnestly. "I hate the feeling of coming through the doorway too. Don't worry, girlie, it wears off quickly enough."

Even as he spoke, Sarah's colour was returning. She turned her head slightly to smile at the *piskie*. "I'm okay. It was just a bit of a shock. I kept walking forward, expecting to bump into something, and then *bam*. Teleported."

Welkin laughed.

"Shall we?" Jack said, indicating the tunnel cutting straight through the surrounding earth. We nodded and set off after him. Talbot fell in behind us, claws clicking on the cobblestones with each long stride.

The path was wide enough for Sarah and me to walk together. Welkin stayed on my cousin's shoulder, hands curled around one lock of red hair. He chattered animatedly, pointing out the stargems embedded in the roof and telling her the same theory Jack had shared with me about how the tunnels were created—that a giant worm or serpent had gnawed its way through the earth, crisscrossing the entire globe in its quest for some unknown object. Or maybe just because it was hungry.

"It's not true that the tunnels don't go under the seas and oceans," he confided in a whisper that kept his words from exactly none of us. "But the tunnels that cross the oceans are filled with water, and black things live there. Water-borne *duinesidhe* and … other things."

"Like what?" Sarah's eyes were wide.

"Squid-like monsters, all tentacles and teeth. Protected by armour made of barnacles and wearing seaweed shrouds. They could swallow a boat in a single bite, and their eyes glitter with evil intelligence."

"You have seen them?" Jack's voice was flat, releasing me from the spell the *piskie's* words wove.

"Well, no, not personally," Welkin huffed. "We *piskies* aren't exactly water creatures, you know. I heard it from a reliable source. A siren."

Talbot snorted.

"If they're so big, how do they fit into the tunnels?" Sarah asked. Her aura spun between wonder and amusement at the little faerie's antics, although she managed to keep her expression polite. "They're big, but not *that* big."

"Some tunnels are bigger than others." Welkin said. "This one, for example, is about average size. I've seen ones so small you could barely crawl through them, and others so big the ceiling is hidden in darkness. I really wouldn't want to meet the creature that dug one of those."

I listened to their conversation with half an ear, the rest of my attention wandering. My heart soared at the magically twinkling lights above our heads, the charged atmosphere. I'd always loved thunderstorms, even when I was small, and that static, pre-storm feeling crackled in the air—so much so that when I glanced at my arms I was surprised that the hair wasn't standing on end.

My skin was starting to glow faintly, though.

"Uh, Sarah?" I said, interrupting Welkin in the middle of a tale about mermaids—scaly fish creatures who laid eggs. "There's something I forgot to tell you."

"Mmm?" she said, distracted.

"I sort of glow. Inside the *sidhe*."

"*Glow*?" That got her attention. She stared at me for the space of several heartbeats, almost going cross-eyed with the effort. Then she swore. "Damn, you *are* glowing!"

"It will get brighter as we get to the *sidhe* proper," I admitted. "Jack says it's just another lucky thing about being part *aosidhe*."

Sarah ran a finger along my forearm and then studied the tip as though expecting the glow to rub off. It didn't. "You could almost read in the dark without a torch."

"If I'd brought a book, sure."

"That reminds me," Jack said, "Isla's light won't be enough to fully illuminate the tunnels once we get past the *sidhe*, and not all tunnels are lit. Talbot, would you mind running ahead to get some torches for us?"

The black hound gaped at us briefly. His tongue lolled out, long and pink. Then he trotted up the tunnel, disappearing into the gloom.

When we emerged into the *sidhe*, I stopped short. Sarah paused beside me. Jack drew several steps ahead of us before realising we weren't following; he turned back with a frown.

Sarah looked down into the valley with a faint smile, presumably taking in the same view of a quaint, eclectic village that had bemused me on my first visit, or contemplating the strangeness of a hollow space where a mountain should be.

I stared up at the sky.

Last time I was here, perpetual night had blanketed the *sidhe*, with no moon or stars to leaven the dizzying blackness. Except, as we'd left, a fat crescent moon had started to rise in an eerie reflection of the real world's night.

As Gall had foreshadowed, that change hadn't stopped with the addition of a midnight sky.

Looking up was like gazing through a filter at midday. The sun was bright, though not bright enough to burn the eye; the light it shed was buttery yellow rather than a stark and unforgiving white. The sky was muted too, some of that summer brilliance stripped away.

The copy was imperfect but somehow lovelier, like a child's rendering of the sky rather than the harsh reality.

Gall had attacked me because I'd brought the sun to his *sidhe*, lighting up a home that had only ever seen the gentle illumination of stargems. Would he be able to adjust to a cyclical day and night, or to the phases of the moon?

ISLA'S OATH

And how was Talbot's garden of night-blooming flowers faring?

"You should not feel guilty," Jack murmured.

"Are you reading my emotions now?" I gave him a sideways look.

"Your expression gave it away." He unpicked the bandana's knot, which sat at the base of his neck, tucking the fabric in his pocket. Then he rubbed his ears with both hands for a moment. Sarah stared.

"I changed the *duinesidhe's* home without permission. How could I not feel bad?"

"Did you do it deliberately?" Jack asked.

"No, but—"

"Then do not dwell on it."

I let the subject drop, although I still felt I owed some of the *duinesidhe* an apology. Especially Gall. Next time I saw him I'd say sorry. Assuming he wasn't trying to kill me.

Talbot loped back up the path, holding a canvas tote bag in his teeth. A faint glow emanated from the bag, painting the black fur on the underside of his fuzzy chin with yellow light. If he were any shorter, the bottom of the bag would have scraped the ground.

"Thanks." I smiled when he reached us. He gave me an odd look, dropping the bag at my feet. I picked it up gingerly—the handles were soaked with doggy drool—and handed out the contents. They were torches of a sort, short sticks with brightly coloured spheres attached to the tops. The spheres' sides were made of plastic latticework; through the holes, I saw each contained several stargems. The small chips of quartz glowed like fireflies, trapped in their little cages.

As I handed Sarah her torch she started to giggle, almost doubling over. Welkin squeaked a protest, fluttering his wings for balance. "They're cat toys!" she gasped. "You know, the ones that usually have a bell in them? Magical, glowing cat toys!"

She was right. Someone had cracked them open along the central seam, replaced the contents, and glued them back together.

Jack shrugged at my amused look, although a smile curved the corner of his mouth as he looked down at the torch in his hand. Sarah's laughter was infectious. And slightly hysterical. I looked hard at her aura, but it only showed signs of great mirth, not of impending insanity.

Although what would that look like, anyway?

Jack led us along the outer wall of the *sidhe*, our feet whipping through lush, emerald-green grass that had never known the touch of a lawnmower. The contrast to the sunburned grass that had crunched under our feet outside, full of clinging seeds and prickles, was striking. I stayed beside Sarah. Her laughter slowly faded to hiccoughs and fell silent.

"It's hard to imagine we're inside a mountain," she murmured after a couple of minutes. "The exterior walls of this cave sort of look like the sides of a mountain themselves. Like we're in a valley surrounded by cliffs."

"I don't think we are though. Inside a mountain, I mean. If we were, people would have noticed by now."

She raised an eyebrow at me. "The way they notice the door I couldn't see?"

She had me there.

"The doors are a portal to another place," Welkin said. "I don't know why, but they're always in the sides of mountains or hills. Like caves."

"No circles of mushrooms?"

"Not that I know of." He shrugged tiny shoulders.

Jack glanced back at us over his shoulder. "Perhaps it is because, if they were on the ground, humans might accidentally fall into them." He looked good without a hat or bandana on. The pointed ears still caught my attention, but not as much as they used to. I was getting used to them. Instead, I noticed the depth of his eyes, the incredible softness of his hair, how quick his lips were to smile.

Realising the train of my thoughts, I felt my cheeks burn with a blush. Fortunately, no one noticed.

"Maybe," Welkin was saying. "All I know is I've flown up to try and find the roof inside a *sidhe*, and had to turn back before I succeeded. I don't know any other *piskie* that's done it either." He grinned. "It's actually a *piskie* pastime. We call it trying to touch the sky."

The tunnel entrance Jack led us to was very similar to the one through which we'd arrived. The perfectly circular opening looked like a stormwater pipe—if pipes were made of packed earth rather than concrete. "This will take us in the right direction. Then it will be up to Welkin and Talbot to get us to Aghi." To his credit, only the twitch of his eye showed how uneasy he was at relying on the capricious *piskie*.

He led us into the darkness.

At first, the tunnel was identical to the previous one: a long, straight cylinder evened out along the bottom edge by the addition of a cobbled path. After about twenty minutes of walking, the number of stargems lessened until they vanished altogether. Sarah, Jack and I held our torches aloft, although at first mine was redundant. As we drew further away from the *sidhe*, though, the glow of my skin faded until it was barely noticeable and the torch I held cast a wider circle than I did.

Talbot moved ahead of us, vanishing into the gloom.

When we first got to the edge of the cobbled path, I sighed with relief. The stones had started to jar my feet with each step, even through the soles of my shoes. When they gave way to compacted dirt, my feet were grateful. But walking on the curved earth presented its own challenges. I placed my feet carefully in the centre, not wanting to twist an ankle—especially not here, far away from ice packs and compression bandages.

Judging from the way Sarah had her arms spread slightly for balance, she shared my concerns. Jack, on the other hand, strode along easily, one hand in his pocket, the other holding his torch steady.

The corridors' sameness meant the occasional variations were much more striking. A few times we encountered strange graffiti, drawings or messages painted or carved into the walls—sometimes legible, sometimes not. The styles varied from cave paintings to something resembling the street art at the city bus interchange. Elsewhere, a painted Celtic knot encircled the tunnel. It was like looking at an Irish-style wedding ring from the inside. Although Jack assured us it was safe to touch, Sarah and I both stepped gingerly over the gold-hued, intertwining cords. At another point, a stream of opaque water poured from a crack high in one wall and ran for a few feet along the floor of the tunnel before disappearing into a cleft on the opposite side. We managed to pick our way past that, only getting a little damp. I wrinkled my nose at the water's musty smell.

That smell was pleasant compared to the one we encountered shortly afterwards.

Talbot appeared in the corridor before us. His tail was still, low to the ground, and he had one paw lifted as though poised to flee. His aura was the jaundiced green of anxiety. "Something's wrong," I murmured to the others. Talbot nodded slowly.

"What is it? Something is coming?" A shake of the head. "Something is ahead of us?" He nodded yes. "Something dangerous?" Yes.

"I'll fly forward and check it out," Welkin volunteered, stepping from Sarah's shoulder into the air. "I won't be long."

"Be careful," my cousin whispered.

He waved and shot away, wings a blur of silent motion. I hadn't realised how fast he could fly when he really wanted to.

"Can *piskies* see in the dark?" Sarah asked.

"No," Jack replied. "They navigate via air currents. One explained it to me once."

"I hope he doesn't fly into trouble he can't sense."

"He will be fine," the hob admitted grudgingly.

Jack's confidence in Welkin was soon vindicated when the little *duinesidhe* whisked back up the corridor. He had drawn his pin and held it diagonally across his torso in a defensive gesture. It should have been comical given his stature. Instead, it made my heart skip a beat.

"What is it?"

"*Sluagh.*" His normally piping voice was barely a whisper.

"What-ah?" Sarah said before I could.

"S*loo*-ah. More than one would be my guess. They

travel in haunts. Like a herd, but for—"

"*Sluagh.*"

I looked at Jack. "What are they?"

"They are *duinesidhe.* They can create fear in their target. Fear enough to kill, especially when many *sluagh* are involved." He turned to Welkin. "Are they in our path?"

"No. This tunnel intersects with another. The air from the new tunnel carries the scent of them. They're in an open space—probably a cave." He glanced at Sarah and me. "They are creatures of air, after a fashion. They like open spaces."

"So we should be able to sneak by?" Jack asked.

The little *piskie* took a deep breath and then nodded.

"You don't have to come with us," I told Welkin. I held out a hand and he alighted delicately, copper pin flashing in the light from Sarah's torch. "Our agreement is pretty clear about dangerous situations."

"Yes, well, you girls need me," he said, puffing out his chest. Then he shrugged. "Believe me, if they come after us I'm out of there. But I think we can get past them."

Talbot, who watched all this with silent interest, lolled his tongue with amusement. Then he squared his shoulders—an interesting gesture for a dog—before turning and padding silently down the tunnel, slow enough for us to keep up.

The walk to the intersection was harrowing. I kept imagining sounds. A whisper in the too-still air. The flap of predatory wings. The creak and scuff of footsteps behind us. Sarah was just as jumpy as I was, while Talbot and Jack thrummed with nervous tension, ready to act at a moment's notice. Every noise we made seemed a thousand times louder in the silence. Even a soft step on dirt was as loud as an avalanche when your blood thundered in your veins and all your senses were heightened.

I knew we were approaching the tunnel before Talbot stopped and stared back at us, the whites of his eyes showing. I could smell the *sluagh*. Their odour was a rank combination of wet leather, musty fabric, and a curious, dry smell that reminded me of a dirty birdcage.

We listened for several long moments but couldn't hear anything other than our own breathing. Jack, Sarah and I put our torches into my backpack so the only light was the glow from my skin, which was so faint that, while I could see my hand in front of my face, I couldn't see the lines on my palm.

We crept forward.

The maw of the tunnel gaped to my right as I inched past. The ceiling was about two feet lower than that of the tunnel we were in. Jack and I wouldn't need to duck if we went in there, but it would be a near thing for Sarah.

On the edge of hearing, a clicking sound echoed up the tunnel, reminding me of cicada song. When I'd heard the insects at the coast, it was the sound of summer. Here, in the dark, it sent a jolt of fear through me.

I wasn't the only one that sped up, in a hurry to leave the chattering *sluagh* behind us.

Once the tunnel was well behind us, Talbot stopped abruptly. I bumped into his furred rear, squeaking in surprise.

"What is it?" Sarah's voice was tight with anxiety.

"I ran into Talbot. Sorry," I whispered.

"We can probably get the torches out now," Jack said in a more normal voice. "If the *sluagh* had heard us, we would know. They are not quiet hunters."

"Right." I looked at the hound. "Is that why you stopped?"
He nodded.

"You could warn a girl next time," I grumbled, a little unfairly. What was he supposed to do? Bark at me?

With the re-emergence of the torches, the shadows receded. But our glancing encounter with the *sluagh* cast a pall over our party. Welkin no longer chatted animatedly with Sarah, instead sitting on her shoulder with a sombre expression. She gripped her torch so hard I thought that, if a *sluagh* manifested before her, she might belt him with it. Jack's shoulders were tight with stress, and he kept casting worried looks my way. He drifted closer, until we walked side by side.

Neither of us spoke. But his presence was a comfort.

More tunnels. More side tunnels, of varying sizes— none of which carried the same air of foreboding as the *sluagh's* tunnel. Some carried faint scents, of grass or water or dry eucalypts. Pleasant smells. Although I wasn't unfit, I also wasn't used to walking for hours. My thighs were protesting and my feet ached by the second time Talbot appeared from the shadows. He wuffed quietly and shook his head, barring our way.

Welkin exhaled gustily and flew ahead without being asked.

"What do you think it is this time?" Sarah asked me quietly.

I shrugged, peering at her in the dimness. "How are you feeling?"

"Tired. I know the others couldn't, but I really wish we'd taken the car."

"I was thinking the same thing," I admitted.

"It feels like we've been in here forever. We're not going

to come out and find a hundred years have passed like Rumpelstiltskin did, are we?"

"Wasn't that Rip Van Winkle?"

"Maybe?" She wrinkled her nose. "I don't know. But if I grow a huge beard I'm going to be pretty angry."

I laughed softly.

When the *piskie* returned he was calmer than the last time; at least, he hadn't drawn his sword. "This tunnel opens out into a *sidhe*. It's occupied by a herd of *karkadann*." He landed on top of Sarah's torch, his shadow looming like a giant butterfly on the tunnel roof. She and I must have looked baffled, because he elaborated. "They're like horses, with long horns on their heads."

"A *unicorn*?" Sarah and I gasped together.

"Maybe if a unicorn got a whole lot meaner." He grinned.

"They are extremely territorial," Jack added. "And have keen hearing and eyesight. We would be better off finding another way. Talbot?"

The hound glanced up.

"Can you smell the *powrie* yet?"

Talbot nodded.

"Oh, for Pete's sake, Talbot!" Sarah stomped her foot, drawing a bemused look from the *duinesidhe*. "If we all turn our backs and promise not to peek, will you change forms and talk to us?"

There was a long pause, during which I had enough time to wonder if she'd offended the *puca*. Finally, he nodded again, his wagging tail stirring the still tunnel air.

I didn't peek. I suspect Sarah would have, if she could have done it discreetly. As it was, she couldn't even check out his shadow—we were holding the light sources, so it fell behind us.

"He's close," Talbot said over the rustle of fabric on skin. "Living on the other side of the *karkadann sidhe* would be my guess. He might be using the herd to slow trackers down. It's what I'd do if an *aosidhe* were after me."

"So what do we do?" I asked.

"Like Jack said, find another way. That last tunnel, the one that smelled of bushland, leads to a portal. We should be able to find our way to him in the above world. Okay, you can turn around."

"What makes you think we'll be able to find him?" I asked as I turned.

Talbot shrugged, smoothing the hemline of the T-shirt restlessly. "The *powrie* can't get through the *karkadann* herd any more than we can. He must have another way in and out. Either a portal or another tunnel."

"Okay. Let's do it."

We backtracked to the side tunnel, which was mercifully only five minutes back the way we'd come. The tunnel itself was much smaller, only three feet from floor to ceiling. We would have to crawl. My hands grew sweaty and my breath short as I stared at the dark mouth of the entrance. It swam before my eyes.

My claustrophobia. *Now* it showed up. Great.

Talbot entered the tunnel first, on hands and knees, followed by Sarah. Welkin flitted along beside my cousin. I hesitated, watching the shadows from Sarah's light swing back and forth as she crawled along. The light dwindled.

Jack waited beside me. "Isla?"

"I just want to get out of here." The urge to feel the sun on my face and taste fresh air was overwhelming.

"From the feel of the air, the portal is not far. But you have to come this last distance. I cannot carry you in such a confined space."

"It's the confined space part I'm worried about." My voice broke on the last word.

He took my hand, placing it against his cheek. Even through the fear, my heart turned over in my chest. "You are safe. I will keep you safe. You know I am telling you the truth. You can see how I feel."

I could. The baby pink of compassion twisted together with the pulsing blue of a deep and abiding trust—bound together by a darker pink. I knew what that colour meant too.

It was the same colour as the roses Dominic had bought me the evening before. *Love.* My heart thundered in my ears for a different reason then.

"Okay." I took a deep breath, as though it had to last me a lifetime, and entered the tunnel, abused muscles aching as I crawled along. I kept my gaze firmly fixed on Sarah's torchlight rather than on the alarmingly close ceiling, and tried to breathe normally.

Jack crawled into the tunnel behind me. At first, knowing he was at my back made me feel better. Then I had an alarming thought. "You better not be looking at my butt back there."

He laughed softly.

The scent of sun-baked eucalypts grew stronger and I increased my pace, impelled by the idea of being free of the interminable tunnels at last. I only stopped when I reached Talbot, Sarah and Welkin. Beyond them a bush landscape shimmered. I could almost taste the dust in the air.

"The coast is clear. Are you ready?" Talbot asked me.

I glanced back to confirm Jack had reached us. He smiled at me. "Let's go."

CHAPTER SIXTEEN

The portal emerged from a tall outcrop of lichen-covered rocks. We crawled on hands and knees into slanting afternoon sunlight, filtered through the leaves of towering trees. The heat was stifling after so long in the cool tunnels.

The others moved around, talking softly. For a long moment I stood still, drinking in the fresh air, enjoying that my gaze could roam to the hilly horizon, which was swathed in grey-green. A faint breeze barely stirred the air, still enough to carry the invigorating scent of the eucalypt forest, a scent like crushed pine and mint mingled with the sweetness of honey.

We were high on a ridge, giving us a good view of the valley through the rough-barked trunks of the trees. The national park's landscape resembled a crumpled piece of paper that someone had tried but failed to smooth flat, marked with the shadowy creases of valleys, and a more sinuous shape in a darker green that had to be the river. It snaked through the hills like a child's squiggly drawing, sometimes doubling back on itself in its meandering journey.

"Isla, check this out," Sarah called. I found her standing behind the portal, staring at a mound of grass.

"What?" It seemed like perfectly ordinary grass to me.

"If there was really a tunnel, it should pass through this space." She waved one hand through the air behind the mound.

"It's in another place. Like an alternate dimension or whatever."

"Well, yeah, but now I can see that for myself."

I rolled my eyes. "Sarah, in three hours we walked a distance that would have taken us that long to drive. There's no way they were regular tunnels."

"My feet feel like I've walked for days," she moaned.

"Mine feel fine," Welkin quipped from where he was sitting atop a speckled granite rock. She swatted at him and he laughed.

"There you are," Jack said, coming around the outcrop with the *puca's* clothes slung over his arm. He handed them to me and I shoved them into my backpack. "Talbot is changing into a hound again. He thinks the *powrie* will probably be living near the river. It needs to hunt, and that is where the animals will come to drink."

"Not much big game out here," I said.

"Kangaroos," Sarah commented darkly. "And maybe feral pigs or dogs. I guess if he's trying to avoid attention he'd be sticking to the park, not going after livestock."

"On the bright side, at least we'll be walking downhill."

Complaining good-naturedly, we set off down the slope after Talbot, whose nose was again to the ground, busily cataloguing the forest scents. He walked slower now than he had at Mount Taylor, ranging back and forth for a scent trail that didn't belong.

I was glad we were taking it slowly. Although I wasn't born in Australia, I'd grown up here, and my gaze scanned the ground as thoroughly as Talbot's nose did. Red-bellied black snakes and eastern brown snakes were common, and both had potentially fatal bites. I grimaced. Dying would be one way to avoid the problem with Everest, but I'd be leaving Jack to face the *aosidhe's* wrath without even my dubious protection.

Best not to get poisoned and die.

The undergrowth beneath the stringybarks was sparse. The high oil content of the dropped eucalyptus leaves discouraged dense scrub, but we still had to pick our way through and around patches of bristly heath, and wattle shrubs taller even than Sarah. Here and there, we passed patches of round kangaroo droppings, which— as much as I avoided them—reassured me that we probably weren't in the *powrie's* main hunting ground yet.

"You said there was a swarm of *piskies* out here," Sarah said to Welkin, who was perched on top of her head, chest-deep in the copper-gold and bleached blond sea of her hair. "Do you think we might see them?"

"Uh." The *piskie* looked sideways at me, a glance I only caught because the sun glinted off his sky-blue eyes. "No. Not really. No."

"Why not? The *powrie*?"

He shifted uncomfortably. "Not exactly."

"He means me," I sighed. Sarah's wide eyes met mine. "The *piskies* can sense *aosidhe* energies in the air or something. And they don't like them. It's me they're avoiding."

ISLA'S OATH

"They've never met you!" She scowled. "They should at least meet you before deciding they don't like you."

I poked my tongue at her. The others laughed.

The Tarlo River was low in its bed but still flowing freely. It tumbled over glistening rocks, glittering like cut crystal in the hot sun, foam swirling across its surface. The air filled with a fine spray. As we emerged from the shade of the trees onto the riverbank, Sarah and I paused, enjoying the feel of misted water on our faces. Jack waited beside us, eyes scanning the line of trees on both banks.

His caution was a sobering reminder that we were seeking a creature who had already proven himself dangerous. Although we weren't out here to hurt him, he didn't know that. I drew my eyes away from the shimmering water with a sigh.

For several minutes Talbot ranged along the bank, nose so close to the ground I worried he'd cut it on something. Then he picked his way across a tumble of wet rocks to do the same on the opposite shore, before vanishing behind a shrub. His voice floated across the water, pitched to carry.

"He's definitely been here, but his scent is a few days old. Welkin, can you give us an idea of which way to try first?"

"Sure thing," the *piskie* replied, shooting into the sky so quickly our eyes couldn't follow him.

"Do you think Talbot is worried about being naked out here?" Sarah whispered to me. "What if he gets bitten by something somewhere private?" She gestured vaguely downwards.

"Why don't you ask him?" I said sweetly. At that moment, Talbot, back in hound form, reappeared from the trees. Something about the set of his ears made me think he'd probably heard Sarah. She clearly thought so too, because her cheeks turned pink. Then she lifted her chin and winked at the *puca*.

"Should we be talking so loudly?" I asked Jack. "What if Aghi hears us coming?"

"Talbot would be able to smell him if he were close enough to hear us. There is not much of a breeze to carry his scent far, or our voices for that matter. Talbot knew that when he called across to us."

"Oh." That made sense. I felt uneasy at not being able to tell for myself whether it was safe to talk. On the other hand, given we'd come out here on Talbot's assurance that he could do this, it seemed silly to start doubting him now.

Besides, Jack trusted him, and I trusted Jack.

Still, I must have frowned, because Jack put his hand on my shoulder, earning a raised eyebrow from Sarah when his caress lingered. "We will be quieter from here on out, though," he reassured me.

By the time Welkin returned, Talbot had recrossed the river and was licking water from between his paws in a way I would have found charming if he wasn't a part-time biped. Instead, the idea of drinking the river water made me feel a little ill.

"Looks like we've come in at the bottom end of the park," Welkin said breathlessly. "If the *powrie* is avoiding the farmland, he has to be upstream."

"Are you okay?" Sarah held out her hand for him to land.

"Yup." He grinned fiercely as he alighted. "There was a kookaburra who thought I looked like a tasty treat. I tweaked his tail feathers."

He was so pleased with himself Sarah and I had to

laugh—although I did feel sorry for the hapless bird.

We made our way upstream, Talbot often moving so far ahead of us that we lost sight of him between the trees. Even though we kept our conversation quiet, neither Sarah nor I were experts at sneaking through bushland. We made a racket with every step.

Jack, on the other hand, moved like a cat.

Trying to move quietly left me taut with nerves and increasingly irritable. Every time a twig snapped underfoot, my cousin and I both jumped, shooting each other apologetic looks. Flies buzzed around us, attracted by our perspiration; we swatted them away vigorously. I wished I'd thought to grab a hat or sunscreen, but when you're planning a trip via subterranean tunnels in an alternate dimension, you don't necessarily think of sun protection. We followed the river but stayed back from the water, under the broad shade of the eucalypts. Sarah and I were both pale; if we weren't careful, sunburn was inevitable.

"Look there," Jack murmured, pointing.

Talbot waited for us by a broad, flat rock that marked one of the river's many hairpin turns. His stance—and aura—were uneasy. When we reached him, he indicated a patch of ground under the trees with a nod of his head. Rusty red stained the grass and scattered leaves. Blood. The drone of flies grew louder.

Sarah and I stood back, nervously holding hands, while Jack bent over almost double to examine the stains. "I'd say he killed something here and then carried it off." He touched a spot of blood tentatively with one finger. "Fairly recently too. This is tacky. It should make him easier to find."

"Wh-what was it?" I swallowed hard, visions of Cavall's

severed head filling my thoughts.

"Probably a kangaroo. There are a few pieces of grey fur here." Jack sounded sure. But, as he turned his back to wash the blood from his finger, scrubbing it with wet sand at the river's edge, I glanced surreptitiously at Talbot. The *puca* nodded, and I exhaled softly with relief.

We moved faster after that. Talbot had a stronger scent to follow, his feet striding through the loam.

After several minutes, a glimpse of colour caught my eye. I turned. Through the trees uphill from us I saw an aura, red, black and yellow. It moved quickly.

Towards us.

"Look out!" I cried as something long and sharp flew straight at us.

Jack shoved me, hard. I fell sideways into Sarah. We landed on the ground in a tangle of limbs. Welkin shot into the air, cursing. Talbot ran past us, feet thundering.

Jack cried out with pain.

"No, no, *no!*" A voice—Aghi's voice—cried. "*Aosidhe* slaves, get away!"

Rolling onto my stomach, I glanced at Sarah to make sure she was okay. She met my gaze and swore even more colourfully than Welkin had. Her cheek was already swelling, grazed, and she had leaves in her hair. But her eyes were clear.

Up the slope, Jack and Talbot closed on the *powrie.* Talbot's lips were curled back in a fierce snarl. Blood streamed down one of Jack's arms; the tip of a crude spear, broken now, protruded from his bicep.

He'd put himself in the way of a spear intended for me. My blood ran cold.

Now I'd met another *powrie*, I could see that Aghi was

big for his kind. His muscles, where they showed through the ragged tears in his clothes, bulged like a bag full of walnuts. His hair was greasy and grey, and his red-hued eyes darted around in panic. He didn't want to fight us.

Jack spoke, his voice cold. "Stand down and we will not hurt you." Maybe he wasn't the best spokesperson for our group at the moment. His tone made it clear he was hoping Aghi didn't stand down.

"I won't let your *aosidhe* take me!" Aghi wailed. In his aura, fear was winning out over the fury that had needled him into attacking us.

Jack spoke slowly, as though talking to a recalcitrant child. "We do not work for Everest."

Aghi blinked, puzzled. "What you talking about? Everest?"

I pulled myself to my feet, wincing. "Everest. The *aosidhe* who's hunting you." I took a step forward and the *powrie* recoiled, tripping over a fallen tree. He landed hard on his back, legs sprawled up over the trunk at an awkward angle.

Under other circumstances, it would have been funny.

"Isla?" Sarah murmured beside me. "I don't think Everest is the *aosidhe* he's afraid of."

She was right. Aghi's expression when I stepped towards him transformed into blind panic. He scrambled backwards, leaves rattling beneath his huge fingers. Jack and Talbot darted forward to pin him in place. The *puca* stood on his chest and glared down at him. With a grunt, Jack yanked the blackened tip of the spear from his arm. He held it, coated with his blood, at the *powrie*'s throat.

"Are you okay?" I asked Jack, alarmed at how much blood dripped from his arm.

He nodded curtly, furious eyes fixed on the *powrie*. "I will heal. What do you want us to do with him?"

"Hold him still."

"What are you doing?" Sarah asked. Her voice was high with panic. "Stay away from him."

"It's my fault he's like this. I have to fix it."

It was true. When Aghi, Cavall and Moray attacked my father's farm, they'd captured Jack and me with embarrassing ease. Aghi had restrained me, and I'd clumsily thrust all of my terror into him, forcing him to let me go. He'd fled, howling, into the night.

"It's your fault he's an unwashed monster?" my cousin asked, not understanding.

I clenched my jaw and didn't reply, moving to stand before the *powrie*.

I wasn't completely foolish; although I needed skin contact, I didn't want to get close to those powerful arms. Aghi could crush my ribcage in seconds—Gall was puny by comparison. I kept the log between us and, wrinkling my nose, reached out to touch one hairy shin.

Aghi pulled away, screaming as though I'd scalded him. But I wasn't the clumsy amateur, new to my powers, that I'd been even a few months ago. Quick as thought, I drained the fear and rage from him, replacing them with the light blue of serenity.

Well, most of the fear. I still wanted him to be wary of us.

The forest was silent in the wake of the *powrie*'s scream, the wildlife frightened into hiding. That was the only reason we were able to hear Aghi's whispered words. "What did you do?"

"Yes, what did you do?" Sarah said, bewildered.

ISLA'S OATH

"I took your fear and anger away," I said.

"Is this what that feels like?" Aghi said. He raised one meaty hand to his forehead, rubbing it. His fingers left tracks in the dirt on his face.

"Um. Yes, I suppose so."

Jack sensed my confusion. "It is like I have told you before, Isla, *powrie* are always violent. It was not hyperbole. It is in their nature. Some say the *aosidhe* have bred them for it for thousands of years." He kept his gaze fixed on the prone giant before him, the point of the spear unwavering.

"Always violent? That's terrible," Sarah said.

"Save your compassion for someone who deserves it," Jack said.

"You don't like the *powrie* very much, do you?"

"No."

I interrupted before an argument broke out. "Aghi, Jack was telling you the truth before. We don't want to hurt you. We just wanted to ask you a question."

"What?" Aghi stared at the hob and then craned his neck to look at me. "I don't understand. I hurt you. Why you not want to hurt me?"

"Because I know you were working for someone else. I just want to know who."

"Moray. He hired me and Cavall. You should ask Cavall. He smarter than me."

"Cavall is dead," Jack said.

The *powrie*'s eyes widened until we could see the whites all around his peculiar irises. "You killed Cavall?"

"Not us. Everest. The *aosidhe* we mentioned before."

Aghi squirmed in the dirt, a curious gesture for a seven-foot-tall ogre. The fear in his aura flickered brighter,

221

beginning to eat away at the artificial calm I had induced. The anger followed behind, smaller, like a worm in an apple. "Is he coming for me too?"

"Yes," Jack said. The *powrie* whimpered, and the hob spoke over him, his voice reasonable but his eyes hard. "It would be best if you answered Isla's question quickly. Then you can flee. If you leave now, you may get a sufficient head start to beat Everest's hounds. Who did Moray work for?"

Aghi took a shuddering breath and gasped, "It was him, okay? It was Everest." The words hit me like a punch to the stomach ... but, at the same time, I wasn't surprised. "Moray was his vassal, part of his court. I swear to you, it the truth. If he after me too, he never stop. He kill me ... you gotta let me go. Please." Those red-tinged eyes rolled to me, begging for mercy. "Please, lady."

There was no reason to keep him. "Swear you won't attack any of us, and you can go."

"Okay. Yes. I swear I won't attack any of you, or that little *piskie* up in the tree neither. Now please let me go."

The oath settled over all of us, feather light; Sarah shifted uncomfortably, muttering under her breath. Jack and Talbot stood back, positioning themselves between the *powrie* and the two of us as the great creature hauled himself to his feet. He didn't hesitate, barrelling uphill through the trees like a boulder rolling in reverse. Branches cracked and hung in his wake.

"Do you believe him?" Sarah was the first to speak.

"He swore it was true. So yeah. Besides, it makes sense."

Jack threw the spear tip into the nearby heath. I pulled Ryan's T-shirt out of the backpack and, after hesitating a moment, ripped it into strips. I'd buy him a new one. "Here, let me." I bound the wound on his arm, which still bled sluggishly.

"It will heal. Do not fret," Jack murmured, although his sapphire eyes met mine, warm with gratitude. I smiled back, and he turned to Sarah, speaking more loudly. "Isla is correct. That it was Everest is logical. When Moray did not come back, Everest came out here to look for him."

Welkin flew down from the tree, straightening his shirt. His expression was faintly embarrassed, but I didn't blame him for hiding when the fight broke out. He was so tiny. What could he do? "Most *aosidhe* wouldn't come all the way out here to look for a hob."

"That is true. However, Moray was sent out here to retrieve Isla's father. If Everest wanted him badly enough, he would have come out here for that."

"Uncle David?" Sarah frowned. Welkin landed on her shoulder and began to pick twigs out of her hair.

"They probably think he is valuable to Melpomene," Jack said, giving me an apologetic look.

"Will he try and elf shot him again then?" She frowned. "Elf shoot him? Whatever the term is?"

"I doubt he cares about your uncle anymore," Jack said darkly. "Now he knows about Isla. She is much more powerful leverage."

"Thanks. I think. I guess that means he does know who my mother is, after all..." I trailed off, stomach churning with horror as a thought crystallised in my mind.

The only way to save Jack was to lose him.

The idea left me cold inside, as if I'd swallowed an ice brick the size of my car. I took a slow, painful breath. "We need to get back to Canberra, get Evie, and then get both of you as far from Everest as we can."

"Run?" Jack blinked.

"Yes, run." My voice was hoarse. I swallowed and continued. "He's going to kill you if we don't. I'll drive you both down to Melbourne. You'll be harder for Fintan to track that way, especially with the steel in the car frame. It'll throw them off. Once you're there, you can hop a ferry across to Tasmania." I smiled weakly. "You get to be closer to Antarctica after all."

"And then what will you do?" His voice was calm despite his aura being a mess of disjointed colours. The electric purple of shock swirled through an anxious yellow that looked like bile, all overlaid with a heavy grey that matched the heaviness in my heart.

"I'll come back here. Everest is trying to use you as leverage to get me. I have to make sure he doesn't take losing that out on my family."

He clenched his jaw. "No. I will not leave you to deal with him alone."

"Jack," I said softly. "You don't have a choice."

CHAPTER SEVENTEEN

*J*ack's eyes widened as he realised what I was saying. I'd order him to obey me if I had to. Then they narrowed. I didn't need to read his aura to know how angry he was. "Very well." He turned and stalked back towards the river, his back as stiff as a board. Tears prickled my eyes as I watched him walk away.

Sarah took my hand. I started. For a moment, I'd forgotten she and the others were there. If my heart wasn't too busy breaking, I might have been embarrassed. "I'll come on the car ride to Melbourne with you. So you don't have to drive back on your own." Her gaze was full of compassion.

"Thanks."

She squeezed my hand in response.

A roar split the air like a crack of thunder, full of outrage and spite. It was followed, a second later, by a high-pitched sound I didn't recognise, similar to the angry squeal of a pig. But from something much, much larger. Talbot's head shot up, nose quivering as he scented the air, and Welkin darted up through the boughs of the trees so that he could get a clearer view.

Jack turned back to us, hand extended towards me. "Isla—"

"*Karkadann!*" Welkin yelled. "*Run!*"

"To the river! Go!"

Talbot shot past Sarah and me, a furred black bullet. We crashed down the hill in his wake, shoes slipping on loose rocks and scattering fallen leaves. Branches whipped across my arm, leaving thin scratches. The river wasn't far, but, as the shrieks and rumble of hooves grew closer, it seemed much farther.

When we reached the shoreline, the *karkadann* were almost on us, looming shadows under the trees. "We have to cross," Jack urged, taking my arm. Talbot had already splashed up the opposite bank, fur dripping.

Sarah's hand tore from mine. I pulled free of Jack's grip, running to her side. Her sneaker was wedged between two worn river rocks.

"Help me!" she cried, face white with pain and fear. I picked at the laces with trembling fingers, hoping to loosen the shoe enough to pull her foot free.

"Isla!" Jack darted between us and the onrushing herd. Welkin buzzed overhead, wringing his hands.

Six *karkadann* burst from the trees and into the sunlight, their appearance so extraordinary that, for a heartbeat, I stopped and stared. They paused, glaring back at us with eyes a deep, glittering blue. They were horse-like only in the same way a donkey is horse-like; their coats gleamed pure white in the blazing sun, except for their faces, which were the garnet red of venous blood.

ISLA'S OATH

Long, elegant legs ended in feathered hooves, which scattered loam as they stomped the ground. Tails like a donkey's lashed in agitation.

The most extraordinary thing was the two-foot-long, tricolour horn, set between ears pressed back against broad skulls. The base was ivory, the middle jet-black, and the sharp point a vivid crimson, as though dipped in fresh blood.

And, unlike horses, I could read their auras. They were universally outraged. Furious.

The largest of them, a stallion, lowered his head and charged.

I screamed, yanking at Sarah's foot. She screamed too, whether from pain or terror I didn't know. We were about to be trampled.

Jack braced himself. The stallion swung its huge head, striking him in the chest with its long nose. The hob flew through the air and landed in the water, disappearing beneath the surface with a splash of foam.

"No!" Unable to restrain the suicidal impulse, I leapt to my feet and glared at the *karkadann*, matching his outrage note for note.

The stallion danced to a halt before me, hooves clattering on stone. A questing, curious tendril of thought touched my mind as I gazed up into his eyes. His ears flicked forward.

I glanced over my shoulder. Talbot was hauling Jack from the water onto the opposite bank, teeth locked into the back of his shirt. My heart started beating again.

Now just to get Sarah and me out of this.

"He won't kill you out of hand," Welkin stage-whispered from a foot above our heads. "Not if you're, you know—"

"What?"

"Virgins."

Awkward.

Not daring to touch the stallion, I reached out with my power, projecting my regret that his herd had been disturbed, hoping I was concealing my terror well enough that he wouldn't sense it. I was sure Aghi had riled the *karkadann* up—either unable to attack us himself due to his oath but desiring revenge, or hoping to delay us in case we decided to change our minds about harming him.

Of course, now I did want to change my mind. *Focus, Isla. That horn could kill you any second.*

I felt the creature's fading outrage. Puzzlement.

It was working. A smile tugged the corner of my mouth. I added to my thoughts a sense of admiration, and the stallion shook his head and blew out his nose, his mane flowing. Vain creature.

"Are you all right, Sarah?" I asked, keeping my gaze on the *karkadann*.

"What's going on?" There was panic in her voice.

"I'm talking to it. Sort of."

"Can you get me out of here?"

I slowly stepped around Sarah so I didn't turn my back on the stallion. Then I knelt down beside her.

Her ankle had twisted when she caught her foot between the rocks. Swollen, it bulged inside her sock as if someone had replaced the joint with a golf ball. Her face was wet with tears, although she choked back her sobs. Her wide eyes fixed on the looming *karkadann* whose shadow fell over us.

"We might have to cut your shoe off."

"Oh god."

ISLA'S OATH

"It's okay. It'll be okay." I squeezed her hand, drawing the edge from her fear.

Both of us squeaked when the stallion stepped forward, lowering his head down between us. He carefully touched the curved side of the horn to Sarah's ankle. The tip left a scratch on the sandstone beside her shoe. I gulped, realising how sharp it was, thankful the stallion had hit Jack with his nose, not his horn. My hands shook as I realised how close the hob had come to being impaled.

"It's gone. The pain is gone." Sarah's voice was full of wonder and gratitude, which I echoed to the stallion. It blinked and then rubbed its horn against my arm, where the wattle had scratched me. The skin healed in its wake. It felt tingly and cool, as though I'd used a sports rub.

With the swelling removed, we were able to take Sarah's foot from the shoe. I tugged the sneaker from the fissure and she put it back on gratefully.

"Are you okay, Isla? Sarah?" Jack was standing midway across the river, thigh-deep in flowing water. Talbot was beside him, head high, submerged from the shoulder down.

"Yes. The *karkadann* healed Sarah. Maybe it will heal you too, if you come over."

Jack hesitated. "I am not sure that is a good idea."

"Just try it."

Jack drew closer to the bank. The stallion squealed and ducked his head, brandishing his horn threateningly.

Flitting back and forth between us, Welkin laughed like a chiming bell. Jack's expression was thunderous as he glared up. "I'm pretty sure our hob friend isn't a virgin," the *piskie* said. "Talbot either."

"What about you?" Jack said coldly.

"Um. I'll just stay up here out of reach."

"You do that."

I turned to the stallion, letting it see my feelings for Jack. Affection. Possibly love. I indicated Talbot and Welkin with a broad gesture, indicating that they were friends too.

The stallion nickered, letting me see how dubious he felt about that, and stepped back a little.

Now he had retreated I could see past him to the rest of the herd. They had withdrawn into the shade of the trees, watching us with a mix of interest and wariness. Most of them were female, although there was one smaller male, probably a yearling.

The largest of the mares—although she was still smaller than the stallion, and more fine-boned—had a direct gaze more intelligent than the rest. She watched as I asked Jack and Talbot to leave the water. This time, the stallion didn't stop them, although he did keep his horn lowered, ready in case they tried anything.

Jack's sodden shoes squeaked on the rocks as he walked over to us, checking Sarah's ankle and then running warm fingers over my healed arm. His touch tingled too, although in his case I was sure it was in my head.

"I had heard they could heal with a touch, but I had not believed it," he said, his tone betraying a hint of jealousy. I guess his healing power seemed paltry by comparison. His blue eyes met mine. "Isla, can you extract us from the herd so we can leave?" I saw his underlying anger, re-emerging in his aura now the orange blaze of panic was receding.

So did the *karkadann*. The lead mare left the rest of the herd, clopping forward to stand with her mate. The stallion touched her nose briefly with his and then took a step back.

"Can everyone try to think calm thoughts?" I murmured to the others.

They all nodded.

Heart in my throat, I stepped towards the mare, keeping my hands at my sides. Now wasn't the time for a misunderstanding.

"Hello," I said, projecting calm, trying not to stare at the lethal tip of her horn. "Would you mind if I touched you so we can talk properly?" Her eyes tracked my movements and she leaned towards me as I came to stand near her shoulder. Taking that as an invitation, I reached out and scratched her warm fur.

Her feelings washed over me. The *karkadann* were intelligent—not as intelligent as a human, no, but cleverer than, say, a dog. The mare's emotions were much more complex than those of the stallion, or perhaps I was just more deeply exposed to them by the physical contact. I felt her pride in her herd and affection for her mate. Her indignation that the smelly *powrie* they had tolerated on the edge of their territory for so long had disrupted their peace. A benign tolerance for Sarah and me, overlaid with curiosity about me, because no human had ever *talked back* before. Vague irritation at the fluttering *piskie* above our heads. Dislike of Jack and Talbot, and an acknowledgement that Jack was my mate—

Shocked, I pulled away from her, eyes wide. She gave me a reproachful look and I scratched her again. Prepared now for the wave of emotions, I was able to notice and marvel at the fine, soft fur of her coat, the hard sinew of the muscles underneath. I wished I could see the herd run; I suspected they'd be faster than regular horses.

The nicker that time sounded suspiciously like a laugh.

Feeling clumsy by comparison, I tried to communicate back to her. My regret at Aghi's actions in upsetting the herd, and my wonder at how lovely and clever the *karkadann* were. Underlying that was my desperation to get us—all of us, not just Sarah and me—back to our *sidhe* as quickly as we could.

I had only intended to convey our desire to leave. However, the mare put her nose into my hair and took a deep breath, and then lay down on the rocks, indicating her back with a tip of her head.

After a moment, the stallion lay down beside her and did the same thing, looking from me to Sarah expectantly.

"I think they want us to get on."

"I can see that," Sarah replied dryly. "Where do they plan on taking us?"

"Home. Back to the Canberra *sidhe*." That meaning was clear from the mare's thoughts. She knew of the Canberra *sidhe* and could get us there quickly.

My cousin's expression was dubious. "Don't get me wrong, I like the idea of not walking, but I've never ridden a horse bareback before, let alone an angry unicorn. And what about Jack and Talbot?"

"Talbot may be able to keep up," I said. The *puca* made a sound in his throat to get my attention, and then shook his head. He was still dripping wet; unlike a normal dog, he hadn't shaken all over us. I appreciated his restraint.

"Does it matter if he can't?" Welkin asked, landing on Sarah's shoulder now the danger seemed to have passed. "No offence, Talbot, but your deal was to help them find Aghi and they've done that. Do you actually care if you get back quickly?"

The *puca* shook his head again, emphatically this time.

"I don't feel right leaving you," I said to the *puca*. "Will you be okay on your own?"

He nodded, his aura flushed with relief. Although I'd known from the start that he hadn't actually wanted to help me, his reaction hurt a little. I'd thought we were if not friends then at least friendly.

"Okay." I turned to the mare, who watched patiently. "What about Jack?" I gestured to the hob, in case she couldn't understand my words.

She eyed him, and I got a clear sense of distaste at the idea of a wet thing on her back. Bad enough that he wasn't a virgin. Trying to ignore that last thought, I handed Jack the backpack. "Change into Ryan's tracksuit pants. She'll let you ride her if you're dry."

Giving the rest of the *karkadann* herd a wide berth, Jack made his way into the trees to change. Talbot gave us a final nod of farewell and trotted back towards the tunnel entrance we'd arrived through, pausing to shake vigorously once he was out of range. The droplets glittered in the air like crystals before raining to the ground.

When Jack emerged, he was barefoot, wearing only the too-long pants with the hems rolled up. His clothes were draped over one arm; he'd wrung them out but they were still sodden. The shoes dangled over his bare shoulder by their knotted laces.

I'd seen guys my age shirtless before, at the pool or beach, or in gym class before I'd finished school. Except for when it had been Dominic, I'd always found it uncomfortable, never knowing where to look. Now I found it hard to look away. Jack's torso was as pale as his face and arms, with no tan line—and no real tan. But instead of looking pasty he seemed to glow in the sun, a statue made from sculpted ivory. His muscles were sleek and lean, the physique of someone who walked everywhere. At first I thought his chest was hairless; then I saw the faintest shimmer of honey-blond hair, as fine as the hair on his head. What would it feel like to touch?

"Down, girl," Sarah whispered. I hastily bent to retie my shoelaces, pretending I wasn't staring.

The *karkadann* mare's amusement was palpable.

Sarah took my backpack and stuffed the wet clothes and shoes into it. "I'll wear this since Welkin is riding with me and he's little. You can ride with Jack." I glanced at her, catching the sad look in her eye. I was grateful for the extra chance to spend time with the hob before he left.

Before I made him leave.

I squared my shoulders and took a breath. The sooner Jack left, the safer he'd be.

The others watched anxiously as I approached the mare. The beautiful creature followed me with her gaze as I gingerly stepped over her broad back and sat behind her neck, legs in the crease between her barrel and shoulder muscles. "Can I hold onto your mane?" I asked, visualising my hands wrapped in that white hair. I got a feeling of assent back from her, so I wound my fingers through it. "Let me know if it's too tight."

Having seen my success, Sarah was quick to follow, sliding onto the other *karkadann*. Welkin still sat on her shoulder, twisting his fingers through her hair in much the same way she did the stallion's. She murmured adoring praise to the creature and his ears swivelled back to listen. Could he understand her, or was he just picking up the tone?

Jack was the last to mount. The mare shifted uneasily at his scent but didn't object as he sat behind me, thighs pressed against mine and arms wrapped around my waist. Even though one of his arms was injured, his grip was strong and reassuring.

I shivered.

He mistook it for nerves. "We will be fine," he said, his breath tickling my ear. "If the stories are to be believed, the *karkadann* have an exceptionally smooth gait."

"That's a relief," I squeaked, heart pounding in my ears.

There was a sudden flurry of motion as we rocked backward and then forward. As quickly as that, both *karkadann* were on their feet. Sarah's wide-eyed gaze met my own. I had just enough time to wonder whether this was a terrible idea before the entire herd began to walk up the hill through the trees. Their strides were long—if we were on foot, we'd have been jogging to keep up.

The mare led the way. Thankfully, she was intelligent enough—or we were lucky enough—to avoid low-hanging branches. Perhaps, with such long horns, the *karkadann* were used to needing a bit of extra clearance.

I glanced back over Jack's shoulder. The stallion had fallen in at the rear, the other mares and the colt ranged out in between. My cousin was barely visible through the trees.

"Jack?" I said, looking down at his arm where it encircled my waist.

"Yes?"

The words came out a whisper. His keen ears caught them anyway. "Please don't be angry at me for trying to protect you."

He hesitated for a long moment. "I am meant to protect you, not the other way around."

"You're not my slave."

"I know. But I will not leave you to face Everest on your own. Please, Isla, do not try to force me to." His tone was fierce. I bit my lip and didn't answer; I couldn't. I'd rather he hate me forever than see his head in a bag.

When we reached the portal, a large opening set at the bottom of a cliff face, we had to duck our heads. I clung to the mare as the inevitable dizziness swept over me, hoping I didn't lose my balance and fall under those sharp hooves. Jack's warm arms held me steady, even though he had every reason to be angry with me.

Belatedly, I realised Sarah wouldn't be able to see the door and hoped the sight of the *karkadann* passing through solid rock didn't alarm her ... and that she didn't throw up all over the stallion. She'd looked pretty green last time.

On the other side of the portal, a high-ceilinged tunnel showed signs of Aghi's occupation. Spears lined one wall, the tips a fire-hardened brown. The half-dressed carcass of a grey kangaroo sat by a charcoal-filled pit—I averted my gaze from the mound of ash-grey fur and red flesh.

At least there were no flies in here.

The *karkadann* seemed to find the sight as distressing as I did, because as soon as they were all through the portal the mare increased her pace to a swift walk. Now we would've been sprinting to keep up.

"Sarah?" I called back. "Are you okay?"

"Just peachy," she replied after a long pause. I could hear Welkin's voice. His tone was reassuring, although

ISLA'S OATH

I couldn't hear what he was saying under the arrhythmic thudding of dozens of hooves on dirt. I'd have to trust the *piskie* would fly forward and tell me if there was a problem, because there wasn't much else I could do from here.

This tunnel was once the same perfect cylinder as the others I'd seen. The heavy traffic of the herd's movements had trampled the floor flat. Deep grooves from *karkadann* horns marred the walls.

My skin's increasing glow told me we were approaching a *sidhe* before we emerged from the tunnel. I still gasped when the roof fell away behind us.

The *sidhe* was ethereal. Its basic shape resembled the Canberra *sidhe* before I'd accidentally changed it—a huge cavern with a pitch-black sky and walls like the steep side of a mountain. Except no one had terraced the valley, or ruined its perfection with ramshackle buildings. Hills rolled gently, carpeted with lush grass and bobbing yellow flowers that resembled daisies—if daisies had glowing stamens at their hearts. Insects swarmed between the daisies, underbellies glittering with luminescent pollen. The scene looked like tiny, earthbound stars with plump spaceships meandering between them.

"It's beautiful," I breathed.

"Yes," Jack agreed.

We had plenty of time to drink in the view, because the mare crossed the entire length of the valley. The rest of the herd fell away to graze and do whatever else *karkadann* do in their leisure time, while the stallion trotted to catch up to us, falling in beside the mare. Sarah bounced around on his back like a sack of potatoes, gasping with relief when he slowed to a walk.

"My thighs are going to be sore by the time we get home," she said.

"Mine too. I'm just grateful that my feet won't get any worse."

"It's funny," she said after a moment. "One of my feet is really tired and achy, and the other one feels fine. I'm all lopsided. I guess when he healed my ankle he made my foot better too." She patted the stallion's neck fondly. He nickered and she drew her hand back, startled.

"I don't think he minds," I reassured her.

"Oh. Good." She gave him another pat, more tentative this time.

"Do you think you can get the torches out of the backpack? They're in the front pocket. It's going to be dark once we get out of here. We don't want to fall off because we didn't see a corner coming."

"What corners?" Sarah snorted. "Those tunnels are all straight as." But she swung the backpack around in front of her so she could reach the pocket.

"Some people claim the tunnels are not actually straight," Jack said in a subdued voice. "That it is just how our minds reconcile something that is beyond our capacity to understand."

"I dunno, my mind is pretty big." Sarah grinned, leaning precariously across to hand me a torch. I stuck it in a pocket so the plastic ball on the end poked out. It was uncomfortable, although not as uncomfortable as falling off the *karkadann's* back would be. I wanted both hands available to hold on if I needed them.

"It actually makes more sense than the idea that the tunnels are all perfectly straight," Welkin said, eyeing the glowing insects with a faint smile on his face. "They always connect with one another at right angles too. If they *were* gnawed out of the earth by giant worms, why would they have connected them that way?" He hesitated. "I'll be back in a second."

The *piskie* zipped down into the grass, landing on the centre of one of the glowing daisies. After a momentary pause to see if it would bear his weight, he jumped up and down, stirring the pollen up. Soon it coated his body from the waist down. "Look at me." He laughed. "I'm one of those movie fairies. You know, the ones with the glitter and flying boats."

He picked another daisy and, struggling with the awkward size of it—relatively speaking—flew back to Sarah. "A flower for your beautiful hair."

"Why, thank you," she said, tucking it behind her ear. His infatuation was so adorable I had to smile. Especially as it seemed to be keeping her mind focused.

The tunnel at the other end of the cavern had a low ceiling. I still had a foot of clearance above my head, but I fought the urge to duck as the mare entered it. My claustrophobia grumbled and I breathed deeply until the urge to flee screaming had passed.

This tunnel was more boring, and my mind soon wandered. If I weren't so terrified of falling and dying, I might have nodded off. Fear is a wonderful motivator.

"This is as far as we got in this tunnel before," Jack said after a few minutes. "Where we turned back."

"You can tell?"

"What, can't you?" Sarah's voice was heavy with sarcasm.

"Not exactly, no."

A questioning thought touched my mind. At first, I

thought the mare was contributing to our discussion. Then she sent me a complex emotion, a feeling of freedom, of flashing hooves and whipping mane.

"Are you guys up to the *karkadann* cantering?" I asked, unsure of whether I was myself.

"I am," Jack added. His presence at my back was reassuring. If I lost my balance, he would steady me.

"Um. I think so," Sarah said. "Just no trotting please. I thought this fellow's spine was going to cut me in two earlier."

I tried to communicate the request to the mare, but wasn't sure I'd succeeded until she increased her pace to an easy canter. The stallion fell in several lengths behind: a sensible precaution when you're face is equipped with a deadly weapon. At first, the pace terrified me, and I clenched my thighs and fists in panic. But the mare's thoughts were soothing, and I slowly relaxed. The wind of our passage rushed past me, blowing my hair back into Jack's face until, laughing, he snared it and tucked it down the back of my shirt.

Behind us, Sarah was laughing too.

Jack heard the sound first. Barely audible over the ruckus we were making, a clicking noise escalated to a higher-pitched whine. It was like a thousand crickets screeching in a deafening chorus.

"The *sluagh*!"

The *karkadann's* consternation was palpable. Had they not known about their neighbours?

"Hold on!" I yelled, sensing what they were about to do.

The easy, three-beat canter escalated into a four-beat gallop. It felt like flying. Through a downpipe. In the dark.

We approached the *sluagh* tunnel and I tensed, expecting

something to leap out at us. But we shot past it, as quick as thought.

Then Sarah screamed.

The *sluagh* erupted from the darkness several lengths behind us, a roiling cloud of fur and teeth. They were short, perhaps five feet tall—or they would have been if they were standing. Instead, they flew on leathery, batlike wings. Glancing back, I caught a glimpse of hate-filled, black eyes. Webbed fingers extended towards us, covered in oily, dark-grey skin. Their mouths gaped to issue that screeching chatter, framed by grimy teeth.

Fear rolled over us in an icy wave, and Sarah screamed again. This time I screamed with her. My heart beat wildly in my chest.

"Isla!" Jack yelled in my ear. "You can stop them. Concentrate!"

I closed my eyes and sensed the *sluagh's* awful power as a palpable force. They could generate terror in their targets, motivated by a powerful malice to destroy anything that loved and laughed. That force grasped at us, a clumsy hand, hoping to make our limbs seize up with fear, to send the *karkadann* crashing to the ground so we would topple off their backs.

And then they would feed.

"They hate." My lips moved in a whisper. No one heard me.

They gathered their power and struck again. The wave wasn't the sickly yellow of fear but instead blazing orange streaked through with black, like the glow of a firestorm on the horizon, stained with tendrils of smoke. I'd seen the orange before, in the boy on the beach who was mortally afraid of bluebottles. So afraid he couldn't move.

What the black meant I didn't have time to contemplate.

I gathered up the terror. Given the way my heart skittered within the confines of my ribcage, trying to absorb it might kill me. Instead, I flung it back at the haunt. My skin flared brightly, casting stark shadows on the tunnel walls.

The *sluagh* screamed, a disturbingly human sound. The cloud trembled and faltered, falling further behind us. I saw one shape tumble to the ground, limp-winged, before the haunt disappeared from view.

"Go, Isla!" Sarah yelled. "You got one!" Welkin clung to her ear with both arms. We were moving faster than he could fly.

A keening sound arose behind us; after a couple of seconds, it transitioned into a shriek of pure rage.

"I think you made them angry!" the *piskie* cried as the sound of flapping wings started again, pierced by furious, insectile chatter. They didn't risk attacking us with fear again, but they weren't going give up. Especially now.

That headlong flight through the tunnel took on a nightmarish quality. I tensed to maintain my seat on the *karkadann's* back, gearing up for another attack by the *sluagh*—not knowing if or when it would come. My limbs trembled with exhaustion.

Jack's arms tightened on my waist. "I have you," he murmured in my ear, and my heart swelled.

I loved him. The realisation came over me, as slow and inevitable as dawn light. And, as much as I wanted this hellish ride to be over, when we got back to the *sidhe* I would lose him forever. There was no other way to keep him safe.

Tears burned my eyes, streamed down my cheeks. Clinging to the mare's mane, I was unable to wipe them away. Her sympathy was a balm.

Sarah cheered when we reached the point where the opaque stream crossed the tunnel. We were almost home. The *karkadann* were tiring from their headlong gallop and the *sluagh* gained ground, inch by inch. They were visible again, a fluttering shadow at the edge of our circle of light.

Fear swallowed my grief. "What do we do if they follow us into the *sidhe*?" I called over the thunder of hooves.

"They do not like bright light. Your sun will drive them away. If it has not set yet."

My sun. The thought would have made me smile under other circumstances. Now I was desperate to know the time. I couldn't look at my watch without letting go of the mane. "If it has, maybe I can make that light again."

"Be cautious. It drains you."

Would I be able to drive the *sluagh* away, or would they slaughter everyone in the *sidhe*?

The golden ring of Celtic knotwork flashed by so quickly I barely noticed the design. But the effect on the *sluagh* was dramatic. They shrieked with outrage, stopped short by an invisible barrier, unable to cross over. Soon the sounds of their chittering and flapping diminished into the distance, fading like a nightmare after the dreamer awakens.

"Huh," Jack said, sounding surprised. "Is that what that thing is for?"

I laughed with relief at Jack's comment. Things still surprised my all-knowing hob.

The spill of late afternoon sunlight—even the muted sunlight of the *sidhe*—into the tunnel filled our hearts with joy. The *karkadann*, weary now, slowed to a walk, sides heaving with each laboured breath. They too were relieved at the idea of a cool drink and a slow trip back to their own *sidhe*. How long would the *sluagh* wait in the tunnel for us before they gave up and returned home? Would the *karkadann* have to travel through the outside world to get back to their valley?

"So, Jack," Welkin drawled from behind us. "I believe you owe me something."

I felt Jack stiffen behind me. "I do?"

"Yes. You need to admit that I'm useful and say sorry. Remember?"

"I will never hear the end of this," Jack muttered in my ear. Then he spoke more loudly. "Yes, Welkin, you are that rarest of creatures, a useful *piskie*. I apologise from the bottom of my heart for ever implying otherwise."

"Apology accepted." Welkin said solemnly.

I shivered. Was I reacting to the exhaustion? But when I looked down at Jack's bare arms, wrapped around my waist, I saw goosebumps.

"Did it just get colder?" Sarah said.

And then we emerged into the *sidhe* and saw a small group gathered on the path that cut through the village.

At the centre of the crowd was Everest.

"Damn," I whispered.

CHAPTER EIGHTEEN

The verdant grass I'd noticed earlier—was it really only this morning?—was silvered with frost. It glittered in the gentle afternoon sunlight as though coated with pixie dust.

"Isla!" Everest's voice carried up the valley. Despite his pleasant tone, a shiver that had nothing to do with the sudden cold ran down the length of my spine.

I slid from the mare's back, tired legs almost buckling under me as my shoes hit the ground. I steadied myself against her side. Jack and Sarah followed; my cousin was little better than I was, but Jack seemed unaffected by our mad ride. "You might want to get out of here," I murmured to the mare, patting her shoulder. It trembled under my fingers. "This probably isn't going to end well."

The mare touched my mind, tentative, offering aid. I was grateful, but knew I couldn't accept it. They were exhausted, and Everest had no mercy. Cavall could have attested to that ... if he had a head. "No, thank you. Get back to your herd." I looked across at Jack. "Is there another tunnel they can take?"

He nodded to our left, away from Everest. "Two entrances that way is one that heads towards Sydney. It will bring them closer to their *sidhe*. Once it is dark they can cross overland to reach the national park."

I tried to convey this to the mare with a few thoughts, layered over my deep regret at not providing them the hospitality we should have—especially given their heroic efforts in keeping ahead of the *sluagh*. She whickered a breath, sweet and warm in my hair. Then, delicately, she touched her horn to the outside of each of my thighs. A brief heat spread through my aching muscles, washing the fatigue and cramps away like waves sweeping a sandcastle from the shore, leaving that cool sensation in its wake.

She did the same for Sarah, who stood frozen, wide-eyed and trembling. Then, with a glance down at Everest, she led her mate along the edge of the *sidhe* towards the tunnel Jack had indicated. Occasionally the pair snatched up a mouthful of frosted grass as they moved swiftly away.

I turned to my cousin. "Sarah…"

"No way." She shook her head vehemently. "Don't you dare suggest I leave too. I'm not going."

"But—"

"If you even say it, I'll hit you." She balled her fist and held it up to show she was serious.

I gave her a quick hug. Although I would have preferred she take the tunnel back to Mount Taylor and home, her support warmed my heart. "Thank you."

"Me too," Welkin added. His voice quavered, and he shrank back into Sarah's hair until all I could see of him was a pair of wide blue eyes.

"You don't have to—"

"Melpomene's daughter!" Everest called. Even though the words were polite, impatience was evident in his tone. "Will you grace us with your presence?"

"We're coming," I called back, looking at Jack, who hugged his arms to his bare chest. "Are you okay?"

"I wish I had a shirt on," he said, giving me a sweet smile. "And some shoes." His aura was choked with despair like ashes, a feeling I shared. How had Everest found the *sidhe*?

I took his hand in one of mine, and Sarah's in the other. Together, we walked down the slope towards the path.

As we grew closer to the centre of the *sidhe*, the frost thickened underfoot until not even a hint of green showed beneath—the kind of hard frost we only saw in Canberra in the depths of winter. We walked gingerly so we wouldn't slip. Given Jack's relative state of undress, it didn't seem right to complain about being cold, but I couldn't stop my teeth from chattering.

I was so busy concentrating on my footing that Sarah was the first to notice. Her gasp drew my gaze sharply to Everest—and the gathering around him.

The group stood on the path at a distance from the buildings, as though they found them distasteful. Given who was involved, they probably did. The *aosidhe* stood out, radiating an energy that drew the eye like a lodestone. He wore his ubiquitous black slacks and shirt, with tooled leather boots to match; his coat was made from silver fox fur that seemed to make his eyes glow.

I blinked. They *were* glowing. Not the gentle skin illumination he and I both had—funny how I was starting to take that for granted—but more brightly, like a pair of cold flames.

Shannon stood behind and to one side of him, head high and eyes glittering with triumph and malice. Ariel and Fintan were on his other side. The hob's expression was gleeful, whereas the *puca's* head hung wearily. All three of them were dressed for the conditions, in heavy coats, gloves and scarves.

Between Ariel and Fintan, on their knees, were two prisoners.

One was Evie. She wore jeans and a plain shirt whose neckline was loose enough that we could see the brass collar fastened around her neck, secured with a heavy padlock. Her hands stretched behind her back at an awkward angle, and her single eye raked over us, taking in Jack's lack of attire and my presence with a flat resignation that belied the fury in her aura. She blamed me for the *aosidhe's* presence. I didn't need her to speak to see that.

The other prisoner—

—was Dominic.

He knelt, loose limbed and unbound, on the frosted path. He seemed oblivious to the cold, to the icy water soaking into the knees of his jeans. His gaze skittered around, unfocused. I wasn't sure he was taking anything in; his aura was a disjointed jumble of colours I hadn't seen before.

It didn't look sane.

Then he saw me and smiled. Those chocolate-brown eyes I adored, even now, were utterly trusting. "You came!" He tried to stand. Fintan placed a leather-gloved hand on his shoulder and shook his head. Confused, Dominic subsided. I nodded reassuringly at him, swallowing my panic. He hung his head like a lost little boy.

Jack's words came back to me from less than two weeks ago. *It is a great risk to a human, bringing them into the sidhe.* I clutched his hand fiercely. What was being here doing to Dominic's mind?

"Where is everyone else?" I whispered to Jack. "The rest of the *duinesidhe*?"

"Hiding or fled," he replied. "Would you not do the same?"

I halted about twenty metres away from Everest and smiled, trying not to look utterly terrified. The expression felt glued on, flaking around the edges. "I didn't expect to see you here."

"Would you believe that I missed you?" the *aosidhe* said with a dazzling grin. He really was the most beautiful person here; even as much as I hated him right then, my heart stuttered as his gaze settled on me. In an instant, his expression hardened. "No? Well, when Shannon told me you had left the area, I was worried you might be trying something foolish. Like running. I wanted to make sure that you had a reason to come back." He stroked Dominic's hair the way I might pat Hamish. My stomach churned.

"I just had something I wanted to look into. You know, before I left."

He raised one of those elegant black eyebrows, radiating scepticism. "And were you successful?"

I nodded, swallowing hard.

"I am so pleased."

"It was you," Sarah blurted.

"Shh!" I tried to silence her, but her cheeks were flushed with anger.

"You sent the elf shot, and you sent people to attack Uncle David!"

"Indeed?" Everest's teeth flashed whitely as he looked back at me. "You found Aghi, did you?" I nodded. The *aosidhe* gave Fintan a dark look that promised future retribution.

The *puca* glanced from Evie to Dominic; although his emotions were frustrated, his expression stayed neutral. I guessed Everest wasn't the sort of master that accepted *I was busy kidnapping other people for you* as a valid reason for not having completed a task.

"Well, then." Everest shrugged, the fox fur shimmering. "Yes, I suppose that is true. I did not intend to cause your father permanent harm, you understand. Quite the opposite. I am sure he would be grateful for a chance at a reunion with his estranged wife." He pursed his lips. "I am sorry he could not be here today. He has fortified himself inside that iron-riddled compound of his."

I bit back a sigh of relief. At least one of my loved ones was safe. Did he have Ryan and Aunt Elizabeth with him, or had Everest not bothered with them? At least I'd managed to protect the identity of my *aislinge*, if nothing—and no one—else.

Everest's fingers tightened on Dominic's hair. The *aosidhe* wasn't wearing gloves, so his hand stood out amidst my boyfriend's dark locks. "Never mind. My clever Shannon found out about this boy and discovered the entrance to your rather pathetic *sidhe* too. Handy, having a finder for an *aislinge*—that is how I discovered where your father was hiding in the first place, you know." The blond woman preened at her master's praise, cheeks flushing. He didn't notice. "And so here we are. I think you were planning on not swearing to me, correct? And helping Jack evade justice? Please do not lie. It is so tiresome."

"Well, I wouldn't want to be a bore," I muttered, irritation a tiny flame in the darkness of my terror. Beside me, Sarah choked back a hysterical laugh. I took a breath and spoke more loudly. "Of course I was," I admitted. "I couldn't trust you to let Jack live or to leave my family alone."

"Oh, Isla," he sighed, placing his free hand over his heart as though I'd wounded him. "Of course I would have. Now? Well." His gaze flickered over Jack dismissively and then lingered on Sarah. "Is this ... your sister? She has the red hair of your father's family."

I shook my head, answering reluctantly. "My cousin."

"Very pretty." He tapped his chin with one tapered finger. "She will come with us when we return. To keep you company, of course. An *aosidhe*—even a lowly half-breed—should have attendants. She would also make a suitable reward for my followers. Ariel does love redheads, and your family owes him some compensation for what happened to Moray."

Ariel stood up straighter at the mention of his name, green eyes sharpening to match his smile. Everest glanced at him. "Given the *karkadann's* assistance, I would wager she is a virgin."

"Leave her alone!" Welkin burst forth from the concealment of Sarah's hair, flying straight at Everest's eyes. His copper pin flashed in his tiny hand.

Moving with blinding reflexes, Everest swatted him from the sky. Welkin's body fell limply, a speck of colour on the pallid frost.

A flicker of movement caught my eye, and I saw Sarah palming the haematite necklace. She'd taken advantage of the *piskie's* distraction to unfasten it from her neck. Tears flowed down her cheeks as she rushed to Welkin's inert form and scooped it up, cradling it to her chest with one hand. "You monster!" she gasped.

"Yes. By your standards, frequently. Ariel?"

Flexing his leather-sheathed fingers, the hob strode forward, grabbing Sarah's hair. With a snarl, she flung the necklace at Ariel's face, holding one end. The chain lashed out like a miniature whip.

The beads struck his cheek. He cried out, stepping back and clutching his face with one hand. I charged at him, grabbing his sword arm and pushing it backward before he could draw the blade from its sheath. I didn't know how to use the weapon, but I'd bet Jack did. "Dominic! Run!"

He scrambled to his feet and turned, lumbering straight into Shannon. The two of them fell in a tangle of limbs. Fintan darted over to help the *aislinge*. Jack lunged, grabbing the tail of his leather coat and using it as leverage to swing him around.

"*Enough!*" Everest roared. A breath of unexpectedly warm air puffed out from him, causing tendrils of fog to swirl and dissipate. His eyes flashed more brightly. He strode over to where Evie knelt, still bound, on the path, and placed his hands roughly on either side of her face. "Stand down, or I will snap this hob's neck. I mean it." We froze. "All of you, come and kneel here. Ariel, bind them."

His left cheek already blistering, Ariel shoved Sarah over to Evie's side. She fell heavily to her knees on the path, biting her lip to keep back a cry. He crushed her hand in his glove until she dropped the necklace, kicking it away from her with the toe of his boot. "You will pay for burning me, bitch," he snarled, plucking the glowing daisy from behind her ear and crushing it. Glowing pollen rained down.

"Bite me," she muttered. Tears glittered in her eyes and her aura was awash with fear.

He smiled, running a finger along her jaw line. "This is why I like redheads."

Shannon steered Dominic to Sarah's other side. He looked confused again. "Should I still run?" he asked me.

I shook my head, heart in my throat, and he knelt.

Jack had fallen motionless when Everest threatened his sister. Fintan tried to grab him, but he shook the *puca* off and came to kneel beside Evie. "Just kill me," he said, glaring up at Everest. "I am the one who committed the crime. These others have nothing to do with it. Kill me and let them go."

Everest laughed. "Arrogant little hob. As if I care what you did to Cacodaemon! This was never about you."

"I know," Jack replied, his gaze finding mine. I hesitated several feet from the others. He was urging me to run—I could see it in his eyes. In his aura, love and fear warred for supremacy.

Jack. Sarah. Dominic. I couldn't leave them.

Everest turned to me, trusting Ariel to secure his prisoners. "Come here, Isla."

I shuddered as I approached the *aosidhe*. My leaden feet dragged on the ground. The frost was melting in a circle around Everest, the air warming noticeably as I drew closer to him. "Your power is cold," I said stupidly, thinking about his frigid hotel room. Not air conditioning after all.

"Heat," he corrected me, his gaze running over my

face, lingering on my lips, my throat. His smile was self-satisfied, heavy-lidded. I was almost in arm's reach now. "I draw it from objects and can release it at will. I can do the same thing to people too. I am told it can be ... intoxicating."

I stepped inside the circle of his arms; he curled one around behind my shoulders and used the other to caress my cheek. His fingers were hot but left a tingling tracery of cold on my skin. An unexpected heat stirred elsewhere in my body. "See? Intoxicating." he breathed. He blinked slowly. "You are quite the unexpected morsel."

"No!" Shannon gasped. Then she covered her mouth with her hands, mortified.

"Silence, *aislinge*." His words were cool, carrying an underlying threat. "You have no claim over me. Do not think you do." Tears brightened her eyes.

I was grateful for the interruption. It gave me a chance to get a hold of myself, shake off the temptation of his touch. The way Shannon cringed away from his gaze like a whipped animal was all the reminder I needed: Everest was a monster.

I took a half-step back, as far as I could go with his arm around me. "Let everyone else go and I'll come with you."

"I think not. You have proven quite elusive, and how else am I to guarantee your good behaviour?"

"I could swear an oath to you."

Jack and Sarah gasped. Dominic glanced from me to Everest, a frown creasing his forehead. "Isla?"

"It's okay, Dommie," I said. And although it wasn't, he believed me.

Everest's eyes widened as he read my expression, looking between me and Dominic. He threw back his head and laughed. "You have made your boyfriend your thrall? You really are your mother's daughter, Isla, binding men's hearts to you. I shall have to be cautious."

Self-loathing welled inside me. I knew, down to the depths of my soul, that Everest was right. What I'd done to Dominic was as bad as what Melpomene did to my father. Never mind the fact I'd already decided to set things right with Dominic. I was as bad as her. As bad as all the *aosidhe*.

Eyes burning with tears, I turned away from him—and my gaze met Evie's.

She hated me. Her gaze reflected my own disgust at my behaviour. Her expression was afire with it. But she was impatient too. As I looked at her, despising myself, she spoke softly. "You are your mother's daughter. So *be* your mother's daughter."

Be your mother's daughter.

I turned to face Everest, looking up into his lambent gaze. "Let us go."

He laughed, and I despised him.

I placed my palms on his too-cold cheeks and attacked him with all my fear and hatred.

With Aghi, Gall and Evie, striking out with my emotions had been like turning on a tap. This was more like breaching a dam. The two emotions poured out of me in a colossal wave, flooding into him in froth the colour of blood and bile. Terror about what I was becoming, and at the fate before us if I failed. Anger at my own foolishness, and at this arrogant monster for treating us like playthings.

Everest sneered, silver eyes glittering with malicious delight. "Really, Isla? I have lived with those feelings since I was a child. You will have to do much better than that."

I'd struck him as hard as I could.

I've failed.

My eyes widened. I had one weapon left.

I gathered the self-loathing eating at my heart and thrust it into him like a spear. My revulsion at what I had done to Dominic. My shame at being able unable to save my family. Even the crushing self-doubt every teenager feels—I spared nothing. All of it, turned against me, turned against him, like acid poured into an open wound.

Everest screamed.

He had never known anything other than a deep and abiding faith in his own self-worth. The black tsunami of doubt and bitter remorse knocked that faith aside, obliterating it as though it never was. Only despair remained.

"*Noooooooooo!*"

He fell to his knees, tears streaking his beautiful features. One tentative finger touched his cheek; his silver eyes stared at the droplets with disgust and confusion.

The air around him—around us—grew abruptly hotter. The frost melted with a hiss of steam. The teardrop evaporated as though it had never been.

"Run!" Jack yelled.

I stepped back from the weeping *aosidhe*, feeling hollow inside, an empty cup. My skin glowed brightly, like a thousand fireflies.

Everest glowed like the molten mouth of a volcano.

Jack ran forward, grabbed my arms to steady me. "We have to go!"

Ryan's painting. A figure wreathed in a sea of flame. The recollection gave new energy to my limbs, freed my tongue. "Get Evie. The rest of you, why aren't you running? *Move!*"

ISLA'S OATH

Ariel hesitated, looking at his weeping master. Everest's skin glowed more brightly from within—bright enough that we each cast a second shadow. Smoke streamed from his mouth, ears, nose—even from the corners of his eyes and the gaps around those perfectly manicured fingernails. He stared up at us, and his eyes boiled.

Ariel fled.

Jack scooped up his sister. I hauled Sarah to her feet, grabbing Dominic with the other hand. Fintan, to my great surprise, ran after us, not his companion.

"Master!" Shannon screamed, darting back the other way.

"Shannon, no!"

She threw herself onto Everest, cradling his head between her breasts. She closed her eyes, expression serene.

For a moment, it was beautiful.

The flames burst from the *aosidhe's* pores, swathing them both in a blanket of fire. Shannon clung to Everest, her scream curling higher and higher, intertwined with plumes of greasy black smoke.

It was a long time before she fell mercifully silent. And longer still before the fire burned itself out, leaving nothing but ashes and bones.

Once the fire had guttered and died, some of the *sidhe's* other residents came out to help tidy up: a few hob and *puca* I'd never seen before, and several short, golem-like creatures made of stone and earth, who levered up the fractured pathway stones that had been shattered by the intense heat. The only *powrie*, Gall, regarded me fearfully and stayed well away.

In fact, almost everyone stayed cautiously out of reach. I'd made an *aosidhe* self-immolate. I could understand why they didn't want to give me a hug and a high five.

The frost had evaporated with Everest's conflagration, leaving most of the *sidhe* unaffected—although Talbot was going to have to tend some of his more fragile exotic flowers when he got home.

Evie was unhurt, although she was sore from having her hands bound to the backs of her ankles for several hours. Strangely, out of everyone in the *sidhe*, she was one of the few that didn't seem afraid of me. "You did a good thing," she told me as I watched a pair of *puca* sweep up the charred mess. One of them was Fintan, who avoided eye contact with everyone. "When the nightmares come, remind yourself of that."

"Thanks." Tears stung my eyes. I told myself it was the residual smoke.

She put her hands on her hips and stared at me until I squirmed under her gaze. "I still do not like you," she said and, with that parting shot, limped away.

Jack came over, cradling his arm carefully against his chest. Someone had found him a T-shirt, but it was several sizes too large. Sarah followed him. "Are you okay?" he asked, studying me with concerned sapphire eyes.

"Yes," I said. "Are you?"

"I will heal. Welkin only sustained a broken arm and a concussion. He is asleep now."

Sarah had the *piskie* cupped in her palm. He was whole, and appeared slightly damp. "He *licked* him," my cousin said with great disgust.

I shrugged. "Hey, whatever works."

ISLA'S OATH

"Welkin was courageous. Stupid, but courageous," Jack said.

"He did it so I could get the necklace off," Sarah protested. "It was his idea."

"Then I retract the part about stupidity." He bowed slightly.

I reached out to touch Jack's arm and then stopped when I saw him flinch. "Will you be okay?" I brushed a hand along his cheek instead.

"Yes. Always." His eyes were earnest, I was relieved to see. His gaze—and aura—were completely unafraid. I wasn't sure I could have dealt with fear from him right then.

"Um, Isla? I hate to interrupt, but..." Sarah nodded past my shoulder to where Dominic sat beneath one of the streetlamps, staring up at the glittering stargems with wide eyes and a passive smile. We had fastened the haematite necklace around his neck. It didn't seem to be helping. "We should get him home. And there's something you swore you would do once the situation with Everest was dealt with." She chose her words carefully, unaware that Jack already knew what I'd done to Dominic.

"Do you think it can wait till I've had a chance to sleep?" My voice came out whinier than I would have liked, but I was beyond tired. Even my hair ached.

"You swore to undo what you did 'as soon as Everest was gone'," she said, making air quotes with her free hand. "Swore it. And he seems to be pretty conclusively gone. I wouldn't risk it if I were you."

Jack frowned, looking between us. "Do you need my assistance to get him home?"

"No. Stay here. Look after your sister." I hesitated,

adding tentatively, "Maybe you could come by tomorrow, if you're feeling better?"

"Of course." He smiled.

Today had already been horrific. And it was going to get worse, because once I healed Dominic I was going to break up with him ... if he didn't beat me to it. As much as I cared about him, I had done him a terrible wrong—and I'd finally recognised my heart belonged elsewhere. I ached for him, for what could have been.

But, as we herded a compliant Dominic back towards the exit to the *sidhe*, towards home, I felt a faint smile curve my cheeks.

"What are you grinning about?" Sarah asked me.

"I'm looking forward to tomorrow."

THE END

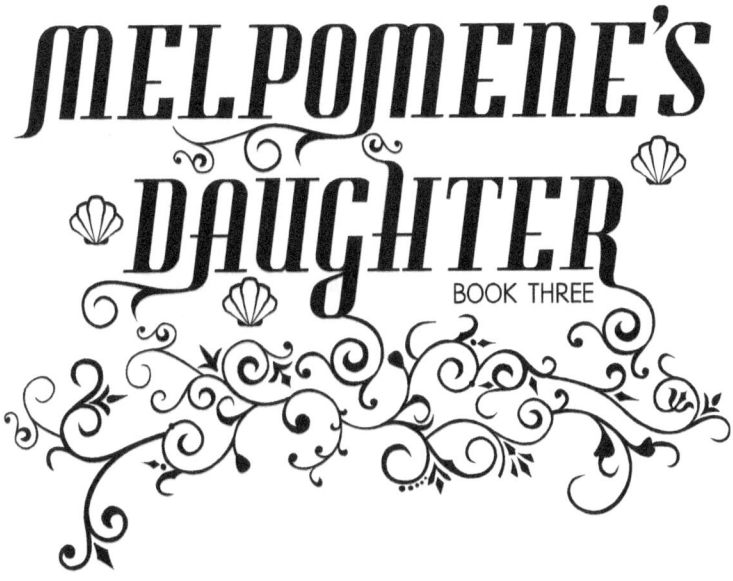

MELPOMENE'S DAUGHTER

BOOK THREE

Isla struggles to embrace her fae nature while preserving her humanity in the final, exciting instalment of the Isla's Inheritance trilogy.

Isla has spent months persuading the Canberra fae that she isn't a tyrant like her mother, trying to prove that—despite her mixed blood—she's human, not a monster. That she's one of them, not one of the high fae who enslaved them.

But a vision of a fresh-dug grave warns that someone is going to die.

When the Old World fae once again move against her family, seeking revenge for old wrongs, Isla will stop at nothing to keep those she loves safe. She just wants to be left alone. But to win that right for herself, her family and all Australian fae, she must cross the oceans and take the fight to the country of her birth.

Isla must prove she really is Melpomene's daughter after all.

Read on for an excerpt of *Melpomene's Daughter*

ΜΕLPOΜΕΝΕ'S DAUGHTER

When Aunt Elizabeth nagged me about getting a job, I doubted this was what she had in mind.

I stood behind Talbot's cottage, coppery autumn sunlight drifting down from the artificial sun above. An artificial sun I'd accidentally created two months before. I was inside the *sidhe*, the magical land under the hills— or perhaps in another reality accessed via portals into the hills. I wasn't clear on the physics. Either way, it was where Canberra's *duinesidhe*, or faeries, lived.

Before me was a wide space. The cottage was at the far end of the eclectic village, so there was nothing but grass between the back of his home and the cliff-like boundary of the *sidhe* beyond. I stared at the field, biting my lip. The amount of space I had to fill was daunting.

"You can do it," Jack murmured beside me. I glanced at him, reassured by the trust in his wide sapphire eyes and, visible only to me, in his aura. "Here." Our fingers brushed as he handed me a piece of paper.

Sketched on the paper in my cousin Ryan's distinctive

artistic style was a fantastical tree. He and Talbot had spent hours working together on the picture, with all the intensity and desire for accuracy of a police sketch artist and his witness.

Talbot's requirements were very specific.

I closed my eyes and pictured the drawing in my mind—the spiralled trunk that reminded me of seashells I'd found on the beach as a child; the large, flat leaves shaped like hearts; the huge, spreading branches; the flowers like tiny points of light.

When I was sure I had the image right, I *pushed*, projecting it outward and onto the empty field before me.

For several heartbeats, nothing happened. Someone shifted nearby. An anxious whine sounded in the back of a throat.

Then the *sidhe* took hold of the idea, pulling it from me like a child sucking juice through a straw. My knees trembled, but Jack was ready. He caught me around the waist and helped me stand. I gritted my teeth and concentrated, brows furrowing, eyes scrunched closed.

Timber creaked, and irregular thudding arose from around us as the ground shook. Talbot swore.

Silence fell.

Jack spoke quietly, his breath tickling my ear. "It is done."

I opened my eyes and stared. Even though I knew what the tree was meant to look like, my jaw fell open as I looked up ... and up.

The tree towered, the leaves of its domed crown glimmering like emeralds, lit all around with gently glowing flowers. Talbot sprang forward into the deep shade beneath the boughs, bare feet whisking through the grass as he dodged clods of displaced earth. He reached up and plucked a bloom from a low-hanging branch, inhaling deeply, his dark-skinned nose twitching in his pale face. When he smiled, I sagged with relief. Jack grinned.

"Here," Talbot said, returning to my side and placing the flower in my palm. "Smell it."

The bloom was a soft pink, radiating gentle light like a Disney fairy. I sniffed it, the pollen tickling my nose. "Strawberries. And musk."

Talbot beamed. "It's perfect."

"Have you checked the other colours?" Each type of flower was meant to smell different, a cornucopia of delights for a *puca* such as Talbot. Like the rest of his species, he was a shapechanger; his other form was a long-eared hound dog. He collected scents the way I collected beads for the charm bracelet that glittered on my wrist.

"Not yet," Talbot said, turning back to the tree.

"Can we finish up here first?" Jack said, indicating me with a tip of his head as he gave the *puca* a significant look.

"It's okay," I protested, although the waver in my voice undermined me.

"You need to rest."

"Well, how about I rest in the shade of Talbot's new tree? Just till he's happy he got what he's paying for."

Jack pursed his lips, but I frowned at him until he relented and we set out across the grass. I leaned on his shoulder. Making changes to the *sidhe*, a place made of magic, wore me out—even for a half-blood *aosidhe*, one of the ruling fae race, making changes had a price.

Jack led me to the huge trunk. I sank down into the soft grass with a grateful sigh, leaning against the bark. "Would you like to take some energy from me?" he asked, looking down at me.

"No."

"You should."

"I won't." We'd had this argument before. I believed taking emotions from others, feeding on them like some storybook psychic vampire, should be reserved for emergencies. I'd prefer to never have to do it at all. Jack, on the other hand, didn't like to see me suffer.

He was a good boyfriend.

The thought made me smile as I gazed up at him. He looked even more mysterious than usual in the green twilight beneath the tree. His golden hair, tapered chin and large eyes suggested his elfin heritage while still being close to human; the long, pointed ears on the other hand weren't even close. In the outside world, the human world, he concealed them under bandanas or hats. Here in the *sidhe* he was able to leave them unhidden.

I preferred them that way.

"What are you smiling at?" he said, sitting beside me.

"You." I leaned forward and kissed him softly, enjoying the warmth of his lips against mine, his hand curling in my hair.

We both jumped when footsteps thudded above. I looked up. Talbot walked along a broad, low branch, bare toes clinging to the wood. "I've got peppermint and chocolate, and this white one here, what's this? It smells fresh, like your skin, Isla."

Jack scowled, but I couldn't help laughing at the *puca's* enthusiasm. "It's moisturiser. Try the darker brown one. It's coffee. My favourite."

"Wonderful!" Talbot dashed away.

"This is such a weird idea," I murmured to Jack, running my fingers over one of the trunk's curves. The upward spiral narrowed as it grew, like a giant unicorn's horn. Or a *karkadann's*. I'd never seen a real unicorn, but the *karkadann* I'd met a couple of months ago were similar in appearance to the mythical creature, if more bloodthirsty.

"There is a tree much like this in one of the Old World courts. Talbot used to serve there, before he escaped to Australia."

"How many *duinesidhe* here are refugees from Europe?"

"Maybe half." Jack looked away, expression grim.

Regret made me wince. "You're safe now." He'd had to kill his *aosidhe* master to free himself and his sister from continued enslavement and torture. The idea my boyfriend was a murderer didn't bother me as much as it would have a few months ago. My mother's people weren't the kind, noble high elves you read about in children's books: they were vain, cruel and self-centred. Although I'd only ever met the one, he'd lived up to everything I'd been warned about—and Jack wasn't the only one with blood on his hands. I shuddered. Jack hugged me tighter, his preternatural warmth easing the sudden chill.

A voice from beyond the field cried, "What is *this*?"

ACKNOWLEDGEMENTS

I owe so much to everyone who helped during the process of writing (editing, re-editing, releasing, promoting or re-releasing) *Isla's Oath*, whether it was with a bit of advice, assistance or just a chance to decompress. Thanks for putting up with how distracted I get when I'm drafting.

As always, to my alpha reader, Peter—who would provide advice on anything except "the girly bits"—thank you. Luckily Jennifer Anderson, my fantastic editor, was more than happy to pick up the slack. Thanks also to the rest of my cheer squad: Ali and Craig, Karen and Mikey, Barbara and Nathan, my work colleagues, my sister Kristy, and the Aussie Owned and Read girls—especially Stacey Nash, who was simultaneously debuting on this crazy ride for her own books, and held my hand (virtually) while I hyperventilated over what I was getting into.

We're old hands now. No more hyperventilating here. *hides the brown paper bag behind the couch*

To the BC09 girls, and my friends on Twitter and

Facebook, who've also provided a ton of virtual support: I couldn't have done it without you. Anyone who says social media friends aren't real has never met you wonderful folks (although, admittedly, in a few cases neither have I).

A special mention goes to Sharon, who came up with the name *Isla's Oath* back when I was just calling the manuscript *Book Two*. Your title is *so* much snappier! And, as always, thank you to Kim from KILA Designs, who designed the trilogy's current, stunning covers and did the amazing interior layout you see before you.

Finally, to Nathaniel, my bright little boy and the light of my life: I love you to the moon and back. No, the sun! No, infinity! I'm sorry the books don't have pictures. xo

ABOUT THE AUTHOR

Cassandra Page is a mother, author, editor and geek. She lives in Canberra, Australia's bush capital, with her son and two Cairn Terriers. She has a serious coffee addiction and a tattoo of a cat—which is ironic given her cat allergy. When she's not reading or writing, she engages in geekery, from Doctor Who to AD&D. Because who said you need to grow up?

www.cassandrapage.com

www.ingramcontent.com/pod-product-compliance
Lightning Source LLC
Chambersburg PA
CBHW050015180626
46810CB00002B/423